I'M OFF
+
ONE YEAR

Jean Echenoz was born in Orange, France, in 1947. He studied organic chemistry in Lille and then the double bass in Metz before he turned to writing. His first novel, *Le Méridien de Greenwich* was published in 1979. His second, *Cherokee*, was awarded the Prix Médicis in 1983, and was followed by *L' équipée malaise* (1987), *L' occupation des sols* (1988), *Lac* (1989), *Nous trois* (1992), *Les grandes blondes* (1995), and *Un An* (1997). *I'm Off* won the Prix Goncourt in 1999.

Guido Waldman is the translator of *Lake* by Jean Echenoz. His other translations from the French include La Fontaine's *Tales in Verse* and Guilleragues' *The Love Letters of a Portugese Nun*. He has also translated *The Decameron* and *Orlando Furioso*. His translation of Alessandro Baricco's *Silk* was awarded the Weidenfeld Prize.

D1638878

Also by Jean Echenoz in English translation

Lake

Jean Echenoz

I'M OFF

+

ONE YEAR

Translated from the French by Guido Waldman

VINTAGE

Published by Vintage 2002

2 4 6 8 10 9 7 5 3 1

I'm off first published with the title *Je m'en vais* by
Les Éditions de Minuit, 1999

I'm off first published in Great Britain by The Harvill
Press 2001

One Year first published with the title *Un an* by
Les Éditions de Minuit, 1997 and in this translation
for the first time by Vintage in 2002

Vintage
Random House, 20 Vauxhall Bridge Road,
London SW1V 2SA

Random House Australia (Pty) Limited
20 Alfred Street, Milsons Point, Sydney,
New South Wales 2061, Australia

Random House New Zealand Limited
18 Poland Road, Glenfield
Auckalnd 10, New Zealand

Random House (Pty) Limited
Endulini, 5A Jubilee Road, Parktown 2193,
South Africa

The Random House Group Limited Reg. No. 954009

www.randomhouse.co.uk

A CIP catalogue record for this book
is availabl from the British Library

ISBN 1 860 46950 7

Papers used by Random House are natural, recyclable
products made from wood grown in sustainable
forests. The manufacturing processes conform to the
environmental regulations of the country of origin

Printed and bound in Great Britain by
Bookmarque Ltd, Croydon, Surrey

Contents

I'M OFF

1

"I'M OFF," FERRER SAID, "I'M LEAVING YOU. I'M LEAVING you everything, but I'm going." And as Suzanne's eyes wandered to the floor and stopped for no reason at a power point, Félix Ferrer dropped his keys on the hall table. Then he buttoned his overcoat before stepping outside and gently closing the door to their suburban home behind him.

Once outside, without a glance at Suzanne's car whose misted-up windows held their peace beneath the street lamps, Ferrer set off for the station, Corentin-Celton, a walk of some 600 metres. Around nine o'clock on the first Sunday evening in January the Metro was pretty well deserted. The only other travellers were a dozen lone men of the type that Ferrer seemed to have become in the last twenty-five minutes. As a rule he would have been glad to find a section of the carriage with nobody seated opposite him, as it were a little compartment all to himself, which was his preferred option when travelling on the Metro. Tonight he did not even give it a thought, brooding as he was – though less than expected – on the scene he had just been through with Suzanne, a difficult woman. He had been expecting a more vigorous reaction – shrieks mingled with threats and resounding insults – so he was relieved, but also put out by this very sense of relief.

His suitcase contained little more than his spongebag and some changes of underwear; he set it down beside him and looked fixedly ahead, mechanically deciphering the advertisements for dating agencies, estate agents and floor coverings. Further in, however, between Vaugirard and Volontaires, Ferrer opened his case and took out an auctioneers' catalogue for

3

traditional Persian works of art, leafing through it as far as Madeleine, the station where he got off.

Around the church of the Madeleine, electric garlands, strung above streets even emptier than the Metro, held up stars that had gone out. The window displays of the luxury boutiques reminded the absent passers-by that life went on beyond the year-end festivities. Alone in his overcoat, Ferrer turned down along the side of the church till he reached an even number in Rue de l'Arcade.

To find the access code for the building his hands clawed their way in beneath his coat, his left hand towards a diary slipped into an inside pocket, his right towards the glasses stuck into a breast pocket. Then, once through the front door, neglecting the lift, he resolutely tackled a service staircase. He reached the sixth floor less puffed out than I should have expected him to be, and stopped before a door badly repainted a brick-red, its frame showing signs of at least two attempts at forced entry. There was no name on this door, just a photo pinned to it, a photo rucked up at the corners and showing the lifeless body of Manuel Montoliu, ex-matador recycled as a peon after a beast named Cubatisto had opened his heart like a book on 1 May 1992. Ferrer gave two gentle taps on this photograph.

While he was waiting, the fingernails of his right hand dug lightly into the inside of his left forearm, just above the wrist, at the point where a number of tendons and blue veins intersected beneath the whitest skin. Then the young woman whose first name was Laurence, deeply tanned, with very long hair, aged not more than thirty, height not less than one metre seventy-five, opened the door and flashed him a wordless smile before shutting the door behind them. And the next morning around ten o'clock Ferrer left for his atelier.

2

SIX MONTHS LATER, AGAIN AT TEN O'CLOCK, THE SAME
Félix Ferrer got out of a taxi in front of Terminal B,
Roissy-Charles-de-Gaulle Airport, beneath a naïve June
sun shrouded towards the north-west. As Ferrer had arrived very
early, the check-in desk was not yet open for his flight, and he
had to spend a good three quarters of an hour pacing up and
down the halls pushing a trolley laden with two bags, one large
one small, and his overcoat, now on the thick side for the season.
Once he had had a second coffee and bought some paper hand-
kerchiefs and soluble aspirin, he looked for a quiet spot in which
to bide his time undisturbed.

If he had some difficulty finding one, this was because an
airport does not exist of its own accord. It is simply a place of
passage, a colander, a fragile façade in the middle of a plain, a
belvedere ringed with taxiways on which breathless rabbits
pumped full of kerosene leap about, a turntable infested with
draughts that carry a large variety of tiny bodies from sources
beyond counting – grains of sand from every desert, specks of
gold and mica from every river, volcanic or radioactive dust,
pollens and viruses, cigar-ash and rice-powder. To find a quiet
corner in such a place is not all that easy, but eventually, in the
basement of the terminal building, Ferrer discovered an inter-
faith spiritual centre with armchairs in which one could calmly
sit and think about nothing in particular. He killed a little time
there before checking in his bags and going to loaf about in duty-
free where he purchased no alcohol, no tobacco, no perfume,
nothing. He was not going on holiday. No reason to weigh
himself down.

A little before one o'clock he boarded a DC-10 in which some music of the spheres, turned down low in order to soothe the passengers, kept him company as he settled in. Ferrer folded his coat, shoved it along with his bag into the overhead compartment, then installed himself in the tiny square metre of space allotted to him by the window and saw to organising his space: seat belt buckled, papers and magazines placed to hand in front of him, glasses and sleeping pills within easy reach. The seat next to his happened to be unoccupied so he could use it as an annexe.

After that it is always the same, one waits, one listens to the recorded announcements with half an ear, one follows the safety demonstration with a distrait eye. Eventually the aircraft begins to move, at first imperceptibly, then faster and faster, and takes off on a north-westerly heading, towards the clouds – one passes through them. Later Ferrer, leaning against the window, could make out through these clouds a stretch of sea adorned with an island he could not identify, then a stretch of land with a lake in the middle of it this time, but he did not know its name. He dozed, gave a listless glance up at the screen for the credits introducing films he found it difficult to watch to the end, distracted as he was by the comings and goings of the air hostesses, who perhaps are no longer what they once were, he was as alone as could be.

Two hundred people compressed inside a fuselage make for a greater isolation than ever. One might imagine that this passive solitude could be the occasion for taking stock of one's life, for reflecting on the meaning of the factors that go to shape it. One tries for a moment, one makes the effort, but one tends not to persist with the disconnected interior monologue that results from it; so one gives up, hunches down in one's seat, grows sleepy, one wouldn't mind sleeping, one asks the hostess for something to drink – it'll make one sleep all the better – then for another to swallow the hypnotic pill. Then sleep.

Leaving the DC-10 at Montreal, Ferrer had the impression of an unusually broad scattering of airport staff beneath a sky vaster than others, then that the Greyhound bus was longer than other coaches, but the motorway seemed of a normal size. Arriving in Quebec, he took a taxi – a Subaru – to the port, Quay 11, the Coastguard office. The taxi set him down in front of a board on which was written in chalk DESTINATION: ARCTIC and, two hours later, the Canadian Coastguard icebreaker *Des Groseillers* cast off for the North.

3

FOR THE LAST FIVE YEARS, RIGHT UP TILL THE January evening that saw him walk out of the house at Issy, Félix Ferrer's daily routine, save for Sunday, had followed the same pattern. Up at seven-thirty, ten minutes in the toilet in the company of some printed matter or other, anything from a treatise on aesthetics to a humble prospectus, then getting breakfast for Suzanne and himself, with a scientific dosage of vitamins and mineral salts. Then came twenty minutes' callisthenics as he listened to the news round-up on the radio. This done, he would wake Suzanne and air the house.

After that, Ferrer would go into the bathroom and brush his teeth to bleeding-point without ever looking in the mirror, but leaving the tap running the while, using up ten litres of the municipality's cold-water supply. He washed himself invariably following the same order, left to right and bottom to top. He always shaved in the same order, invariably the right cheek then the left, then chin, lower lip, upper lip, neck. And as Ferrer, in thrall to this immutable sequence, asked himself each morning how to escape from this ritual, the very question had now become an integral part of the ritual. Without ever having arrived at a resolution to the question, he would set out for his atelier at nine o'clock sharp.

What he refers to as an atelier is one no longer. It vaguely answered the description in the days when Ferrer called himself an artist and conceived of himself as a sculptor, but it is nothing more than the back room of his art gallery which can serve its turn as his studio and has done so ever since he turned to the handling of other people's art. It is on the ground floor of a small building in the IXth arrondissement, in a street not at all predisposed towards the presence of a gallery: it is a busy shopping street, fairly popular for this quarter. Right across from the gallery is a large building site in the early stages of development: for the present, deep bores are being sunk for foundations. Ferrer comes in, makes himself a coffee, takes two Efferalgan, opens his mail, bins most of it, fumbles about a bit among the papers gathering dust and possesses his soul in patience until ten o'clock, fighting valiantly against the idea of a first cigarette. Then he opens the gallery and makes a few phone calls. About ten past noon he is back on the phone in search of a lunch companion – he never fails.

From three o'clock, for the rest of the afternoon until half-past seven, Ferrer remains at the gallery; at that point he rings Suzanne always with the same message, "Don't wait dinner for me if you're hungry." She always does wait, and at ten thirty Ferrer would be in bed with her, every other night they have a row, and at eleven o'clock lights out. That's how it had been for the past five years until this last 3rd January when there had been a sudden change. Not everything, however, was going to change: in Laurence's cramped bathroom, for instance, he had to admit, not without a slight sense of disappointment, that he continued to wash from left to right and from bottom to top. But he would not live at her place all that long, one of these days he would go back to live in his atelier.

This atelier, constantly several vacuum cleanings in arrears, featured as a bachelor pad, a place where a hunted man could hole up, a bequest stuck in limbo while the heirs are at each others' throats. Five sticks of furniture ensured a minimum of comfort, plus a small safe, though Ferrer had long forgotten the number of the combination lock, and a kitchenette measuring one metre by three contained a dirt-spattered cooker, a refrigerator, empty save for a couple of withered vegetables and some shelves holding tinned goods beyond their sell-by date. The fridge was very seldom used so a natural iceberg invaded the freezing compartment, and when it turned into shelf-ice Ferrer would proceed to an annual defrost with the aid of a hair-dryer and a bread-knife. The chiaroscuro depths of the wc had been colonised by tartar, saltpetre and purulent plaster, but a wardrobe concealed six dark suits, an array of white shirts, and a battery of neckties. The point is that when Ferrer is doing his gallery-owner thing he makes it a rule to be impeccably turned out: he comes across with all the sober austerity of a politician or a bank manager.

In what passed for a living room there was nothing to recall the previous artistic activities of the gallery owner, except for a couple of posters advertising exhibitions at Heidelberg and Montpellier. Saving also for two blocks of marble, disgruntled and pockmarked, which served as coffee table or to stand the television on; the secret of the shapes that were one day supposed to emerge from them is something they were destined forever to keep to themselves. They might have been a skull, a fountain, a nude, but Ferrer had already given up.

4

IT WAS NOW AN ICEBREAKER A HUNDRED METRES LONG and twenty in the beam: eight traction engines coupled together developed 13,600 HP, maximum speed 16.2 knots, draught 7.16 metres. Ferrer had been shown to his cabin: furniture bolted to the bulkhead, sink with pedal-operated tap, video screwed to the extension of the single bunk, and Bible in the drawer of the bedside table. Plus a small fan, a paradox in view of the heating, which was turned up full blast and generating a thirty-degree fug, as tends to be the case in all polar installations, be they ships, tractor cabins or buildings. Ferrer unpacked his things into the cupboard and kept within reach, by his bunk, a book all about Inuit sculpture.

The crew of the *Des Groseillers* comprised fifty men along with three women whom Ferrer spotted at the outset: a compact young coloured girl who had charge of the mooring cables, a nail-biter in charge of the accounts, and a nurse with an ideal nurse's build, discreet make-up, delicate suntan, not much on beneath her smock; her duties extended to the library and the video collection; and her name was Brigitte. As Ferrer was soon in the habit of dropping in on her to borrow books and videos he was to realise in a day or two that Brigitte at eventide went to join a square-jawed radio officer with a slim nose and handlebar moustache. Not much hope in this quarter, therefore, but we should see, we should see, it's early days.

The first day, on the bridge, Ferrer met the people in command. The captain looked like an actor and his first mate like a compere, but that's as far as it went; the rest of the officers, senior and junior, rang no particular bells. With the introductions over, conversation soon dried up and Ferrer sloped off to look over the huge, warm body of the icebreaker, progressively solicited by her smells. At first glance she was clean as a whistle and did not smell of anything in particular, but on further investigation it was possible to pick up, in the following order, phantom wafts of diesel oil, burning fat, tobacco, vomit and compacted garbage cans, then, on further exploration, a floating, flaccid, foul swash of damp or condensation, brackish drains, querulous plumbing.

Tannoys buzzed with orders, giggles came from behind half-open doors. Following the companionways, Ferrer ran into crew members of various kinds without speaking to them; stewards or engineers little accustomed to the presence of non-professionals on board, and in any case too preoccupied. In addition to their functions in running the ship, most of them were busy all day in vast engineering or electrical workshops, crammed with enormous machines and tiny, delicate instruments, down in the bowels of the vessel. The only one he managed to have a moment's conversation with was a bashful sailor, a vulnerable, well-muscled young man, who drew his attention to some birds of passage. The ptarmigan, for instance, the eider from which eiderdowns are made, the fulmar, the petrel, and I think that was about the lot.

That was about the lot, the high-fat meals happened at fixed times, and there was only a brief half-hour every evening when the bar was open to dispense a beer or two. After the first day of exploration, with the misty day that followed time began to fray. From his cabin scuttle Ferrer watched Newfoundland slip by to starboard before the ship coasted along the Labrador shoreline as far as Davis Bay then Hudson Strait, without ever being aware of the engines' rumble.

The still air that bathed the high, purple, ochre-brown cliffs was frozen, therefore heavy; it bore down with all its weight on an equally motionless sea, of a sandy grey-yellow colour. Not a breath of wind, not a ship, soon scarcely a single bird to animate it with the smallest movement, not a sound. The cliffs were deserted, dotted with moss and lichen like ill-shaven cheeks, and dropped sheer to the water. Through the even layer of fog it was possible to imagine rather than see the edges of the glaciers descend from the summits at their imperceptible speed. The silence remained intact until the pack ice was reached.

As this was relatively thin to begin with, the icebreaker started by forcing a passage head-on. Soon enough, though, it became too thick for her to be able to continue in that way. She began then to try running up onto the ice in order to crush it under her weight; but the pack ice would shatter, fissuring in all directions as far as the eye could see. Ferrer went down into the hull, separated from the impact by sixty millimetres of metal, and listened from close by to the sound this produced: a tape-recording of a haunted castle, all dragging chains, screeches and growls, low rumbles and sundry scrapings. Back on the bridge, however, all he was to hear was a constant light cracking, like some material that tears without resistance above the head of a silent, motionless nuclear submarine resting peacefully on the sea-bed, with people in it who are cheating at cards as they vainly wait for their orders to be countermanded.

On they went, the days passed. They met with nobody else except, once, for another icebreaker of the same make. They hove to for an hour on the other's beam, then pressed on when the skippers had exchanged charts and fixes, but that was all. These are regions that no-one ever visits even though they are more or less claimed by a good number of nations: Scandinavia because that is where the first explorers hailed from, Russia because she is not that far away, Canada as being in the offing, and the United States because because because. Two or three times abandoned villages were to be seen on the Labrador coast, originally built by the central government for the benefit of the natives, and fully equipped, from the power station to the church. But they were not adapted to the needs of the locals, who tore them down before deserting them in order to go and commit suicide. Next to some gutted barracks carcasses of dried seals were to be found here and there, dangling from gibbets, the only reminder of the stores thus kept out of reach of the polar bears.

All this was interesting, it was empty and majestic, but after a few days it was a tiny bit tiresome. It was then that Ferrer started haunting the library, getting out classics of polar exploration – Greely, Nansen, Barents, Nordenskjöld – and all manner of videos – *Rio Bravo*, *Kiss Me Deadly*, of course, but also *The Check-out Girls* or *The Voracious Alumna*. These latter he borrowed only once he was sure of Brigitte's liaison with the Radio Officer: once he had abandoned hope of making out with the nurse, he was no longer bothered about discrediting himself in her eyes. Vain scruples: it was with an even smile, full of maternal indulgence, that Brigitte logged out indifferently *The Four Horsemen of the Apocalypse* or *Let's Get Stuffed*. Her smile was so reassuring and permissive that Ferrer soon had no hesitation about dreaming up every other day some affliction that was easy to fudge – headaches, twinges – in order to go in search of treatment, be it a pill or a massage. It worked all right, at least to start with.

5

WHAT WAS NOT WORKING SO WELL, SIX MONTHS earlier, was business at the gallery. The thing is, at the time I'm speaking of, the art market was not all that brilliant nor, be it said in passing, was Ferrer's last electrocardiogram. He had already had some cardiac alerts, a mild coronary whose only consequence was to make him stop smoking, a point on which his specialist, Feldman, had shown himself intransigent. Thenceforth, if his life punctuated with Marlboros had seemed to him up to that point like climbing a knotted rope, once he was denied cigarettes it was like forever climbing the same rope but bereft of knots.

These last years Ferrer had assembled a small pool of artists whom he regularly visited, occasionally advised, obviously disturbed. Not sculptors, given his own antecedents, but painters, of course, like Beucler, Spontini, Gourdel and especially Martinov who these days was on the up and up and who worked only in yellow; and also a few people in the plastic arts. Eliseo Schwartz, for instance, who specialised in extreme temperatures and created closed-circuit bellows (Why not insert valves, Ferrer proposed, just one or two?), and Charles Esterellas, who installed here and there little mounds of icing sugar and talc (Wouldn't you say all this is somewhat lacking in colour? Ferrer ventured to ask), Marie-Nicole Guimard, who went in for enlargements of insects' stings (And why not take a look at the same idea with caterpillars? Ferrer imagined. And snakes?), and Rajputek Fracnatz, who worked exclusively on sleep (Go easy on the barbiturates, though, suggested Ferrer anxiously). But for one thing, nobody was all that taken with such works at times like these, and for another these artists, not least Rajputek, when he was startled out of his sleep, eventually made it clear to Ferrer that his visits were not welcome.

In any event none of this stuff was selling all that well any more. Gone were the days when the telephones were constantly bawling, faxes endlessly spewing out, art galleries the world over demanding news of artists, artists' opinions, artists' biographies and photos, artists' catalogues and projected exhibitions. There had been some quite giddy years, amusing in their way, when there was no problem taking care of all these artists, obtaining for them scholarships in Berlin, residencies in Florida, teaching posts in art schools at Strasbourg or Nancy. But now the fashion seemed to have had its day, the seam was exhausted.

Unable to convince enough collectors to buy these works, and noting, besides, that ethnic art was gaining ground, Ferrer had finally, some time back, shifted his field of activities. He somewhat distanced himself from his plastic artists, while definitely continuing to look after his painters, especially Gourdel and Martinov – the latter in full flight, the former on the way out – but now he envisaged concentrating on more traditional practices, Bambara art, Bantu art, art of the Plains Indians, that kind of thing. To advise him on his investments he had secured the services of a competent pundit called Delahaye who remained on hand at the gallery three afternoons a week.

In spite of Delahaye's professional qualities, his outward appearance worked against him. Delahaye was all curves. Curved backbone, flabby face and scrubby asymmetrical moustache that irregularly masked the whole of his upper lip to the point of disappearing back inside his mouth, and certain hairs even grew up into his nostrils against the current as it were; the thing was overgrown, it had a factitious air, one would say a false moustache. Delahaye's gestures flowed, they were rounded, his gait and his mental processes were equally sinuous, even the earpieces of his glasses were twisted, the lenses lived on two different floors, in a word nothing in him was rectilinear. "Do stand up a little straighter, Delahaye," Ferrer would sometimes tell him crossly. The other would not oblige. Ah well, can't be helped.

The first months after leaving Issy, Ferrer took full advantage of his new rhythm of life. He disposed of a towel, a dish and half a cupboard at Laurence's, and to begin with he was to sleep every night at her flat in Rue de l'Arcade. Then, little by little, the system broke down: it was to become every other night, then every third, and soon every fourth, and Ferrer spent the rest at his gallery, on his own at first, then less so, until the day when Laurence told him: "Right, off you go, now, hop it. Collect your clobber and shove off."

"O.K.," said Ferrer (fact is, I couldn't care less). But after a cold night of his own company in the back room of the gallery, he was up early and off he went to push open the door of the nearest estate agents'. This crummy studio, it can't go on. He was invited to look at an altogether different apartment in Rue d'Amsterdam. "It's your typical Haussmann thing, if you know what I mean," said the agent: "mouldings on the ceiling, parquet floors, double living room, double entrance hall, glass-panelled double doors, tall mirrors over marble fireplaces, vast passages, maid's room, and a three-month deposit." "O.K.," said Ferrer (I'm taking it).

He moved in. It took a matter of a week to buy a few sticks of furniture and sort out the plumbing. Feeling ensconced at last, one evening, in one of the armchairs he was running in, a glass in his hand, an eye on the television, there was a ring at the door and there stood Delahaye, unannounced. "I'm only stopping for a moment," said Delahaye, "I just wanted to raise something with you – if I'm not interrupting." Given his diminutive stature and corpulence, which prevented him in principle from hiding any person or object behind his back, it did seem as if this time there were some presence behind Delahaye, in the darkness of the landing. Ferrer lightly rose on tiptoe. "Yes," said Delahaye turning round, "forgive me. I'm with a friend, she's a bit introverted. May we come in?"

There are people, as anyone can observe, with a botanical physique. There are those who evoke foliage, trees or flowers: sunflower, bulrush, baobab. As for Delahaye in his sloppy attire, he evokes those grey, anonymous plants that grow in towns between the cracks in the paving of an abandoned warehouse forecourt, in a crack defacing some decayed façade. Consumptive and colourless as they are, they maintain a discreet but tenacious hold on life, knowing that they have but a minor role, but perfectly capable of hanging onto it.

If Delahaye's anatomy, his body language, his fuddled elocution evoked stubborn weeds, the girl accompanying him hailed from a different part of the vegetable patch. Victoire was her first name, a pretty, silent plant at first glance, that looked like an uncultivated species rather than something pleasingly ornamental, datura rather than mimosa, not so much a blossom as a thorn, in a word she did not look terribly accommodating. Be that as it may, Ferrer realised at once that he was not going to take his eyes off her. "Of course," he said, "come on in." Then, listening to Delahaye's confused outpouring with but half an ear, he did all he could to make himself intriguing without appearing to try, and to catch her eye as much as possible. A waste of effort: at first glance he seemed a long way from scoring, but you never know. In any event, what Delahaye had to report that evening was not without interest, though it could have been better related.

On 11 September 1957, he explained, in the far north of Canada, in the region of Mackenzie, a small freighter called *Nechilik* was caught in the ice off the coast, at a point which to this day has not been exactly determined. She was on passage between Cambridge Bay and Tuktoyaktuk when she was caught in the pack ice, and she was carrying a load of pelts – fox, bear, seal – as also a cargo of ancient local artefacts deemed to be extremely rare. Running aground after hitting a reef, she was trapped at once by the ice. Fleeing the paralysed vessel, at the price of many a frostbitten limb, the crew made their way with great difficulty to the nearest base, where some of these members had had to be amputated. In the weeks that followed, even though the cargo represented a considerable value on the market, the isolation of this region had discouraged the Hudson Bay Company from trying to salvage the ship.

Delahaye reported these facts about which he had just been informed. He had even been given to understand that it should be possible on diligent enquiry to obtain a more exact fix on the location of the *Nechilik*. This was all, of course, not a safe bet, but if more precise information were forthcoming, the operation could prove to be of greater interest. In fact, as a rule, the steps towards the discovery of a work of ethnic art or of an antiquity number four or five. For a start it is usually a dead-end hole where the object is discovered; then it is usually the local chief who has control of this kind of traffic in his patch; then it's the specialist in the artefact concerned who gets involved; lastly it's the gallery owner who generally provides the final link in the chain before the collector. All this little crowd, of course, gets richer and richer, the object at least tripling in value at each stage. Now in the case of the *Nechilik*, if some initiative turned out to be feasible, all these middlemen might be sidestepped by going into action directly in the locality: that way a great deal of time and money would be saved.

But that evening Ferrer, truth to tell, had paid scant attention to this recital, being too much taken up with this girl Victoire, little reckoning that she would have moved in before a week was up. Had he been so advised, he would have been delighted, even though he would no doubt have harboured a touch of concern. But had he been told that each one of the three people gathered in his flat this evening was about to disappear in his or her own way before the month was out, not excluding himself, he would have been considerably more alarmed.

6

THE DAY THEY CROSSED INTO THE ARCTIC CIRCLE this crossing of the line would normally be celebrated. Ferrer was given notice of it in an allusive manner, in a mocking and vaguely threatening tone, as if for an inescapable initiation. He ignored the threat, however, supposing this rite to be reserved for the equator, the tropics. But no: such things are celebrated just as much in the cold.

That morning, therefore, three sailors disguised as succubi stormed, yelling, into his cabin and blindfolded him, then rushed him at the double through a network of corridors as far as the sports hall, which was draped in black for the occasion. His blindfold was removed; on a dais in the middle Neptune sat enthroned in the presence of the captain and some junior officers. Complete with crown, toga and trident, and with diver's flippers on his feet, Neptune, played by the Chief Steward, was flanked by the nail-biting woman in the role of Amphitrite. Rolling his eyes, the God of the Oceans bade Ferrer prostrate himself, repeat after him a string of gibberish, measure the sports hall with a short ruler, retrieve a ring of keys with his teeth from the bottom of a bowl of ketchup, and other innocent tribulations. The whole time that Ferrer did as bidden it seemed to him that Neptune was discreetly cursing out Amphitrite. Thereafter the captain delivered himself of a brief discourse, then presented Ferrer with his diploma of passage.

This done, and the Arctic Circle crossed, a few icebergs began to heave into sight. But only in the distance: icebergs are objects that vessels prefer to steer clear of. Sometimes scattered as they floated on the current, sometimes in a motionless group like a flotilla at anchor, some of them were smooth and glistening, immaculate ice through and through, while others were dirty, blackened, yellowed by the moraine. Their contours suggested the profiles of animals or geometrical shapes, and in size they varied between Place Vendôme and the Champs-de-Mars. And yet they seemed more discreet, more eroded than their fellows in the Antarctic which moved about thoughtfully in great tabular blocks. These ones were also more angular, asymmetrical and baroque, as if they had tossed and turned a great deal in a bad night's sleep.

At night, when Ferrer too was sleeping badly, he would leave his bunk to go and kill time up on the bridge with the men on watch. Vast and empty as a station concourse at daybreak, the bridge was glassed in on every side. Under the somnolent control of an officer, two helmsmen took four-hour tricks before the consoles, echo-sounders and radar screens, their eyes glued to the steering compass. Ferrer settled down in a corner on the thick carpeting. He looked out at the scene lit up by powerful projectors, not that there was anything to much to look at, after all, nothing except an infinity of white on black, so very little to see that sometimes it was all too much. To keep busy he would look at the chart table, the Global Positioning Satellite indicator and the faxed weather reports. Rapidly initiated by the men of the watch, he would kill time by running through every waveband on the radio receiver: the complete sweep took a good fifteen minutes, which is always that much time got through.

In fact there was only one event, when for technical reasons the vessel hove to in the middle of the ice pack. As a ladder had been put down – on the rungs the ice formed miniatures in the shape of mountains – Ferrer climbed down to take a look around. Silence, endless silence, not a sound but those of his footsteps muffled by the snow and the soughing of the wind, once or twice the cry of a cormorant. Moving off a little way in spite of the recommendations made to him, Ferrer noticed a family of sleepy walruses, snuggled up to each other on an ice floe. These were old, monogamous walruses, bald and bewhiskered, their hides all scored in combat. They were accompanied by their mates and, opening an eye from time to time, a cow would fan herself with the tip of a flipper before nodding off again. Ferrer returned on board.

Then things resumed their course, their endless course. There was, however, a way to fight off boredom: time could be sliced up like a sausage. You cut it up into days (D minus seven, D minus six, D minus five before arrival), but also into hours (I'm feeling a touch peckish: H minus two before dinner), into minutes (I've had my coffee: generally M minus seven or eight before I head for the toilet), and even into seconds (one turn round the bridge: S minus *c.* thirty; between the time it takes to decide on it beforehand and to reflect on it afterwards, you've got through a whole minute). In a word all it takes is to count, as in prison, to give a time-value to everything you do – meals, video, crosswords, strip cartoons – to strangle tedium at birth. Equally, though, you can do nothing at all, spend the morning in yesterday's T-shirt and underpants on your bunk reading, putting off until later the business of getting washed and dressed. As the ice pack projects a blinding and brutal whiteness through the cabin scuttle, which invades the entire area without affording the tiniest shadow by scialytic effect, you hang a towel over the aperture, and you wait.

Even so there is the odd distraction, however paltry: the regular inspection of the cabins by the Chief Engineer and the Safety Officer, boat drill, and the timed donning of the buoyant thermostatically controlled survival suit. There are also the visits, as frequent as possible, to Brigitte the nurse, you can take your chances on a little canoodling while the Radio Officer is on duty, you may compliment her on her abilities, her looks, her tan – a paradox in this climate, but it transpires that, to avoid depression or worse, a collective agreement has provided that in regions deprived of sunshine the female staff is entitled to four hours a week under the ultraviolet rays.

The rest of the time is Sunday, a perpetual Sunday, whose felt-padded silence creates a distance between sounds, objects, even instants: the whiteness contracts space and the frost slows down time. You grow sleepy in the amniotic warmth of the icebreaker, you do not even think any more of moving in this stiff-jointed world, after crossing the line you never once set foot in the sports hall, in fact you concentrate essentially on mealtimes.

7

VICTOIRE: PUPIL ALERT IN AN ELECTRIC-GREEN IRIS like the eye of those old radios, a frosty smile but a smile nonetheless – Victoire moved into Rue d'Amsterdam.

She had arrived without much in the way of luggage, just a small suitcase and a bag that she dropped in the entrance hall, as if leaving them there for an hour at Left Luggage in a railway station. And in the bathroom, apart from her toothbrush, just a minute sheath containing three foldable accessories and three beauty-care samples.

There she remained, spending most of her time reading in an armchair in front of the television with the sound switched off. For the rest, she talked little, in any event as little as possible about herself, answering questions with a question of her own. She seemed constantly on the qui vive, even when no external threat justified it for all that this mistrustful air did sometimes risk precisely giving rise to aggressive ideas. When Ferrer had visitors she always behaved as though she were one of them, he expected to see her leave around midnight along with the rest, but she stayed on, she stayed.

Among the other consequences of Victoire's presence at Ferrer's, Delahaye was to be seen dropping by more frequently, looking as scruffy as ever. One evening when he turned up at Rue d'Amsterdam more scandalously turned out than usual, in a shapeless parka flapping loosely over green jogging bottoms, Ferrer thought fit to react just as the man was preparing to leave. Detaining him for a moment on the landing ("Don't take it amiss, Delahaye"), he put it to him that it would be all to the good if he dressed a little more suitably when he came to mind the shop, an art dealer needs to take care of his appearance. Delahaye looked at him uncomprehendingly.

"Put yourself in the collector's shoes," Ferrer had persisted, dropping his voice, as he gave a further push to the timer-button controlling the stair lights. "This collector, he's about to buy a picture off you. He hesitates. And you know what it means to him, buying a picture, you know perfectly well how terrified he is of losing his investment, terrified of being off-beam, terrified of missing a Van Gogh, terrified of what his wife's going to say, and so on. He's in such a twitch he's not seeing the picture any more, right? All he sees is you, the salesman, in your sales-man's outfit. So it's your appearance that he's going to put on the picture, are you with me? If you're dressed like a pauper he's going to invest it with all your poverty. But if you're looking smart as a new pin, that's quite another matter, so it's good for the picture, so it's good for everyone and particularly for us, do you follow me?"

"Yes," Delahaye had said, "I think I see." "Good," Ferrer had said, "well, see you tomorrow." "D'you think he cottoned on?" he asked Victoire after this, with little hope of an answer, but she had already gone to bed. Turning out the lights one by one, Ferrer had reached the darkened bedroom, and the following afternoon he was in the gallery dressed in a chestnut-coloured tweed suit, striped shirt, navy on light blue, knitted tie, brown and gold. Delahaye was already there, five o'clock shadow, same outfit as before except even more crumpled, anyone would think he sleeps in it, take a look at that shirt.

"I think we're getting somewhere with the *Nechilik*," said Delahaye. "The what?" said Ferrer. "That boat," said Delahaye, "you know, the one with the antiques. I think I've got a line on it." "Oh, right," said Ferrer evasively, distracted by the tinkle of the bell on the shop door. "Mind," he whispered, "a visitor. Réparaz."

Réparaz, he knew him, he was a regular. He made pots of

money in business and was bored stiff – it's not always so uplift-ing to have the world monopoly on Smartex. His only moments of moderate amusement were when he'd come to buy some work of art. And he liked to listen to advice, to hear how the market's going, to be taken off to meet artists. One Sunday when Ferrer took him to the studio of an engraver up near Porte de Montreuil, Réparaz, who never left the VIIth arrondissement except to cross the Atlantic in his private jet, was tickled pink to be crossing the XIth. "My goodness, the architecture, the exotic population, unbelievable, I wouldn't mind doing this with you every Sunday. Fantastic! Time well spent," Réparaz considered. In spite of which he was one of the world's vacillators. At the moment he was smooching around a big Martinov, a yellow acrylic, on the pricey side, going up close, then standing back, then going up close, etc. "Now watch this," muttered Ferrer to Delahaye, "just you watch. I'm going to talk him out of it, that's something they love."

"Well," he said, moving across to the Martinov, "you like it?" "H'm, it has something," said Réparaz, "there's something about it. It strikes me as, well, you know what I mean." "Of course, I'm right with you," said Ferrer. "But the fact is it's no great shakes, between you and me, it's nothing near the best in the series (it's a series, you see), besides which it's not completely finished. Quite apart from his being frankly a bit on the expensive side, Martinov." "Oh? Right," said the other. " Seems to me that that yellow really has something." "You're right," agreed Ferrer, "it's not bad, I won't deny it. But even so, it's a bit pricey for what it is. If I were you, I'd sooner take a look over there," he went on, pointing to a work consisting of four aluminium squares painted light green and juxtaposed, propped up in a corner of the gallery. "Now there's something interesting. Before long it's going to appreciate quite a bit but it's still affordable. And look at all the light in it, you can't miss it, the luminosity."

"Even so, there's not all that much to it," said the mogul. "I mean, there's not much in it to look at." "At first glance," said Ferrer, "that's how you might see it. But at least when you step into your home and you have that on your wall, it doesn't assault you." "That's true. I'm going to think about it," said Réparaz as he left. "I'll be back with my wife." "Perfect," said Ferrer to Delahaye. "You wait and see. You can be sure he'll take the Martinov. Sometimes you have to head them off. You have to make them think they got there on their own. Hang on, here's the next."

Aged forty-eight, tuft of hair beneath his lower lip, velvet jacket, smiling, name of Gourdel, a stretcher wrapped in brown paper tucked under his arm, the next was a painter Ferrer had been looking after for ten years. He brought a painting and asked how things were going.

"Not too well," answered Ferrer wearily. "You remember Baillenx who took one of your pictures? Well, he brought it back, didn't want it after all, I had to take it back. Of course there was also Kurdjian, you remember, who was thinking of buying. Well, in the end he's not going to, he'd sooner buy an American. And then you have two hefty pictures that went for auction; they fetched a derisory price, so the fact is, things are not look-ing too good." "Oh well," said Gourdel with a dwindling smile as he unwrapped the stretcher, "here's what I've brought."

"You have to recognise it's a little bit your own fault," pursued Ferrer without a glance at the object. "You really blew it when you moved from abstract to figurative, I had to overhaul my strategy for your work completely. You know the problems it causes when a painter keeps changing the whole time, people are expecting one thing and they're left disappointed. You know that everything is pigeonholed but even so it's easier for me to promote something that does not change too much, otherwise it's a disaster. You know how brittle it all is. Well, you can see for yourself, I don't have to tell you. Anyway I can't take this one, I want first of all to sell the rest."

Pregnant pause, then Gourdel wrapped up his stretcher any old how, nodded at Ferrer and left. On the pavement he ran into Martinov on his way in. Martinov is a young man with an innocently canny look, they stopped to exchange a few words. "He's putting me out with the trash, blast him," said Gourdel. "I'd be most surprised," said Martinov to console him. "He knows what you do, he has faith in you. And he does have some artistic flair." "No," said Gourdel before disappearing into the half-light, "no-one has artistic flair any more. The only people who used to have a little were the popes and the kings. But nobody since them."

"So you saw Gourdel," said Ferrer. "Yes, I just ran into him," said Martinov, "he didn't look on top of the world." "He's quite falling apart," said Ferrer. "The bottom's dropped out of his market, he's nothing, a complete zero. You, you're quite another matter, you're doing famously at the moment. A chap came in a minute ago, he's sure to take the big yellow picture. Aside from that, what are you working on at present?" "Well," said Martinov, "I had my vertical series, I'm going to include two or three in a group exhibition." "Hang on a minute," said Ferrer, "what's all this about?" "Nothing," said Martinov, "it's only for the National Savings Bank." "What's that?" said Ferrer, "you're going to take part in a group exhibition for the National Savings Bank?" "Why not?" said Martinov. "There's nothing wrong with the National Savings Bank." "Personally," said Ferrer, "I find it absurd that you should be exhibiting at the National Savings Bank. Quite absurd. And a group exhibition what's more. Talk of depreciation! Take it from me. O.K. go ahead and do it."

So Ferrer was not in the best of moods when he went on to listen to Delahaye's general account of art north of the Arctic Circle: the Ipiutak school, the Thule, Choris, Birnik schools, the

Denbigh culture, ancient cultures of the early whalers dating back to between 2,500 and 1,000 BC. When Delahaye compared the materials, the influences, the styles, Ferrer paid less attention than when the man was talking figures: it seemed increasingly probable that this story of a wreck abandoned in the cold would be worth the visit, if it turned out to be a fact. For the present it was all unconfirmed, in the absence of more precise information. But we were now towards the end of January and at all events, as Delahaye reminded him, even if there was more information to hand, the weather conditions precluded setting out before the spring, at which point in those high latitudes the daylight makes its appearance.

8

I T WAS INDEED ON THE POINT OF MAKING ITS appearance when Ferrer opened one eye; the scuttle projected a pale blue-grey rectangle on one of the cabin bulkheads. Given the exiguity of the bunk it was not easy to turn towards the opposite wall and, once he had succeeded, he had a bare thirty centimetres of mattress left on which to lie on his side, but at least it was a good deal warmer than previous mornings. He tried to consolidate his position by means of furtive sideways shifts, assuming this to be possible – but all in vain. Then just as he was attempting bolder shifts to win himself a little of this warm space, a sharp reverse thrust flung him backwards and he tumbled out of his bunk.

He landed with all his weight on his right shoulder, thought he had dislocated it, and shivered: the floor of the cabin was all the colder as Ferrer was naked save for his watch. He stood up, making use of all his limbs, then considered the bunk, scratching his scalp the while.

Well, things have changed, so it seems. The unforeseen had come to pass. In this bunk, alone at last and heaving a sigh of relief, the nurse Brigitte turned over before she resumed her snoring, and sank comfortably back into her sleep. Her tan was more sustained and colourful than usual, a bronze that veered towards orange. The fact is, the previous evening she had yet again fallen asleep under the ultraviolet rays, poor thing, she had given herself a tiny bit of an overdose. Ferrer shrugged, shivered again, then looked at his watch – six-twenty – before slipping on a pullover.

He's not feeling all that well, truth to tell, it's a worry. Last time he saw Feldman, the cardiologist warned him against extremes of temperature: great heat or great cold, big jumps in temperature, none of this did a cardiac case any good. "You're not leading a healthy life given your condition," Feldman had said. "There's more to it than giving up smoking, what you need now is to set up a whole regime." So Ferrer took care not to let him know that he was off to the Arctic wastes. He confined himself to some vague mention of a business trip. "All right, then come back in three weeks or a month," Feldman had said, "it'll be time to do a little echocardiogram on you and I'll find reason to stop you playing games." Recalling this discussion Ferrer instinctively placed a hand on his heart, just to check that it was not beating too fast, too slow, too irregularly, but no, it was O.K., it seemed to be doing its stuff.

He was feeling less chilly now, he looked a proper charlie in his pullover, with his poor shrivelled genitals barely bouncing about beneath it. As he waited for something better to do, he glanced out through the cabin scuttle. A distant shimmer suggested the nascent sun reflected for the moment only by the terns with their spotless wings who were wheeling about in the sky above. In this niggardly light Ferrer reckoned that the eroded mass of Southampton Island, grey as a pile of old gravel, was being left to port; they were on the point of entering the channel that led to Wager Bay. Ferrer pulled off his jumper and climbed back into bed.

Easier said than done. Brigitte was decidedly a well-proportioned nurse, but this did not stop her taking up the whole of the bunk: not an inch left to insert so much as an arm. No angle of approach from the side. Taking his courage in both hands, Ferrer chose to approach in a dive, sliding on top of the nurse with all the delicacy at his command. Brigitte, however, started to moan in disapproval. She refused herself, fended him off to the point where he contemplated throwing in the towel, but by luck and by degrees the nurse eventually relaxed. He busied himself – he could only busy himself – with a restricted margin for manoeuvre, the narrowness of the bunk inhibiting most combinations and permitting rather few: the only disposition available is one on top of the other, even if two ways in alternation, and no harm in that. There is no hurry, after all it's Sunday, it's possible to concentrate on the task in hand, to take one's time, and there's no leaving the cabin before ten in the morning.

It was Sunday, a proper Sunday, one could smell it in the air, where a few scattered flights of cormorants stormed about more sluggishly than usual. As he was on his way up to the bridge, he happened upon a group of the crewmen coming out of the chapel, among them the Radio Officer who was ill-disguising his vexation. But Ferrer's goal was now close at hand, anyway, it was only a matter of hours before the Radio Officer was rid of this rival who, on reaching his destination, went up to the skipper and his minions on the bridge and saw to his leave-taking then, back in his cabin, to his packing.

The icebreaker dropped Ferrer at Wager Bay and set sail at once. That day there was an opaque, leaden fog, uniform and pervasive, low as a ceiling, and it hid the adjacent peaks and even the upper structures of the ship, while at the same time energetically diffusing the light. Ferrer went ashore and saw the *Des Groseillers* disintegrate in the fog, her masses dissolving to leave only her contours, then these lines themselves fading out to leave only their intersections, which eventually evaporated in their turn.

Ferrer chose not to linger at Wager Bay: it was nothing more than a cluster of prefabricated huts with rusty corrugated-iron walls pierced by little windows lit with dusty ochre. Among these buildings huddled around a mast, a few sketchy streets were at their last gasp – thin, irregular alleyways, they were

rutted with dirty ice, blocked with snowdrifts, and their intersections were cluttered with dark piles of metal or cement, with
shreds of petrified plastic sheeting. A flag, stiffly outstretched
like washing on the line although frozen in the horizontal,
flapped motionlessly at the top of the mast whose barely
perceptible shadow extended as far as the heliport's narrow
landing pad.

This little heliport was next door to a tiny airport where Ferrer
embarked on a Saab 340 Cityliner, bound for Port Radium;
the plane could carry six people, though apart from himself
there was nobody else on board but an engineer from the
weather station at Eureka. Fifty minutes later Ferrer was meeting
his guides at Port Radium, which resembled Wager Bay like
an ill-favoured brother. They were locals and their names were
Angutretok and Napaseekadlak; they were dressed in padded
eiderdowns in polyester for polar use, aerated underwear,
Day-glo overalls and self-heating gloves. They came from the
neighbouring district of Tuktoyaktuk and were of the same
build, rather stocky and plump, short legs and slender hands,
pentagonal beardless faces, sallow complexion, high cheekbones,
stiff, black hair, gleaming teeth. After introducing themselves
they went on to introduce Ferrer to the sled dogs.

These dogs formed a drowsy pack around a leader in an
enclosure; they were shaggy, dirty, their coats were tawny-black
or verminous yellow; their character was unaccommodating. If
they did not like the men who, liking them not much the better,
never stroked them, neither did they appear to think much
of each other; the looks they exchanged suggested nothing but
cupidity and jealousy. Ferrer would soon recognise that, taken
individually, not one of these animals was all that approachable.
If one of them was called by name, he would barely turn round,
and then only to turn back if he saw that nothing edible was
on offer. If he were urged to get to work he would not respond,

but indicate with a brief sideways glance that it was the pack leader who needed to be addressed. And the leader, a self-important beast, would then put on airs and would make no answer except with a flutter of an eyelid, the peevish eye of a department head at his tether's end, the distrait eye of his secretary attending to her nails.

They set out the same day, see them vanishing into the distance. They are equipped with carbines (Savage 116 FFS All-weather), binoculars (15×45 IS with image stabiliser), knives and whips. Napaseekadlak's knife has an oosik handle, a bone that stands in for a walrus's sexual organ, and whose suppleness, resistance and porosity are ideal for a firm grip. Angutretok's knife is less traditional, a White Hunter II Puma with a Kraton handle.

On leaving Port Radium they engaged first of all in a little defile. On either side snow-encrusted ice had come sliding down to the rocks like a remnant of froth on the sides of an emptied beer glass. They made quite fast progress, each one of them rat-tling about on his sledge, for it was rough going. Initially Ferrer tried to exchange a few words with his guides, especially with Angutretok who had a smattering of English; Napaseekadlak expressed himself only in smiles. But the words, once uttered, echoed but a moment before turning solid: while they remained for an instant suspended, frozen in midair, you had only to stretch out a hand for words to come tumbling out any old how and melt gently between your fingers before being snuffed out in a whisper.

They were assaulted by the mosquitoes from the word go, but fortunately they were very easy to kill. In these latitudes animals have little acquaintance with man, and are quite unsuspecting; you knock them off with a backhander, these mosquitoes, they don't even try to escape. Which does not prevent them from making life unbearable, attacking at the rate of dozens per cubic metre and stinging through your clothing, especially at the shoulders and knees where the material is stretched taut. Any thought of taking a photograph, and their swarming in front of the lens would have blocked out the view – but no-one had a camera, that's not what the trip was about. You blocked the ventilation holes in your cap and moved along beating your sides. Once they spotted a polar bear, but too far off to be a menace.

It was the dogs who posed all kinds of problems. For example one morning, when Ferrer found himself bumped off his sledge by a rutted snow-crest, the vehicle, with no-one in control, went rocking about all over the place. But instead of coming to a halt the brutes, thinking they were free, took off like rockets and in several directions at once. In the end the sledge capsized and got wedged across the trail, immobilising the dogs at the end of their reins and these at once started noisily snarling at each other. Meanwhile Ferrer was trying to pull himself together by the edge of the track, massaging his hip. After getting him back on his feet Angutretok tried to subdue the animals with his whip, but succeeded only in making matters worse; far from simmering down, the first dog to be struck reacted by biting his neighbour, who bit another down the line, who bit another two, who responded in kind, until the whole thing degenerated into a vast battle, into utter confusion. It took no end of trouble to bring them under control. Then they set off again. The Arctic summer was advancing. Night never fell.

9

IN PARIS, AT THE BEGINNING OF FEBRUARY, INITIALLY it was Ferrer himself who might have vanished for good. The end of January had been very busy. Delahaye had kept reverting to the *Nechilik* and the interest it presented, and Ferrer had determined to look into it more closely. He visited museums and private collections, consulted experts, travellers and curators, and began to acquire a good first-hand knowledge of everything to do with polar art and its market value. If what remained of the boat proved to be accessible, there's no doubt that the game would be well worth the candle. Ferrer had even bought two small sculptures from a gallery in the Marais quarter and studied them at length each evening: a sleeping woman from Povungnituk and one from Pangnirtung representing spirits. Although these shapes were unfamiliar to him, he hoped eventually to understand them a little, to recognise their style, the challenges they had posed.

In any case this northern venture remained for the present hypothetical. In spite of his researches Delahaye was making little progress in obtaining information that might pinpoint the whereabouts of the wreck. While awaiting such information, however, Ferrer continued to draw up the broad plans for a prospective expedition. But during these winter days new worries cropped up. The plan for a first Martinov retrospective, after he had given up on the National Savings Bank, water damage in Esterellas's studio which reduced his artefacts made of icing sugar to zilch, Gourdel's attempted suicide, and other preoccupations provoked an unaccustomed flurry of activity. Without even entirely noticing it, Ferrer found himself overburdened with work, like any old rep pushing the latest piece of technology. Such activity was so little within his habits that he never even fully woke up to the fact – and a few days later he would pay the price.

A few days or a few nights because once, during his sleep, a physiological accident occurred: all his vital functions, exhausted as they were, went to sleep at the same time that he did. This did not last for more than two or three hours at the most, but during this time his biological rhythms went on strike. His heartbeat, the air pumping in his lungs, perhaps even his cell replacements delivered only the minimum necessary to assure a barely perceptible survival, a coma of sorts, virtually impossible for the untutored eye to distinguish from clinical death. Nor did Ferrer have the smallest inkling of what was happening inside his body, he didn't feel so much as a pang, at most he experienced it like a dream, and perhaps in fact a dream is what it was. Not such a bad dream either – because he reopened his eyes in a rather cheerful mood.

He woke up later than usual, without having noticed anything. He did not for a moment imagine that he had just been victim of what is known as atrio-ventricular block. Had he been examined, the specialists would no doubt have thought first of all of Mobitz type-II A.V. Block before giving the matter further thought, debating among themselves and plumping for second-degree block of the Luciani-Wenckebach type.

In any case he woke up to find that Victoire was not there. It looked as if she had not come back to sleep. Nothing exceptional about that: it happened now and then that the young woman spent the night at a girlfriend's, generally one Louise, at least that was what she tended to assure him in her remote, evasive manner – and Ferrer was not sufficiently possessive or devoted in his attachment to her to try and find out for himself. Once up, however, he had first assumed that Victoire had chosen a different bed in the course of the night in order to sleep at peace for the simple reason that he snored, he knew he sometimes snored, there was no getting away from it. So he had gone to see if Victoire was sleeping in the end room. No. Never mind. But then, noticing soon enough the absence of her toiletries from the bathroom, then that of her clothes from the wardrobe, then that of her person in the days that followed, he was bound to admit that she had upped stakes.

Within the limits of his available time, he went in search of her as best he could. But if Victoire had ever had any close friends who might have news of her, some kith and kin, some delegate or trustee, she had never introduced them to him. She had very few routines apart from three bars she frequented: the Cyclone, the Soleil, and especially the Central, which was also a haunt of Delahaye's, but the man was not easy to track down at present – he claimed to be fully occupied on the *Nechilik* project. Ferrer had also seen Victoire two or three times in the company of this girl of her own age whose first name was Louise, who rejoiced in a fixed-term contract of employment with French National Railways. He went from bar to bar, saw Louise again, discovered nothing.

So he reverted to a solitary lifestyle – for which he was not cut out. Least of all those mornings when he'd wake up with an erection (which happened most mornings, as is the case with most men) before shuffling about the apartment between the bedroom, kitchen and bathroom. With these comings and goings it was luckily soon no more than a half-erection: but ballasted, almost thrown off balance, by this appendage standing perpen-dicular to the curved vertical of his vertebrae, he'd end up sitting down, opening his post. This was an operation that was almost invariably a disappointment and which generally came to a speedy end with a new sedimentary deposit in his wastepaper basket but which, *mutatis mutandis* if not *nolens volens*, at least returned his appendage to its normal dimension.

No, he's not cut out for the solitary lifestyle, it can't go on. But it's not easy to improvise when one's faced with a sudden void. If Victoire's had not proved all that enduring a presence, it had nonetheless endured long enough to blot out the presence of other women who gravitated towards Ferrer. He always imagined, the simple fellow, that they continued to be there, as if they were spares only hanging around waiting to be needed by him. Well, they were all very much not there, they had not hung around, naturally, they had their own lives to lead. So, as he can't be on his own for long, he'd go poking about here and there. But everyone knows that you don't find a person by looking, better not to seem to be looking, better to behave as if you couldn't care less.

Better to await the chance encounter, especially without seeming to do so. For it is thus, we are told, that great inventions are born, by the unexpected contact of two products haphazardly juxtaposed on a laboratory worktop. Of course it is necessary that these products should actually have been placed beside each other, even if one had not expected to make any such association between them. And of course it is necessary that they be brought together at the same moment, proof that, well before anyone thought of it, the two objects had something in common. That's chemistry for you. One goes all over the place hunting for molecules that one tries to combine: no luck. One sends to the ends of the earth for samples: still nothing. Then one day all it takes is an inadvertent movement, two objects nudged up against each other that have been lying about on the worktop for months, an unexpected splash, a test tube knocked over into a Petri dish and whoops! – the reaction is produced that one has been hoping for year after year. Or perhaps you forget some cultures in a drawer and, bingo! – penicillin.

Well precisely, by just such a process, after long, vain searches during which he pursued his explorations further and further from Rue d'Amsterdam in concentric circles, Ferrer ended by finding whom he was looking for in his neighbour across the landing. Her name was Bérangère Eisenmann. That was certainly not what he had been expecting, the door slap across from his own. Let us not of course forget that such a proximity does not present only advantages, there is the good and the not so good, a question that we would willingly endeavour to look into further if time permitted. But we cannot for the moment develop this angle because a more pressing matter is engaging us: the fact is we have just learnt of Delahaye's tragic demise.

10

THE DOGS WERE GIVING MORE AND MORE TROUBLE. There was the day, for instance, when they came upon the body of a pachyderm caught between two transparent prisms of cutting ice, the corpse had been lying there since God knows when. It was half buried in powdered ice, better preserved than a Pharaoh inside his pyramid: cold embalms as radically as it kills. In spite of the two guides' oaths, exclamations and cracks of the whip, the dogs fell enthusiastically upon the mastodon and after that there was nothing to be heard but panting and the repulsive crunching noise of busy jaws. Once the beasts were surfeited, once they'd made a mere mouthful out of that part of the beast exposed to the air, without even waiting for it to thaw properly, the men had to hang about while the dogs finished their siesta before setting off again. They were beginning to be more than a little fed up with those animals. This would be the last day that their services would be retained. They pressed on, however, in the perpetual daylight that was ever more obscured by the clouds of mosquitoes.

Let us remember that here at this season nothing separates the days, the sun no longer sets. You have to consult your watch to know when it is time to turn in, to put on a blindfold in order to sleep, having first swept the floor of the tent with a gull's wing. As for the mosquitoes, their larvae will have come to maturity in the countless puddles and they attack with a vengeance. It is no longer by the dozen but by the hundred to the cubic metre that they carry out their attacks in close formation, penetrating up your nose, into your mouth, your ears and your eyes as you stride along, treading the permafrost. On the advice of Angutretok, and in flat contradiction to what is prescribed by the Faculty of Medicine as incarnated by Feldman, Ferrer had to take up smoking again even though the taste of tobacco, rediscovered in this cold, made him feel queasy. But it was the only way to repulse the blighters: it was even worth smoking two or three cigarettes together at the height of an assault.

They pressed on along this barely visible track which was marked every two or three kilometres by carefully erected cairns. These were simple stone tumuli stacked up by the first explorers of the region to mark their passage; originally they had served simply as markers to provide a fix, but they could sometimes also contain objects testifying to past activity in the area: old tools, calcified remains of food, redundant weapons and now and then even documents or bones – a skull, for instance, on one occasion, in the eye sockets of which tufts of moss were growing.

It was thus that they proceeded, from cairn to cairn, in reduced visibility, for this was impaired not only by the mosquitoes, fogs also took a hand. Not content with affecting the transparency of the air and thus concealing objects from view, the fogs could also enlarge them considerably. Unlike what is seen in a rear-view mirror, which is always closer than it appears, sometimes the dark silhouette of a cairn looming out of the white immensity seemed to be within touching distance when it was in fact still an hour's march by sledge.

The business with the pachyderm had got the better of the guides' patience. At the first stop after Port Radium, at a place that hired snowmobiles, the dogs were all traded in for three of these vehicles and lightweight trailers were attached. Thus they continued their journey, riding these objects that went farting ludicrously across the Arctic silence like so many mopeds. Leaving behind them on the powdery ice many a splodge of oil and trails of grease, they continued to weave their way between the blocks, sometimes describing long loops to avoid the frozen barriers, and never, ever, passing the smallest tree nor the humblest tuft of grass. The fact is there have been not a few changes in this part of the world over the last 50 million years. Poplars used to grow here, and beech, vines and redwood, but that's all over now. At the most, a couple of days earlier, a little further south, it was possible to notice from time to time the odd bit of lichen, a vague scrap of heather, a puny birch tree or a cringing willow, a small Arctic poppy, the occasional boletus, but that was that, no longer a scrap of vegetation as far as the eye could see.

The rations on which they fed were unvarying, individual portions, a balanced diet, specially devised for this kind of enterprise. But this basic ration was soon improved, on one occasion when they picked up some *angmagssaet* with a view to a fry-up. When a great block of ice fell from a glacier into the sea, a high wave had flung these little sardine-like fish onto the shore; first of all it had been necessary to chase off the seagulls who wheeled silently above the *angmagssaet* and threatened to dive-bomb. On another occasion Napaseekadlak harpooned a seal. Now it is a well known fact that nothing goes to waste in a seal, it is a bit the polar equivalent to the pig: the flesh is grilled, poached, stewed, the blood tastes of egg-white and makes a perfectly sound black pudding, the fat gives one light and heat, its hide is used to make first-rate tent canvas, the bones produce needles, its tendons thread, even the gut is used to make pretty transparent drapes for the home. As for its soul, once the creature is dead, that lives on in the point of the harpoon. Angutretok therefore prepared a dish of seal's liver with ceps on the brazier beside which Napaseekadlak had laid down his harpoon, lest the soul feel the chill. And in the course of dinner Angutretok taught Ferrer some of the 150 words relating to snow in the local idiom, from crusty snow to crunchy snow via fresh, soft snow, hard, corrugated snow, fine powdery snow, wet compact snow and wind-scattered snow.

The further north, the colder it got, not surprisingly. Icicles had taken up residence on every hair of Ferrer's face; hair and eyelashes, beard and eyebrows, nostrils. He and his guides advanced behind dark glasses, skirting the craters hollowed out by meteorites from which the natives would over time extract iron to forge themselves weapons. Once they spotted a second polar bear in the distance, all alone on the pack ice, standing guard over a seals' air-hole. Quite wrapped up in his watch, the bear ignored them, but Angutretok thought it suitable to advise Ferrer on the correct procedure if one stumbled upon a bear. No running away: the bear runs faster than you do. Try rather to distract him, throwing some coloured garment off to one side. But if a confrontation seems inevitable, remember as a last resort that all polar bears are left-handed: go in believing in your ability to defend yourself, and you'd do well to approach the creature by its less energetic side. Pretty illusory, but better than nothing.

11

THERE WAS TO BE NO FUNERAL MASS FOR DELAHAYE, simply a service of benediction in a small church out towards Alésia, late morning. When Ferrer arrived, a fair crowd was already assembled though he could not recognise a soul. He would never have imagined that Delahaye had so many relatives or friends, but perhaps all they amounted to were long-suffering creditors. Discreetly he found a seat at the back of the church, not quite the last row nor behind a pillar, but one row from the back and not too far from a pillar.

All these people had just entered, were about to enter, were entering. To avoid catching anyone's eye Ferrer focused on his shoes, but his peace was of short duration: bucking against the incoming tide, a pale, hollow-cheeked woman in a paisley suit came to introduce herself – Delahaye's widow. "Ah," said Ferrer, who did not know, who would never have imagined, that the man was married. O.K. so he'd been married, well bully for him.

However, as the widow informed him, she and Delahaye had not been living together for six years, they lived in separate accommodation, in point of fact not too remote from each other, for they had remained on good terms, phoned each other twice a week, and each possessed, in case of absence, a key to the other's apartment so as to see to the house plants and the post. But after a week she'd been worried by Delahaye's silence and had ended by going round to his place only to discover his lifeless body on the tiled floor of the bathroom. That's always the problem when you live on your own, she concluded with a questioning look. "Absolutely," Ferrer agreed. Delahaye's widow who had, she said, heard a great deal about him – "Louis-

Philippe was very fond of you" – summoned Ferrer to sit beside her in the front row. "Gladly," he said, the liar, and made a reluctant move. But as it was after all the first time, he told himself, that he was attending such a ceremony, this would give him the chance of a closer look at how these things work.

In fact it could not have been simpler. You have the coffin on trestles, set down with the deceased's feet forward. At the foot of the coffin you have a garland of flowers as ordered by the occupant. You have the priest rapt in meditation upstage right and the MC downstage left – the bloated, rubicund look of a psychiatric nurse, dissuasive expression and black suit, an aspergillum in his right hand. You have all the congregation that has just sat down. And when the church, now practically full, falls silent, the priest recites some prayers followed by a homily in praise of the deceased, after which he invites everyone to bow before the cadaver, or to bless it by means of the aspergillum, whichever is preferred. It's short enough and soon it's over, Ferrer is waiting to see everyone bow when the widow pinches his arm, indicating the coffin with her chin while raising her eyebrows. As Ferrer scowls in perplexity, the widow once more raises her eyebrows and thrusts her chin the more emphatically while subjecting his arm to a harder pinch, and giving him a shove. So it looks as if it's up to him to act. Ferrer gets to his feet, all eyes fasten on him, he is not a little embarrassed, but up he goes. He does not know what to do, he's never done it before.

The MC hands him the aspergillum, Ferrer grasps it without being sure he has it by the right end then starts recklessly shaking it about. While having no particular figures in mind he sketches a few circles and straight lines in the air, as also a triangle and a Saint Andrew's cross, making a complete circuit of the coffin under the bemused eyes of the congregation, quite unable to tell when or how to stop, until the congregation begins to mutter and the MC austerely but firmly hooks him by a sleeve to readdress him to his seat in the front row. Now at this point, startled by the clerical grip on his sleeve, Ferrer lets go of the aspergillum he's still brandishing: the thing goes flying off to thud against the coffin that emits a hollow clang.

Later, somewhat agitated as he was leaving the church, he noticed the widow Delahaye in conversation with a young woman; it took him a few seconds to recognise Louise. They turned in his direction once as they were speaking, but looked away when they saw he was watching them. He decided to approach them, and had to force a passage through the church-goers who were lingering in small groups as on leaving a theatre, and who turned as he passed, as though recognising the actor from the aspergillum scene.

Before Ferrer had put any question to her, Louise repeated straight off that she still had no news of Victoire. The widow, before being questioned either, made it abundantly clear that Delahaye's departure created a void that nothing would ever be able to fill; to such an extent that post mortem, she explained rapturously, it seemed inconceivable that Delahaye would not continue to manifest himself. In the meantime, I'll see you again at the cemetery at teatime. Thus convoked, Ferrer could not get out of it. But the fact remains that post mortem, as he returned home to Rue d'Amsterdam, before he set out again for the burial, a big beige envelope without a postmark slid beneath his door quite outside the postman's normal visiting time, and only heightened Ferrer's unease. The envelope bore his name and address, stencilled, and what it contained were the *Nechilik*'s co-ordinates.

The wreck had gone aground in the Gulf of Amundsen, on the northern edge of the Northwest Territories, longitude 118° E., latitude 69° N., more than a hundred kilometres north of the Arctic Circle and not a thousand from the Magnetic North

Pole. The nearest town was called Port Radium. Ferrer looked in his atlas.

The poles, as anyone knows who has tried, are the hardest places in the world to look at on a map. One never gets quite what one's looking for. There are only two options: you can first try to see them occupying the top and the bottom of a classic planisphere, with the equator taken to be the median horizontal baseline. But in this case it's just as if you were looking at them in profile, in a diminishing perspective, always necessarily incomplete, and this is not satisfactory. Or you can go on to look at them from above, as it were a bird's-eye view: such maps exist. But then it is the way they lie in relation to the continents, which one normally sees so to speak face-on, that leaves one thoroughly confused and that's no good either. In a word, the poles do not take kindly to flat projections. Necessitating as they do a multi-dimensional approach, they pose any number of problems for the cartographic intelligence. A globe would be handy, but Ferrer does not possess one. Ah well, he does eventually manage to pick up a few notions about the area: it's very remote, very white, very cold. This done, it was time to set out for the cemetery. Ferrer left his flat and what did he stumble upon: the scent of the woman across the landing.

Bérangère Eisenmann was a big, cheerful girl, highly scented, jolly in the extreme, scented in the extreme. On the day Ferrer finally noticed her, the affair took off within a few hours. She had stopped in for a drink, then they'd stepped out for a bite, "Shall I leave my bag here?" she had said. "Yes, go ahead and leave it," he had said. Then, the first enthusiasm past, Ferrer had started to have his doubts: women too close by can pose a problem, not least if they live across the landing. Not because they are too accessible, which would be all to the good, but because he, Ferrer, becomes much too accessible to them, possibly that does not suit him. True, nothing is for nothing, true, one needs to know just what it is one wants.

But chiefly, in no time at all, the scent was going to pose a problem. Ecstatics Elixir is a terribly acid and persistent perfume, it wobbles perilously on the crest between spikenard and sewer, it surfeits you as much as it assails you, arouses you as much as it asphyxiates you. Each time Bérangère was to call in on him, Ferrer would need to have a good long wash. A relatively ineffectual remedy, this, so much would the scent seem to have seeped under his skin, so he would change the sheets and towels, toss his clothes straight into the washing machine rather than into the laundry basket where they would have made short work of contaminating everything else once and for all. In vain would he air the flat for ages, the smell would take hours to evaporate, not that it would ever clear off entirely. Besides, it was so powerful a scent that Bérangère only had to call him on the phone for the odour to travel down the telephone wires and reconquer the apartment.

Before meeting Bérangère Eisenmann, Ferrer was unacquainted with Ecstatics Elixir. Now he was still inhaling it as he tiptoed towards the lift: the scent passed through the keyhole, the gaps in the front door, it followed him right into his flat. Of course he could always suggest to Bérangère to switch to another perfume, but he dared not, of course he could always make her a present of another brand of perfume but different arguments dissuaded him, perhaps the gift would commit him too much, oh very well, the North Pole, heaven knows, that's the place to be.

But we're not there yet. First we have to go to the cemetery at Auteuil. It's a small rectangular cemetery, bounded on the west by a big blank wall and on the north, along Rue Claude-Lorrain, by an office block. The other two sides are occupied by buildings whose windows overlook the network of intersecting paths and enjoy a splendid view of the graves. They are not luxury apartment blocks though these elegant quarters are littered with them, but rather a sort of upgraded council housing from whose windows, in the silence of the cemetery, miscellaneous scraps of sound come fluttering down like ribbons, noises from the kitchen or the bathroom, the flushing of a toilet, exclamations in radio quiz games, quarrels and children's cries.

One hour before anyone arrived for the burial, a smaller crowd than in the church at Alésia, a man had stepped into the concierge's of one of these blocks, using the Rue Michel-Ange entrance. This man stood very erect, was sparing with words, his face was expressionless and almost mask-like, he wore a grey suit that looked brand-new. "I'm here about the fifth-floor studio flat which is to let," he'd said. "I was the one who called you on Monday about coming to see it." "Ah yes," the concierge recalled, "name of Baumgarten?" "Tner," the man corrected her, "Baumgartner. Can I take a look at it? You stay put, I'll nip up for a moment and I'll tell you if I'm taking it." The concierge handed him the keys.

The said Baumgartner went into the studio, which was on the dark side because it faced north and had beige carpeting; it had a few sticks of dingy, depressing furniture including a gimcrack bench upholstered in brown stripes soiled with suspicious matter and a whole continent of damp patches, a chipped Formica table, net curtains stiff with greasy dust and tacky bottle-green curtains. But the new arrival crossed this studio without a glance, making for the window which he opened just a chink, standing a little back from it, to one side, so he was invisible from outside because half hidden behind one of the curtains. From there he closely followed the burial service. After which he returned downstairs to the concierge and told her no, it wasn't quite what he was after, it was a bit dingy and too damp, and the concierge admitted that the whole place could have done with a sprucing up.

What a shame, Baumgartner explained, it was precisely in this quarter that he was looking, but he had been told of another place not too far off, and the concierge ungrudgingly wished him good luck, and he left to look at this other place, at the beginning of Boulevard Exelmans. Not that Baumgartner would in any event have taken this studio flat in Rue Michel-Ange.

12

THE *NECHILIK* WAS SPOTTED FROM SOME DISTANCE one fine morning, a little elongated lump, the colour of rust, of soot, as it lay on an ice floe dotted with outcrops of rock, an old broken toy on a tattered cloth. She did in fact seem to be pinched in the ice at the foot of an eroded bluff; this was partially snow-covered, but its face broke down in a succession of short bare cliffs. At this distance the wreck did not seem in too bad a state of preservation: its two short masts were intact, stayed by the shrouds that were still under tension and stood patiently upright, and the wheelhouse at the stern still looked solid enough to afford shelter to shivering phantoms. Knowing, however, that this part of the world teemed with hallucinations, and suspecting at first that this boat was just another ghost, Ferrer waited until he was quite close to assure himself of her reality.

Illusion does indeed reign in this sort of climate. Only the previous evening, as they pressed on behind their dark glasses, without which the Arctic sun fills the eyes with sand and the head with lead, this same sun on a sudden was multiplied in the ice-laden clouds by the effect of parhelion: Ferrer and his guides found themselves dazzled by five suns aligned in a row, among which was the true one – with a further two positioned vertically above it. This had lasted for a good hour before the true sun reverted to being once more on its own.

On first sighting the wreck Ferrer signalled to the guides to be quiet and slow down, as if it were a living thing, no less capable of sudden reactions than a polar bear. They slowed down on their snowmobiles and in due course switched off the motors before making a cautious approach, as slow as that of a mine-disposal team, pushing the contraptions by their handlebars before leaning them against the steel hull of the vessel. Then, while the two natives kept their distance from the *Nechilik* which they considered gravely, Ferrer undertook to step on board by himself.

It was a small freighter, twenty-three metres in length, and a copper plaque riveted to the wheel pedestal gave its date of construction (1942), and port of registration (Saint John, New Brunswick). The hull, superstructure and rigging seemed in good condition, filmed with ice and looking brittle as dead wood. What must have been two crumpled pieces of paper, lying once upon a time on deck among the tangles of rope, had become two pink gypsophila on a background of deep-frozen grass snakes, the whole lot trapped in a layer of ice that did not even splinter under Ferrer's boots. He went into the wheelhouse and took a quick look round: an open logbook, an empty bottle, a discharged rifle, a 1957 calendar adorned with a somewhat under-dressed girl, a brutal reminder that seemed to bring home just how extreme was the ambient temperature, somewhere around 25° C below. The pages of the log were frozen together, there was no leafing through it. Through the wheelhouse windows, which nobody had looked through for more than forty years, Ferrer glanced at the whitened landscape. Then he went down to inspect the hold, and found straightaway what he was looking for.

Everything seemed to be present as expected, packed into three large metal chests that had manfully weathered the intervening time. Ferrer struggled to free their lids sealed by the cold, then, after a summary inspection of the contents, went back up on deck and summoned his guides. Angutretok and Napaseekadlak joined him cautiously, respectfully and not without hesitation, moving about the boat as if they'd broken into a person's second home. The chests being heavy, and the iron companion ladder giving access to the hold being supernaturally slippery, it would be the devil of a job to haul them up on deck before taking them off. They secured them as best they could on the snowmobile trailers, then paused for breath. Ferrer said nothing, the two guides chuckled, bandying untranslatable jests. They seemed to take the whole thing very lightly while Ferrer himself was rather moved. Good. That's it, then. Nothing left but to head for home. But how about a quick bite, suggested Napaseekadlak, before setting off.

Ferrer detailed him off to light the fire, and he used his axe to chop up the *Nechilik*'s mizzenmast while Ferrer, followed by Angutretok, went back into the hold to give it a closer inspection. The furs which made up part of the cargo were still there but, unlike everything else, they were not so well preserved, being hard as tropical wood and nearly all their hair had come away from the skin: probably they no longer possessed much in the way of commercial value. Nevertheless Ferrer took away a small white fox fur that seemed to have survived a bit better than the rest, and which he would defrost to present to . . . whom? That remained to be seen.

In what seems to have stood in for the galley it was necessary to dissuade Angutretok from opening a tin of monkey meat that had been going off for close on half a century. Of course it was a pity not to be able to retrieve the few things still on board the *Nechilik* that could have been in worse shape, some pretty little copper lanterns, for example, a Bible in an elegant binding, a superb sextant. But they were laden enough as it was for the return journey, no excess baggage could be contemplated. Once they had eaten, it was time to head back.

Slowed down by the load, they took a long time returning to Port Radium. Like a ratchet that slips without warning, little blades of biting wind got up now and then to cut their momentum and the polar spring opened up unexpected breaches in the permafrost: on one occasion Ferrer fell into one to mid-thigh, it was quite a business to haul him out and dry him and warm him up again. They spoke even less than on the way out, bolted their food, and slept with one eye open, at any rate Ferrer kept his mind entirely on his loot. At Port Radium Angutretok found him a room through second cousins, in a sort of club or hostel built in cement – this was the nearest they came to a hotel in the locality. Still, once alone in this room, once the chests were opened, Ferrer made an inventory of the contents.

It comprised, as anticipated, very rare artefacts from the ancient whaling tradition, deriving from various styles that Delahaye and other experts had introduced him to. There were, among other things, two carved mammoth tusks coated in blue vivianite, six pairs of snow goggles carved out of reindeer antlers, a little whale carved from whalebone, a piece of laced armour made of ivory, a contraption for putting out caribous' eyes, made of caribou antlers, some inscribed stones, some quartz dolls, some cup-and-ball games made from seals' flipper-bones, from musk-ox horn, there were engraved narwhal tusks and sharks' teeth, rings and awls forged in nickel from meteorites. There were also a good number of magical and funerary objects in the shape of pretzels or merlins, made out of polished soap stone or kidney stone, out of red jasper, green slate and flint, blue, grey, black and every shade of serpentine. Plus all manner of masks, and, last of all, a collection of skulls whose mouths were plugged with lengths of obsidian, the eye sockets stopped up with ivory balls made from walrus tusks and encrusted with jet pupils. A fortune.

13

OW, IF YOU'LL PERMIT ME, FOR A CHANGE OF
scene, to join the man who answers to the name of
Baumgartner. Today, Friday 22 June, while Ferrer is
trudging across the ice pack, Baumgartner is dressed in a pure-
wool charcoal-grey double-breasted suit, a slate-coloured shirt
and an iron-grey tie. Although summer has officially begun,
the sky is in keeping with this outfit, rudely spewing out a little
drizzle at intervals. Baumgartner is on his way up Rue de Suez,
served by the Château-Rouge Metro stop, in Paris's XVIIIth
arrondissement. It is one of those little streets close to Boulevard
Barbès, just the place for African butchers, live-fowl merchants,
satellite dishes and cheerful multicoloured fabrics – all-singing,
all-dancing patterns – printed in Holland.

On the even-numbered side of Rue de Suez, most of the
doors and windows of the dejected old buildings are bricked up
in a crazy pattern of rubblework, a sign of compulsory purchase
prior to demolition. One of them is not entirely plugged up:
two windows on the top floor are still faintly breathing. Curtains
sag behind window panes mat with dust – one is cracked across
and reinforced with tape, the other is missing altogether and
replaced with a black dustbin liner cut to fit. Jammed half-open,
the front door gives first onto two assorted letter boxes, anonymous and gutted, then onto a staircase with irregular treads and
walls generously cracked. Here and there the implacable progress
of these cracks is recorded by marks signed with handwritten
dates entered by the city's building authorities.

The stair-light time switch being out of order, Baumgartner
groped his way up to the top floor. He knocked at a door, and

was about to push it open without awaiting an answer when it seemed to open of its own accord and a tall, thin, wizened type of about thirty came bounding out and almost collided with him. In the dark, Baumgartner could only just make him out – equine face, receding hair line, evil smile, aquiline nose, slender crooked fingers, taciturn and no doubt a night owl since he went charging down the unlit staircase without hesitation.

As Baumgartner pushed open the door, he knew he'd rather not close it behind him: the stifling dump into which he'd penetrated was not one to promote good cheer, it was a sort of indoor tip, a waste ground turned inside out like a glove. If four walls enclosed it and a ceiling protected it, the floor could barely be discerned beneath the rubbish, wrappings of mouldy food, piles of rags, tattered magazines and mildewed brochures scarcely readable by the light of a candle-stub stuck in a beer bottle perched on a crate. The atmosphere, overheated by a butane gas-burner, was nothing but a concentrated fug, a compound of mildew and burnt gas. It was unbreathable. By the head of the mattress a radio-cassette recorder, turned down low, emitted some sort of pap.

The features of the young man lying on this purulent foam-rubber mattress, in a knot of blankets and burst cushions, were not all that distinct either. Baumgartner approached. This young man with closed eyes did not look fresh as a daisy. In fact he looked more dead than alive. The radio-cassette recorder served as support for a teaspoon and a hypodermic syringe, a wisp of dirty cotton wool and the remains of a lemon: Baumgartner saw straightaway what was what, but was nonetheless worried. "Hey, Le Flétan," he said. "Hey. Le Flétan." As he leaned over he saw that Le Flétan was breathing, the man must be slightly indisposed, unless it were a case of being too well disposed. Anyway, even in drawing closer, even bringing up another candle, whatever the distance and the lighting, Le Flétan's physiognomy remained imprecise, as if nature had exempted him from possessing clear-cut features. He was a pale individual, rudimentary, his dark attire no less rudimentary, but he did not look unduly dirty. And now he was anyway opening an eye.

Look at him: he was even propping himself up wearily on his left forearm, and extending a hand to Baumgartner, who withdrew his own as soon as possible from those warm, rather clammy fingers, stepped back and looked around for a chair; his eye rested only on a bockety stool, so he gave up and remained standing. The other slumped back on his mattress, complaining that he felt sick. "What I need," he drawled, "is tea, perhaps, except I don't feel like getting up, I'm really not up to it." Baumgartner made a face, but no doubt he could not refuse, evidently he needed the other to pull himself together a little. Distinguishing in the dark beside the sink a speculative kettle, he filled it and put it on the gas burner, then dug out of the tip a cup that had lost its handle and a chipped bowl. These receptacles were out of proportion to each other. Le Flétan, who had closed his eyes again, took turns now between grinning and grimacing. As he waited for the water to heat, Baumgartner vainly searched for sugar and retrieved what was left of the lemon, for lack of anything better, while the radio-cassette continued to kill time. "Well," said Le Flétan when he had drunk his tea, "when are we going to be able to get on with it?"

"A matter of days," said Baumgartner pulling a mobile phone from his pocket, "should be within the month. Now here's what – from now on I must be able to contact you at any time," he said, handing the object to the young man. "You have to be ready the moment we're up and running."

Le Flétan grasped hold of the telephone, while exploring his left nostril with his forefinger, then, having scrutinised the mobile and his finger in turn, "Marvellous," he concluded after this inspection. "What's the number?" "Don't you worry about the number," said Baumgartner, "I'm the only one to know it, and that's the way it has to be. Here's one thing I must tell you right now about this phone. It's not programmed to make calls on, O.K.? It's only for receiving them. It's only for listening to me when I'm the one calling you, are you with me?" "O.K.," said the young man, wiping his nose on his sleeve. "So you keep it by you at all times, of course," said Baumgartner, filling up the receptacles. "Of course," said Le Flétan. "The other thing," he added, "is I could do with a little something on account."

"Naturally," Baumgartner conceded, and dug in his pocket for six 500-franc notes held together by a paperclip. "Good," said Le Flétan, handing back the paperclip. "Of course more would be better." "No," said Baumgartner, pointing at the stuff sitting on the radio-cassette. " I know you, you'll go and blue the lot on your crap." During the negotiations that followed, which ended up with his handing over another four notes, Baumgartner absently straightened out the paperclip until he had a more or less straight stalk.

Later, out in the street, Baumgartner checked to see that no dirt, no wretched molecule suspended in the atmosphere at Le Flétan's, had settled on his clothing. He brushed himself off, however, as if the foul ambient air could have polluted his clothes, even though he had taken care not to brush against anything, all he'd need would be to scrub his hands, and perhaps his teeth as well, when he got home. Meanwhile he repaired to the Château-Rouge Metro station to return to his new abode. It was still a slack period and the Metro was half empty: there was plenty of room to sit down but Baumgartner chose one of the jump-seats.

In the Metro, whatever the degree of plenitude on the train, and even when it is empty, Baumgartner always prefers these tip-up seats to the fixed seating, unlike Ferrer who prefers the latter. On the fixed seats, which face each other, Baumgartner necessarily risks finding himself seated beside someone or opposite someone, more often than not both the one and the other. Which means brushing against others, body contact and suchlike vexations, problems with crossing and uncrossing one's legs, parasitic stares, and conversations one could do without. All things considered, even if the carriage is crowded and he has to stand up to make room, the jump-seat strikes him as preferable from every angle. It is individual, moveable and flexible. It goes without saying that the all-too-rare isolated jump-seat is in his view even better than the kind paired up with a neighbour, for here too there is some risk of uncomfortable promiscuity – though these are less deleterious than the inconveniences posed by the usual seating plan. That's Baumgartner for you.

Half an hour later, back in his new digs in Boulevard Exelmans, he noticed the little wire stub between his fingers, and could not bring himself to get rid of it, so he stuck it in a flowerpot and went to lie down on the couch. He was going to shut his eyes, wouldn't mind a nap, to switch off for twenty minutes, maybe a half-hour if that's O.K. by you, but no, it was not to be.

14

NEITHER HAD FERRER SLEPT A WINK ALL NIGHT. Kneeling before the open chests, he had turned each object this way and that a thousand times. Now he was exhausted, he no longer had the strength to look at them, no longer saw what he was looking at, was deprived even of the energy to rejoice. Creased from bending, he had straightened up protesting, walked towards the window and seen that the day was dawning but no, wrong, at Port Radium the day had not turned in any more than he had done.

Ferrer's room had the feel of a small individual dormitory, which seems a contradiction in terms but that is how it was: bland, empty walls, naked ceiling-bulb, lino on the floor, cracked washbasin in a corner, bunk beds (Ferrer chose a lower berth) broken television set, cupboard empty save for a pack of cards – just the thing, at first glance, for games of patience but in fact useless because lacking an ace of hearts – strong whiff of Lysol and heating all a-stutter. No reading matter but anyway Ferrer had little inclination to read, eventually he dropped off to sleep.

After visiting the *Nechilik* a short breather at Port Radium was called for – moreover at each breath a whirligig spout of vapour, cotton-dense, would escape from your lips before shattering against the iced marble of the air. Once Angutretok and Napaseekadlak had been thanked, paid off and were on their way to Tuktoyaktuk, Ferrer had to wait a good two weeks in this town where the provision for lodging amounted to this room, adjacent to a laundry. Whether this building was a club, an annexe, a hostel or what, Ferrer was never exactly to discover given that the place was always empty and the manager deprived of speech. Or at any rate sparing of words, because perhaps at bottom he was suspicious, tourists being rare in this backwater abandoned by men and by God – the days drag on endlessly, the distractions are few and far between, the weather's filthy. In the absence of any police station or any representative of the public authorities, the resident stranger could be suspected of escaping from justice. It took no small number of days and dollars, smiles and sign-language before Ferrer was able eventually to circumvent this manager's wariness.

Nor was it easy to find among the inhabitants of Port Radium an artisan capable of constructing containers suitable for the cargo he had got off the *Nechilik*. It was all the harder in that in this climate wood was virtually non-existent: it was in as short supply as everything else, but as usual, everything has its price. Ferrer met the supermarket storekeeper who undertook to make over to the required dimensions the solid packing materials for televisions, refrigerators and other domestic appliances. It couldn't be done in a flash, Ferrer would have to be patient – usually staying in, because he did not want to be too far from his antiquities, getting bored witless when he could no longer bear to keep an eye on them. Port Radium really can be the pits, a place where absolutely nothing happens, least of all on Sundays during which tedium, silence and the cold all play their hand at once and to devastating effect.

He might chance to go out to take a turn around the place, but there was not a great deal to see: three times as many dogs as people, and twenty little houses in pastel shades, with sheet-metal roofs, and two rows of buildings fronting the harbour. Besides, given the temperature, Ferrer was never outdoors for long. Through the almost deserted streets he would make a rapid tour on foot, past all these houses built on a circular plan to prevent the cold catching at the corners, to give the smallest possible exposure to the frost. As he made for the landing stage, he went past the dispensary, painted yellow, the green post office, the red supermarket and the blue garage in front of which snowmobiles were parked in rows. And on the waterfront further rows of boats hauled out and chocked up stood waiting for a milder season. The worst of the snow had melted on land, but the pack ice, penetrated only by a narrow channel, still obstructed the greater part of the bay.

In the prevailing peace he happened to observe some signs of activity. Two provident souls, taking advantage of the thaw, were digging holes in the earth while it was malleable, with a view to burying those of their kinsfolk who were to die in the course of the coming winter. Two others were surrounded by prefabricated materials as they erected their house from a kit, closely following the assembly instructions thanks to an explanatory video-cassette; a generator shot up the silence as it supplied power to the outdoor video-recorder. Three children were bringing empty bottles back to the supermarket. Then, down by the harbour, an old metal-built church dominated the quayside where two iron-grey Zodiacs that had forced a passage through the channel were put-putting as they set down a dozen passengers dressed in anoraks and shod in clodhoppers. The frozen lid of the lake had started to come apart in great sheets with simple outlines, like pieces of a beginners' jigsaw puzzle, and beyond there loitered a good hundred icebergs, large and small, streaming water in the pale sunshine. Returning to his quarters, Ferrer passed again the two men putting up their house. No doubt for a change of fare, to give themselves a break, they had swapped the video-cassette that went with the kit for another of a pornographic nature which they stood solemnly watching, motionless and meditative, without exchanging a word.

Those first days Ferrer took his meals alone in his room and there was nobody to try communicating with except for the manager. But chatting with the manager, even once he seemed to have set his mind at rest, was no great shakes. Besides, there's something wearisome about conversing in nothing but signs. During his brief outings, the locals whose paths he managed to cross would always give him a smile. Ferrer would smile back but that's as far as it went. Then, a couple of days before his departure, as he was trying to peer into a house through its yellowing window panes, he noticed a girl in the background, and she smiled at him as the rest did. As with the others, he smiled back but, this time, the girl's parents took matters in hand. A genial couple with evidently nothing else to do, they invited him for a drink; to freshen up the whisky they sent the girl out to snap off a little ice from the nearest iceberg, then they knocked back their drinks as they chatted in pidgin English; next he was invited to stay to dinner – seal mousse and whale-calf steak. But first he was taken on a tour of the house: it was freestanding, had a telephone and television, large stove and modern kitchen, cheap whitewood furniture Scandinavian style, though it is to be found even in the Paris suburbs.

Thus Ferrer fraternised with the entire Aputiarjuk family. At table, he had some difficulty understanding what the father did for a living until he gathered that the man did nothing. He lived off welfare and preferred to go hunting seals in the great outdoors rather than sweat in a cramped office, in a great big factory or on a large boat. In his view fishing was itself nothing but a ghastly way to earn one's crust, while seal-hunting, that was the ticket, the only sport that afforded real pleasure. Ferrer kept his end up in the matter of toasts, and they drank copiously to seal-hunting, affectionately they drank the health of seal-hunters, enthusiastically they drank to seals in general and soon, their emotions stirred by alcohol, Ferrer was being invited to spend the night with them if he felt like it, there would be no difficulty about his sharing the girl's room, and the next day they would recount their dreams as, in this climate, every family was accustomed to do every morning. Ferrer was hard put to refuse, the lamps gave a gentle glow and the radio was pumping out Tony Bennett, it was snug, the stove was purring, everyone was joking, the girl was smiling at him, ah, Port Radium, tell me about it!

15

THUS, AFTER HIS VISIT TO LE FLÉTAN THE OTHER DAY, it was on a jump-seat in the Metro that Baumgartner reached his new address, then a good week elapsed. This abode was not far from Rue Michel-Ange, behind an unappealing gateway on Boulevard Exelmans: three 1930s villas are scattered pell-mell plumb in the middle of a large garden backing onto the Vietnamese embassy.

Now the thing about the XVIth arrondissement is, you'd never imagine how pretty it can be until you see it from inside. You'd be inclined to think it's quite as depressing as it looks, and how wrong you'd be. Those austere boulevards, those ghastly streets conceived as ramparts – or masks – have in fact nothing sinister about them except their appearance: the homes they conceal are unbelievably attractive. The point is, one of the cleverest ruses of the rich consists in conveying the impression that they get bored to death in their quarters, to the point that one almost starts to feel sorry for them, to empathise and pity them their good fortune as though it were a handicap, as if it imposed on them a depressing lifestyle. Well, you're way off beam, no kidding!

On the top floor of one of these three villas Baumgartner pays a high rent for a very large studio flat. The staircase leading up to it is painted a very dark green, verging on black. As for the studio itself, the walls are in brown marbling, the fireplace in white-veined marble, and spotlights are let into the ceiling. Long, almost empty shelves, a long table with a dirty plate on it, a long sofa with a blue cover. The room is so vast that a vast Bechstein shoved away in a corner is but a detail, and the big television set lodged in a different corner looks like a tiny porthole. No other superfluous furniture: just a massive clothes cupboard holding a substantial wardrobe composed of new-looking clothes. Tall windows give onto acacias, carnations, ivy and gravel extending to a roof terrace rimmed with a narrow, hollow guardrail set in earth in which weeds and such things as dandelion grow without enthusiasm.

In the few days since he started living there Baumgartner went out as little as possible. He did very little shopping, and had his meals sent in via Minitel. Withdrawn as he was from the world, it seemed as though he were biding his time. He did virtually nothing all day. He tipped the delivery boys handsomely. Pursuing his bachelor lifestyle, he looked like a man quite capable of coping on his own. Only he was not a bachelor. The proof is, he'd ring up his wife.

The cordless telephone left him free to stride about the flat as he talked. "Yes," he said as he moved from the Bechstein to the window, "well, you know how it is when you're on your own. Mostly frozen foods," he said by way of clarification as he manipulated the television remote control, cutting the sound and running though the programmes: serials, documentaries, games. "Vitamins, no," he said, "actually I did forget them. Anyway," he continued in the interests of precision, but without completing what he was going to say, and now cutting the picture in order to stare out of the window: clouds, convolvulus, magpies.

"That's right, but I never noticed any chemist hereabouts anyway," he resumed, returning to the Bechstein, sitting down at it and adjusting the height of the piano stool. Depressing the soft pedal, he plunked a chord down on the keyboard, the only third he knew. "Well yes, you heard; it's only a baby grand. Look, listen: it would be as well if you find out the moment he's back, you see," he said, standing up and leaving the piano.

As he passed a flowerpot he pulled out the piece of wire he'd stuck into it the other day: he cleaned off the earth and twisted it into a variety of shapes, spiral, zigzag, television aerial.

"Well how the hell should I know?" he burst out. "You could bat your big eyes at him, whatever. Stop it, well obviously, of course you know," he smiled, rubbing the sides of his nose. "But I think I'd do better to keep out of the way for a bit, I don't want to risk running into anyone. I'm keeping the studio on but I'm going to spend a few days in the country. Of course I'll let you know. No, I'm leaving tonight, I'd as soon be on the road at night. Of course. Of course not. Yes, same to you: kiss-kiss!" He switched off, switched on again and punched in the number he alone knew of the mobile he had given to Le Flétan. It rang for a fair while before the man came on the line. "Hallo?" said Le Flétan, "yes I'm listening, oh, hallo there Mister." At first glance, Le Flétan's voice was not fresh as a daisy: it was torpid, sluggish, mushy, no relief features, vaguely somnolent, the vowels dragged the consonants heavily behind them.

And at Le Flétan's, where as usual the light was as dim as could be, the silhouette of the big fellow in dark clothes whom Baumgartner had passed on the stairs the other day was hard at work fumbling with heaven knows what on a pocket mirror with the aid of a Gillette blade by the radio-cassette recorder, it's impossible to make out anything. The big dark fellow smiled a hard smile as he fumbled.

"What?" said Le Flétan, "what's wrong with my voice? No, I'm not on anything, it's just that I was asleep, that's all, I'm never all that fresh when I'm woken up. Aren't you the same? [The big dark fellow silently mimicked an exaggerated burst of laughter, while taking care not to exhale, no matter what, for fear of scattering two little white lines he was concentrating on.] The problem is, I'm going to need a bit more cash up front. [The dark fellow nodded vigorously.] What d'you mean, out of the

69

question? [The big fellow frowned.] Wait! Hang on a minute! Oh blast: he's hung up on me!"

Baumgartner switched off his phone and packed his bag. As he took a little time choosing his clothes, each item a function of the last, and as he took the occasion to inspect each one minutely, he spent more than an hour on the operation but he had plenty of time: he was not leaving Paris before nightfall. He was going to pick up the ring road as far as Porte d'Orléans, from where he would get onto the motorway and thus down to the south-west via Poitiers, where he was to spend the night.

And in the weeks that followed, Baumgartner was to tour the whole of Aquitaine like a lone holiday-maker, changing hotel every third night, sleeping resolutely on his own. He would seem not to obey any particular imperative, or follow any precise plan. Before long he would leave the Pyrénées-Atlantiques département less and less, killing time in the few museums he happened upon, visiting churches each morning, exhausting every tourist site, patronising empty cinemas in the afternoons to see foreign films dubbed in French. Sometimes he'd drive around at a venture for hours on end, with barely a glance at the scenery, half-listening to the Spanish radio stations, and stopping only for a pee by the roadside, against a tree or in a ditch, sometimes too he'd spend the entire day in his hotel room, confronting piles of magazines or television serials.

Baumgartner, who was apparently concerned to be discreet and evidently wanted to pass unnoticed, would take care to talk to as few people as possible, but, if only so as not to lose the gift of speech, he would continue to ring his wife every evening and Le Flétan every four or five days. But apart from that, whether it was the Clos Zéphyr (Bayonne), the Résidence des Meulières (near Anglet) or the Hotel Albizzia (outskirts of Saint-Jean-de-Luz), he was never to approach a soul.

16

HERE WE HAVE A TERRIFIED RABBIT STREAKING across a broad expanse of grass at daybreak. And here we have a ferret called Winston chasing this rabbit who, seeing the threshold of his burrow not far off, imagines, the simple creature, that he's made it, he's safe. But barely has he dived into it, dashing all the way into his refuge, than the ferret hard on his heels catches up with him in this blind alley, seizes him by the throat, pierces his carotid artery and bleeds him dry in the darkness. He takes his time over draining him of blood and slaking his thirst, as witness the slight crackling sounds induced by fractures, and the obscene sucking noises. Once sated, the ferret looks forward to a well-earned siesta and now goes to sleep beside his prey.

Now here we have a pair of technicians employed by the Aéroports de Paris; they are biding their time at the entrance to the burrow. When they reckon that the siesta has lasted long enough they call the ferret several times by name. Winston pops up in a moment; he looks not a little reproachful, and he is dragging the rabbit by the neck in which he has planted his incisors like so many staples. The technicians grasp the body by its ears before shutting the ferret Winston in his cage. As they ask themselves the usual question of how they'll divide up the rabbit, how they'll cook it, in what kind of sauce, they climb into a small electric vehicle and disappear off between the airport runways, on one of which flight No. QN560 from Montreal has just landed, the flight from which Ferrer disembarks, somewhat creaky and aching from jet lag.

He had had to spend longer at Port Radium than anticipated.

The Aputiarjuk family had made him cordially welcome, he had ended up taking all his meals with them, and the daughter of the house came every evening to join him in his room, so he had allowed the making of the crates to drag out somewhat. In fact for some days, truth to tell, such was the solace afforded by the Aputiarjuk household that he had not even given all that much thought to his antiquities. Happy days at Port Radium! But once the containers were ready, there had been nothing for it but to make up his mind to leave. Ferrer was afraid to disappoint, as usual, but the Aputiarjuk parents had not made a scene on learning that he was not to be their son-in-law, and the farewells, all things considered, had been cheerful enough.

Chartering a Twin Otter, the small twin-engined plane used in the polar regions, and dealing with Customs in Montreal, this had all taken a bit of time. Then the day arrived for returning to France and here we are back again. It was another Sunday, early in July, very early in the morning; the night shift had finished sweeping, scrubbing, washing and polishing up the airport, the escalators and travelators had been switched back on in a long concert of murmurs.

At this time of day almost nobody was at work except for the Customs officers and the airport medics, who were much too concerned with a party of Pakistani would-be jewellers and of self-proclaimed tourists from Colombia to spend much time on Ferrer. To them fell the task of X-raying these arrivals then stuffing them with laxatives to make them expel their precious stones and pessaries full of cocaine, then to pull on gloves and repugnantly retrieve these objects; it fell to them also to get on the trail of traffickers in rare spiders and boa constrictors, of cartons of Virginia cigarettes buried inside manioc flour, of fissile material and forgeries. What with the crowd, that morning, Ferrer had little difficulty in clearing through the cargo channel clogged with suspect packages, he passed unnoticed through the barrage of police and excise officers. Then, once he had recovered all his crates, he had to phone for a van to come and load them up. It was to be all the more complicated, being a Sunday, but Rajputek, waking up with a start, eventually agreed to come, though not without grumbling a bit. While waiting for the van to arrive Ferrer went back again to the waiting room in the Spiritual Centre to kill time.

The Spiritual Centre and the Business Centre are symmetrically adjacent to the Shopping Centre in the basement of the airport building, between the escalator and the lift. The waiting room is on the cold side and is furnished with metal chairs, racks stuffed with leaflets in seven languages, tubs in which five species of green house plants are growing. The three half-open doors are stamped with a cross, a star' or a crescent. Seated in an armchair, Ferrer made an inventory of the rest of the accessories: a wall-mounted telephone, a fire-extinguisher, a collection box.

As at this very early stage in the day there were not many people about, Ferrer risked three glances through the chinks. The microsynagogue was almost bare, three chairs surrounding a low table. The same went for the microchapel, with the addition of a pot of flowers, altar, picture of the Virgin, visitors' book complete with ballpoint pen and two handwritten notices: one mentioned the presence of the Blessed Sacrament, the other requested that the ballpoint not be removed. As for the micromosque, it contained a green carpet, a coat rack, and a straw mattress beside which a few Adidas trainers, flip-flops, moccasins and overshoes of North African, Central African and Middle Eastern worshippers kicked their heels.

As the morning advanced the clientele of the Spiritual Centre made their appearance little by little. These comprised not so much air travellers as airport employees, servicing or maintenance staff in blue overalls, security men, often blacks and always well built, walkie-talkies and bleepers at the ready. A few civilian adepts did pass by though: a pretty Lebanese nun, a Bulgarian mother and her grown-up son, a weedy young man with a beard, he looked Ethiopian, and his red eyes expressed agoraphobia, fear of airsickness – before boarding he wanted to receive the Sacrament from a priest, which Ferrer was reluctantly obliged to admit he was not.

The van driven by Rajputek showed up at the end of the morning. Once the crates were loaded, then unloaded at the gallery and carefully deposited in the studio, Ferrer returned home on foot. As he left the gallery to go home he glanced at the building site to see how it was progressing: it looked as if the foundations had finally been dug out, metal sheds had been installed to house men and machines, two big yellow cranes were being erected with the aid of a towering red crane. During the week, the noise threatened to be hellish, still, he'd see.

Meanwhile, this summer Sunday, the silence of Paris called to mind the silence of the ice pack, except that it was not the ice surface that the sun was melting but the tarmac. As he let himself in, after reaching his floor, the absence of Ecstatics Elixir surprised him, as though the urban silence had made everything vanish, equally disposing of the tribe of scents. It transpired, on checking with the concierge, that Bérangère Eisenmann had moved out during his absence. So no woman immediately available any more. Ferrer took it fairly well and, unpacking his things, came upon the fur coat retrieved from the *Nechilik*: it had rotted through and through, the fur was coming away from the skin in tufts, and the skin, in normal temperatures, had turned into a purulent mess of hardened gum. Ferrer decided to toss it out before attacking his mail.

At first sight it was a mountain of post but, once the bills were paid and the announcements, invitations, circulars and magazines thrown out, nothing was left but a summons to the Palais de Justice three months hence, 10th October, for a session with

Suzanne in connection with the divorce proceedings now under way. So he found himself more than ever in a womanless condition but, knowing him, it wouldn't last. Just a matter of time.

17

WELL, WHAT DID WE SAY? NOT TWO DAYS HAVE passed and here's one already. On Tuesday morning, Ferrer had an appointment at the gallery with the expert, who turned up attended by a man and a woman: his aides. The expert was called Jean-Philippe Raymond, some fifty summers, swarthy complexion, knife-edged profile, floating in clothes a size too large. His diction was muddled, his pout was sceptical, his eye was sharp. He moved around cautiously, as if unstable and off-balance, holding on to the backs of chairs as if to the ship's rail in a Force 9. Ferrer had some slight acquaintance with this expert, having already had recourse to his services on two or three occasions. His male assistant walked with a firmer step, helped to this end by the constant extraction of roasted peanuts from the depths of his pocket, and wiping his fingers every five minutes on a transparent Kleenex. As for the female assistant, who must have been getting on for thirty, she answered coldly to the name of Sonia. A hazel-eyed blonde with a pretty face, austere, though suggestive of ice or fire; she was dressed in a black suit and cream blouse, and she kept fingering a packet of Benson & Hedges with one hand, an Ericsson cellular phone with the other.

Ferrer offered them chairs before unpacking the objects brought in from the cold. Once seated, Jean-Philippe Raymond began a sulky inspection of these antiques without vouchsafing any comment, he simply delivered himself from time to time of some esoteric coded signs, strings of numbers and letters. Sonia stood behind him, whispering them into her mobile – though heaven knows who was on the other end – then whispered equally abstruse replies furnished by her interlocutor, then lit another cigarette. This done, the expert and his male assistant pursued an unintelligible discussion while Ferrer, after abandoning any attempt to fathom what they were saying, exchanged ever more glances with Sonia.

These exchanges of intrigued glances are familiar enough; the glances with which two strangers in a crowd who hit it off from the start persist in addressing each other on first sight. They are the briefest of glances but serious and somewhat on tenterhooks, very fleeting but at the same time quite prolonged, the duration seeming to be a great deal longer than it actually is; they slip secretly into the ambient conversations and the crowd notice nothing or at least pretend to. Ferrer's in any event proved disquieting, witness the fact that the assistant Sonia seemed on one occasion to have got her accessories mixed up, speaking for two seconds to her packet of Benson's.

The whole labour of evaluation took a good hour during which time neither of the two men deigned to glance at Ferrer, but when it was done Jean-Philippe Raymond's lips twisted into a disturbingly sceptical smirk. The corners of his mouth sloped floorwards as he lined up a few columns of ciphers in a narrow notebook bound in purple lizard-skin, shaking his head petulantly the while. Ferrer, noting the expression he was wearing, thought that well, that was that: the whole lot's not worth a bean, a wasted journey. But, this done, the expert came out with his figure. The sum, although given before tax and in a disdainful tone of voice, could easily enough match the sale price of one or two small chateaux in the Loire – I'm not talking of any big chateaux in the Loire, please note, I'm not talking of Chambord or Chenonceaux, I'm talking of the small to middling chateaux, something like Montcontour or Talcy, which is certainly not to be sneezed at. "I presume you have a safe," the expert supposed. "Well, actually no, I don't," said Ferrer. "That's to say, yes, I've an old one in the back, but it's a bit on the small side."

"You're going to have to put all this stuff in a safe," intoned Jean-Philippe Raymond. "A large safe. You can't keep it here. And there'd be no harm sorting something out with an insurance broker rather quickly, you don't have a safe but I expect you must have an insurer." "Fine, I'll attend to it all tomorrow." "In your place," said Raymond as he stood up, "I wouldn't leave it till tomorrow, but anyway, it's up to you. Now I'll be on my way, I'll leave you with Sonia to work out my bill, you can sort it out with her." "Sort it out with her," mused Ferrer, "but of course."

"Otherwise, how's business?" asked Raymond indifferently as he put on his coat. "The gallery? It's going O.K.," Ferrer assured him. "I have a few big names," he ventured, to impress Sonia. "But I can't give them a show every two years, the big names, they're too much in demand, know what I mean? And I've got a few little ones, youngsters, who've just arrived, but that's a different problem: the little young ones, they mustn't be over-exposed or they peak too soon, so I show one of their things from time to time, not too often. What would be good," he went on, "would be to give them a show now and then upstairs, if I had an upstairs, anyway, you see how it is, but it's O.K., it's going O.K." He broke off, aware that he was beginning to lose his audience and that everyone was averting their eyes.

Once the bill was sorted out, there was in fact to be no problem inviting Sonia for a meal, she would have been a good deal impressed even if she was not letting on. It was a fine day, it would be good to take a table outside, and the account of Ferrer's journey was bound to interest the girl, indeed to fascinate her – to such a degree that she'd switch off her mobile and light one cigarette after another. Then he would escort her home, a small split-level apartment not far from the Quai Branly. And after settling for one last drink, when Ferrer followed her home, there would turn out to be a girl ensconced in the downstairs part of the flat; the girl's eyes would be smothered by thick lenses as she was absorbed in photocopies of a constitutional-law text on which sat three empty pots of fruit yoghurt as also a small plastic transistor in shocking pink that looked like a toy. The apartment would be possessed by an atmosphere of harmony rather than of violence. Red and pink cushions would be floating on a couch covered in frosty flowered percale. In a dish, under gentle lamplight, oranges would be casting shadows of peaches.

The girl and Sonia exchanged news of Bruno – Ferrer gathered that he was one and three quarters and slept upstairs: the shocking pink transistor was in fact a so-called Babyphone, its function being to receive and transmit any crying he got up to. Then the babysitter took an age to collect up her papers, throw her yoghurt pots into the bin, and disconnect the Babyphone before being off at last, and it was possible for them to fling themselves upon each other and move as though in a clumsy sideways dance, like two crabs enlaced, towards Sonia's bedroom, where a black bra could be unfastened and dropped gently onto the rug in this room like an outsize pair of sunglasses.

Now, after a moment the Babyphone, reactivated on the bedside table, began to emit a succession of sharp sighs and moans, soft at first and in counterpoint with those Sonia was emitting on a more or less soprano register, but eventually hers were overwhelmed to make room for a crescendo of cries, yells, strident shrieks. It was necessary to get disentangled at once, any old how but not without a twinge of conscience, after which Sonia climbed the stairs to appease young Bruno.

Left on his own and tempted to get off to sleep, Ferrer felt it would be practical and discreet as a first step to reduce the decibel count on the Babyphone. But he had little acquaintance with this sort of gadget and no doubt pressed the wrong button, for instead of lowering the volume of shrieks and soothing noises, he altered the frequency which abruptly intruded on that

of the guardians of the peace, whose nocturnal duties of pre-
vention, surveillance and repression he could, henceforth, follow
perfectly. And with no further chance to disrupt the gadget,
Ferrer began feverishly punching every button, looking for an
aerial to twist off or a wire to cut, trying to muffle the sound with
the aid of a pillow, but in vain – each effort only increased its
vociferations, it was growing louder with each passing second.
Ferrer threw in the towel, dived into his clothes and fled, doing
up his buttons on the way downstairs, with not even any need
to make a discreet getaway so thoroughly were the clamours
from the Babyphone invading the aether, taking over the entire
building stage by stage – he would not ring her again in the days
that followed.

One woman who was to phone him the next day, on the other
hand, was Martine Delahaye, his assistant's widow, whom Ferrer
had met in the church at Alésia on the day of the funeral. He
rather had the impression that, despite her mourning attire,
she did not seem to find him uninteresting, but he thought that
he was at the time nothing more than a possible shoulder to
weep on. Well, here she was ringing him towards the end of the
afternoon, on some flimsy pretext, something to do with Social
Security papers that Delahaye might have left at the gallery,
she couldn't lay her hands on them and was wondering . . . "Oh
dear," said Ferrer, "I don't think so, he never left any of his
personal belongings here." "Oh, what a nuisance," said Martine
Delahaye. "I wonder if I could stop by anyway, maybe drop in
for a drink, I'd love to talk about old times."

"That's going to be complicated," lied Ferrer, who had no
thought at all of any involvement with the widow Delahaye,
"I'm just back from a trip and have to leave again soon, you
see, I'm a bit short of time." "What a shame, can't be helped,"
said Martine Delahaye. "Tell me, did you go far?" And Ferrer,
to excuse his fib in his own eyes, gave her a summary account

of the Great North. "Splendid," gushed the widow, "I've always dreamed of seeing those regions." "They're certainly beautiful," wittered Ferrer, "it's certainly very, very beautiful." "Lucky man!" exclaimed the widow, piling it on, "being able to nip off on a holiday to countries like that." "You know," said Ferrer, rather miffed, "it wasn't exactly a holiday. I went on business, if you follow. I was going to look for things for the gallery." "Splendid," she repeated impulsively, "and did you find anything?" "I think I have a few odds and ends," said Ferrer cautiously, "but I'll have to see, I don't yet have a precise valuation." "I'd love to see them," she said, "when will you put them on display?" "I can't really say for the moment," said he, "the date's not yet fixed, but I can send you a notification." "Do," said the widow, "send me a little card, promise?" "Yes," said Ferrer, "promise."

18

FOR THE WHOLE PERIOD THAT CONCERNS US Baumgartner had put up only in comfortable inns and hotels commanding a lavish number of stars in the guidebooks. In July, for instance, he had spent forty-eight hours at the Hotel Albizzia, where he had arrived late afternoon. The rate was 420 francs, breakfast included, and the room was not too bad at first glance, somewhat on the large side but felicitously proportioned; a velvety light crept in through a bay window, sixteen by nine, laced with climber roses. Turkish carpet, multifunctional shower, pay-as-you-view erotic videos, tawny bedspread, and view over a small public garden well stocked with starlings, planted with captive eucalyptus and imported mimosa.

Having built their nests beneath the roof-tiles of the Albizzia, in a hole in the wall, amid the eucalyptus, the ear-splitting starlings expressed themselves as ever by means of whistles, croaks, clicks and take-offs of colleagues, but they seemed also to have enriched their repertoire: adapting themselves to the ambient noises of our times, they were now including the sounds of electronic games, musical car-horns, the jingles of commercial radio stations and, not content with that, they had now added the shrill of the mobile phone with which Baumgartner had called Le Flétan, as he did every third day, before retiring early to bed with a book.

Then, quite early the next morning, he had gone down with a newspaper to breakfast in the empty restaurant. At that hour there was nobody yet about. The clink of utensils and muffled voices came to him from the kitchen, rustling noises, the sound of muted footsteps, nothing of interest; he had pushed his glasses up the bridge of his nose without lifting his eyes from his paper.

But let's take a look at now, a few weeks later on: Baumgartner has put up in a different hotel further north, the Résidence des Meulières, near Anglet. No garden here but a paved courtyard planted with ancient plane trees among which plashes a little fountain, or rather a big jet of water swaying in place as it produces an irregular frothy noise. Most of the time, the sound appears to be trying to mimic scattered bursts of muted clapping, not over-enthusiastic clapping, merely polite. But there are also moments when it gets into step with itself and for a few seconds falls into a rhythm of steady applause, it sounds a mite absurd and binary – encore, encore – the kind of applause unleashed when the audience wants the artist back on stage.

As every day, Baumgartner has rung his wife, but this time the call took longer than usual. Baumgartner put several questions to her, noted down the answers in the margins of his newspaper, then rang off. Pondered. Redialled, this time Le Flétan's number. Le Flétan picked up at once. "Right," Baumgartner told him, "I think we're on. First you're going to hire us a little refrigerator van, not a lorry, right? Only a small van." "No problem," says Le Flétan; "why refrigerated?" "None of your business. Let's say it's so as to avoid defrosting. I'm going to give you a Paris number. I'll be back tomorrow for a few days, and you give me a call as soon as you've done it." "O.K.," said Le Flétan, " I'm with you. I'll see to it tomorrow and give you a call straight after."

19

BUT ISN'T IT ABOUT TIME FERRER GOT HIMSELF sorted out? Is he to be an eternal collector of trivial liaisons, knowing perfectly well how they're going to end, no more imagining this time than on the previous occasions that he's struck gold? It could be said that he's now throwing in the towel at the first obstacle: after the business with Ecstatics Elixir, he has never even thought of finding out Bérangère's new address, and after the Babyphone episode he has made no further effort to see Sonia. Has he simply turned over a new leaf?

While waiting, as he had a little time on his hands, he went back to his cardiologist for a check-up. "We're going to do that little echocardiogram I mentioned," Feldman told him, "come this way." The room was plunged in a semi-darkness punctured by three computer screens but light enough to display three third-rate prints on the walls, two diplomas in angiology awarded to Feldman by foreign societies and a glassed-in frame containing photos of his household, which included a dog. Ferrer undressed and lay down, naked except for his underpants, on the examination bed covered with blue absorbent paper. He shivered slightly even though the room was warm enough. "Let go, relax," said Feldman once he had set up his programme on the machines.

Then the cardiologist proceeded to apply the tip of a black, oblong object, a sort of electronic pencil or something like that, first smeared with conductive gel, on different parts of Ferrer's body, here and there on his neck, groin, thighs, ankles, the corners of the eyes. Each time the pencil touched one of these spots, amplified sounds of arterial pulsations rang out loud and clear in the baffles of the computers, fearsome noises redolent of radar blips, short, violent gusts of wind, the stuttering bark of a bulldog or a panting Martian. So Ferrer listened in to his arteries while, at the same time, flashes of sound waves delivering their pictures appeared on the screen as a succession of peaks filing across.

This all lasted for a fair while, after which: "Not too hot," Feldman concluded; "you can dry yourself off," and he tossed at Ferrer a wad of blue absorbent paper he'd torn off the bed on which the patient was lying. Ferrer wiped himself over with it to mop up all the sticky gel smeared on him. "Not good at all," Feldman pursued. "Needless to say you're going to have to take care now. You're going to have to do something for me: be more careful in following the diet I prescribed. What's more, sorry to be blunt, but you're going to do me the favour of cutting down on your sex life for the time being." "For the present, at any rate," said Ferrer, "you've nothing to fear." "And one more thing," said Feldman. "Mind you steer clear of extremes of temperature, are you with me? Nothing too cold, nor too hot, because, as I've told you, that can be a catastrophe for people like you. Still," he chuckled, "you don't have all that many occasions for them in your line of work." "You've said it," admitted Ferrer without breathing a word about his foray into the Arctic.

At this point we have a July morning, the city is pretty quiet, bathed in an atmosphere of tacit half-mourning, so Ferrer finds himself on his own at an outside table of a café on Place Saint-Sulpice, in front of a beer. From Port Radium to Saint-Sulpice is no mean distance, a good six hours' worth of time zones, and Ferrer is not yet back on local time. Despite the admonishments of Jean-Philippe Raymond, he had put off until the morrow the chores relating to the safe and the insurance cover, he would make the two appointments later, towards the end of the afternoon. In the meantime he'd stashed all the antiquities in a cupboard under lock and key, at the back of the back room which was also bolted and barred. For the moment he was taking a breather, not that anyone really puts his feet up, one talks of it sometimes, one imagines that one's resting or that one is about to rest but it's no more than a small hope one entertains, knowing perfectly well that it won't pan out like that, it simply won't happen, it's merely a thing one says when one's tired.

Though he was completely flaked out, maybe even switched off, Ferrer did not forgo watching the women go by, so under-dressed at this time of year, so instantly desirable it can be almost painful, like a phantom pain in the solar plexus. A person may sometimes be so enrapt by the sight of the passers-by that he could become totally oblivious to himself. Thus Ferrer takes the girls all in, the ravishing beauties and the plain Janes. He relishes the absent look, a trifle haughty, imperious, put on by the ravishing beauties, but he also likes the absent and slightly wild, nervous look adopted by the plain Janes as they scowl at the asphalt at their feet, once they are fully aware that from a café terrace they are being closely inspected by folk with nothing better to do, and judged, moreover, to be somewhat easier on the eye than they take themselves to be. The more so because these too must make love like every other girl, and no doubt this is not at all how they look then – it's been known to happen, nay, perhaps in those circumstances the ravishing beauties and the plain Janes do actually swap places. But his thoughts must not take this turning, Feldman has forbidden it.

At the same moment Le Flétan was making his way on foot towards a massive private parking lot patrolled by massive guardians assisted by great big guard dogs, beyond the ring road across from Porte de Champerret. As he walked, Le Flétan breathed more easily than he had. When his skin itched, here or there, he'd absently scratch himself but it was not unpleasant, he could trudge a long time thus under the sun, he kept going. He passed in front of a little makeshift garage – some work benches, a drainage pit, three cars in differing stages of dismantlement, a winch, the usual things. Then came a parking lot that looked as if it specialised in commercial vehicles, juggernauts, trailers and half-trailers. In the transparent box where he supervised six closed-circuit televisions and two heaping ashtrays the parking lot's security man was a tight-arsed little fellow, as genial as a barn door. Le Flétan told him he'd come for the refrigerator van that had been booked by phone the day before; the man nodded, seemed to know about it, set out for it with Le Flétan in tow.

It was a small white oblong van, as boxy and angular as the hutments at Port Radium; aerodynamic it was not. Above the driver's cabin there was a small motor capped with a round ventilation grille that looked like a hotplate. The security man unbolted the back doors, revealing a large empty space with metal walls; some polystyrene crates were stacked up at the back. Though the inside was clean, no doubt sandblasted, it still gave off a slight odour of congealed fat, of stale blood, tendons and ganglia, no doubt it was normally used for the wholesale transport of meat.

After listening with half an ear to the man explaining how the vehicle functioned, Le Flétan handed him part of the money entrusted to him by Baumgartner and let him push the sliding door to before climbing in. Once the man had left, Le Flétan dug out from his pocket a pair of household cleaning gloves in reinforced rubber, off-white, whose nodular palm and fingers gripped surfaces and prevented slipping. He put them on then turned the starter key and drove away. The reverse gear could have been smoother, but then the gear changes engaged harmoniously as the van moved off towards the outer ring road; we shall take it and leave by Porte de Châtillon.

On Place de la Porte de Châtillon, Le Flétan double-parked

by a telephone box. He got out, entered, lifted the receiver and uttered a few words. He appeared to be given a laconic reply then, bequeathing a few of his molecules to the handset – a gob of earwax blocking a perforation of the earpiece, a drop of saliva in an orifice of the mouthpiece – he hung up and raised an eyebrow. He did not look all that convinced. Indeed he looked somewhat guarded.

20

FOR HIS PART BAUMGARTNER ALSO HUNG UP WITH no particular expression on his face. He did not look dissatisfied, however, as he made for a window of his studio. Nothing much to see. He opened the window: not all that many sounds, a couple of bird songs pursuing each other, a far-off mist of traffic noise. He was back in Paris, then, back in his big studio flat on Boulevard Exelmans with nobody plumb opposite to look at. He had nothing more to do now but wait, kill time looking out of the window, and when night fell, turn his eye to the television. But it was for the moment the window.

The paved courtyard, planted with lime trees and acacias, contained a small garden bordered with hedges surrounding a pool with a vertical jet of water which today was bent, indeed thrown off-balance, by a spot of wind. The trees were enlivened by a few sparrows and two or three jays or blackbirds (female) who kept company with a piece of whitish plastic sheeting, the kind used to bag up bricks, and stamped with the word Bricorama – it was caught in a tangle of upper branches and puffed out by this bit of wind like a small sail, and it vibrated and shuddered like a living thing as it emitted snapping sounds and flute-like noises. Below him a child's bicycle with stabiliser wheels lay knocked over on the ground. Three derisory street lamps placed in the corners of the courtyard, and three CCTV surveillance cameras mounted above the front door of each villa kept watch on this small panorama.

Though the branches of the lime tree blocked off the view between the villas, Baumgartner could espy the terraces with their furniture of striped-canvas deckchairs and tables in teak, the balconies and large bay windows, the sophisticated television aerials. Further off, a row of opulent buildings could be descried, which made for a number of architectural disparities but never mind, nothing clashed: 1910 stood so lavishly beside 1970 that they achieved a harmonious coexistence; money talks loudly enough to drown out the anachronisms.

What the inhabitants of these dwellings seem to have in common is that they are in their mid-forties and earn quite a comfortable living in one audio-visual field or another. Here, in a blue office, we have a plump young woman with big headphones over her ears, tapping onto her computer the text for a housewives' question-time that Baumgartner has been hearing day after day at around eleven o'clock on one of the public-service radio stations. Here we have a little red-haired man with an absent expression and a fixed smile; he seldom prises himself out of the chaise longue on his terrace and must be a producer or something, seeing that there appears to be no end of girls around his place. And here we have a war correspondent for television; she's not often there, spending her life as she does in the world's trouble spots, hopping from one minefield to the next with her mobile phone, from the Khmers to the Chechens and from the Yemenis to the Afghans. As she spends her life sleeping when she comes home, the shutters closed on her jet lag, Baumgartner sees little of her, except on his television screen now and then.

But for the moment he saw nobody. Even this morning, at the back of the Vietnamese embassy, five or six tracksuited diplomats had gone through their t'ai chi as they did every day. But at present there was nothing beyond the embassy railings but a basketball backboard nailed to a tree, an asymmetrical swing and a rusty safe lying on its back, with, in the background, a blank cement wall and an empty chair parked in front of it. It seemed warmer, more humid beyond the railings, as if the embassy produced its own South-east Asian micro-climate.

In any case Baumgartner watched the world from a good distance. He may have observed people but he'd play possum, and greeted nobody except the retired dentist on the ground floor to whom he handed his ample rent each Monday – the floor was rented to him by the week. This had been the arrangement they had made, Baumgartner having warned the dentist from the start that he wouldn't be there all that long, that he would probably have to leave without notice. Most of the time he was closeted in this flat and it has to be admitted that he got more than a little bored, and had to get out for a breath of air from time to time.

And look at him now, just on the way out to stretch a leg and, fancy! here is the war correspondent looking as if she's just woken up and off she goes, yawning, to some editorial meeting. She's one of these big blondes who drive a small Austin, hers is emerald green with a white roof, the radiator stove in, the windows plastered with notices warning that the vehicle is about to be towed away, notices which the police superintendent, a friend of hers, will quash. For here we're in a rich neighbourhood inhabited by not a few people in the public eye, who in their turn know a good few more people in the public eye, these are prosperous quarters and thus haunted by droves of paparazzi.

And as it happens, two of the species had staked out the place from under a porch in Rue Michel-Ange; they were equipped with those large oblong contraptions in grey plastic that look less like cameras than like telescopes, periscopes, surgical implements, or even weapons with infra-red telescopic sights. These photographers were astonishingly youthful and evidently dressed for the beach, in short-sleeved shirts and Bermuda shorts, but they watched the porch opposite grim-faced, no doubt waiting for a superstar to step out on the arm of her new boyfriend.

Baumgartner stopped out of curiosity and waited awhile beside them, discreetly and with no display of interest until he was none too politely invited to clear off. He was not one to stand on the order of his going, he cleared off.

He was idle, almost painfully idle, he pottered off to take a turn round the cemetery of Auteuil, it was but a step away and on the small side, a place where a fair number of Englishmen, barons and ships' captains are laid to rest. Some of the tombstones were broken, fallen to ruin, others were being repaired. One of the funerary monuments that looked like a small pavilion seemed to be in the course of restoration; it was adorned with statues and had the verb *Credo* written where the doormat should be. Baumgartner passed in front of Delahaye's grave without stopping – though he retraced his steps to straighten a potted azalea that had been knocked over. Then he passed before that of an unknown man, doubtless one who was hard of hearing, for *Respects from his deaf friends in Orleans*, the inscription shouted; then in front of the tomb of Hubert Robert: *Respectful son, tender husband, good father, loyal friend*, murmured the inscription. And that was just about that: he left the cemetery of Auteuil and went back up Rue Claude-Lorrain towards Rue Michel-Ange.

Here, as, a little later, the long-awaited superstar had just stepped outside in the company of her new boyfriend, the two photographers undertook to riddle the couple. The boyfriend quivered and beamed, the superstar froze and bade the snappers go jump, and Baumgartner, back from the cemetery and lost in his own thoughts, passed all unwittingly across the frame before going indoors. He poured himself a drink and glanced once more out of the window while awaiting the day's end, which took its time, which indefinitely prolonged the shadows of objects, be they mineral or vegetable, front-door steps or acacias, until they themselves with their own shadows were drowned in a greater shadow which softened their outlines and their colours until it absorbed them, sponged them up, obliged them to fade out and disappear, and that was the point when the phone rang.

"It's me," said Le Flétan, "it went O.K." "Are you sure no-one saw you?" Baumgartner worried. "Not a chance. There was no-one following me. In fact there was practically no-one in the shop either. Seems to me modern art's in sad shape." "Belt up, fat-head," said Baumgartner. "So come on. Where's the stuff right now?" "All in the freezer-van, as intended. It's snugly parked near my place in the lockup you rented. What now?" "We meet tomorrow at Charenton," said Baumgartner. "You remember the address?"

21

EANWHILE FERRER WAS STILL TAKING IN THE sun and still parked in front of a beer – the same and a different one – but if he had not left this quarter on the Left Bank, he had moved and was now installed in a café on the Carrefour de l'Odéon. This is not as a rule the ideal place to stop for a drink, for all that there are always plenty of folk to wait on you; it is a busy, noisy intersection, hemmed in on all sides and riddled with red lights and cars going every which way; moreover it is cooled by the mighty draught funnelled in from Rue Danton. But in the summer, when Paris is somewhat emptied, the outside café tables are not bad to sit at, the light is diffused and the traffic much reduced, and there's a tiptop view overlooking two of the exits from the same Metro station. A few people were going in and out of these exits and Ferrer watched them, taking a closer interest in the feminine half which is, at least in terms of quantity, as we know, superior to the other.

This feminine half may also, he had noticed, be divided into two tribes: those who, the moment one has left them, and not necessarily for good, turn round as one watches them go down the steps into the Metro station, and those who, for good or not, neglect to turn round. So far as Ferrer is concerned, he always turns round the first few times to establish to which category, turners or non-turners, this new acquaintance belongs. Thereafter he proceeds as she does, adapts to her manner, adapts his behaviour to her own, seeing that there is really nothing to be gained by turning round if she does not.

But today nobody was turning and Ferrer made to go home. As there were no taxis free – For Hire sign switched on, parking flashers switched off – and as he had an ample allowance of time, it made sense for him to return home on foot. It was some little distance but nonetheless quite feasible, and a little exercise could only serve to sort out his ideas, for his head was still befuddled by a remnant of jet lag.

And in this confused stage his thoughts, leaving aside memories, focused on the insurer and the safe-merchant whom he had to call, an estimate for a pedestal that needed renegotiating, Martinov, who could do with a relaunch seeing that he was currently the only one of his artists who was going anywhere, then the gallery lighting needed to be radically rethought in view of his new antiquities; which still left the question of whether or not he was going to give Sonia a call.

As to the urban scene, to look at it in order, on his gradual approach to Rue d'Amsterdam, zigzagging along the pavements to avoid the dog turds, notable sightings included a fellow in dark glasses heaving a big drum out of a white Rover, a little girl informing her mother that on second thoughts she'd go for the trapeze, then two young women at each other's throats over a parking space, followed by a refrigerator van making off at a fair clip.

Ferrer arrived at the gallery, to be buttonholed for a moment by an artist sent his way by Rajputek, who wanted to tell Ferrer what he had lined up. He was a young fellow into the plastic arts, wearing a smirking, smug expression – he had masses of friends in the art world and as for ideas, Ferrer had seen them all before a dozen times over. This time, rather than hang a picture on a wall, what you do is etch out the collector's wall itself with acid at the point where the picture is to hang: a small rectangular format 24×30, 25mm deep. "I develop the idea for the work in negative, you could say," the artist explained. "I remove part of the thickness of the wall instead of adding to it." "Of course," said Ferrer, "an interesting idea, but I'm no longer working all that much in this area, at present. Perhaps it's something to think about later on, but not right now. We must talk about it again, leave me your portfolio and I'll be in touch." Once rid of the etcher, Ferrer tried to tackle all the matters pending, with the help of a girl called Elisabeth whom he had taken on trial as a replacement for Delahaye, she was anorexic but dosed up on vitamins, and anyway she was on trial, it'd be a question of seeing how she worked out. To start with he gave her a few minor duties.

Then it was time to make with the telephone; Ferrer called the insurer and the safe-vendor, both would stop by tomorrow. He went over the estimate for the pedestal and phoned the man to say he'd call in later in the week. He did not succeed in raising Martinov, only getting his answerphone, on which he left a message, an ingenious combination of admonishments, encouragements and warnings; in a word, he was doing his job. He spent a long time with Elisabeth contemplating the best way to improve the gallery lighting with an eye to displaying the polar artefacts. The better to flesh out his ideas Ferrer decided to go and fetch a couple of things from the storeroom, to do a dummy run with say, the ivory armour and one of the two mammoth tusks, you'll see what I mean, Elisabeth. Then he went to the back of the gallery, unbolted the door to the storeroom and there it was, plain to see: the cupboard door forced, gaping wide, opening on to nothing any more. This was no longer the time to be asking himself if he was going to ring Sonia.

22

ROPPING TWO FAT SUITCASES SNAPPED SHUT NEAR the door of the now perfectly tidied studio, as if he were about to clear off any minute, Baumgartner slammed the door behind him. Like a harmonic, like the tonality of the telephone bell or the signal for the automatic closing of doors on the Metro, this dry, mat clack produced an almost perfect F which made the strings of the Bechstein baby grand vibrate in sympathy; for ten to twenty seconds after Baumgartner had left, the ghost of a major chord haunted the empty flat before slowly wasting away then dissolving.

Baumgartner crossed Boulevard Exelmans and went down it for a moment towards the Seine before turning off down Rue Chardon-Lagache. In mid-summer the XVIth arrondissement is even emptier than usual to the point that Rue Chardon-Lagache looked from certain angles as if a bomb had hit it. He collected his car from the underground car park in a modern block on Avenue de Versailles, then rejoined the Seine and took the expressway, leaving it before Pont Sully. He found himself back on Place de la Bastille, from where he drove south-east up the full length of the endless Rue de Charenton, all the way to Charenton itself. He thus crossed the entire XIIth arrondissement along its axis, its backbone, finding it a little more inhabited at this season than the XVIth, the natives taking fewer holiday breaks in the former quarter than in the latter. On the pavements denizens of the Third World and those who inhabited the Third Age were particularly in evidence, sluggish, solitary and bewildered.

Once in Charenton, the Fiat turned right into a little artery named after Molière or Mozart, Baumgartner could never remember which, but he knew it ran at right angles to another expressway, beyond which a tiny industrial estate fronted the Seine. This estate consisted of rows of warehouses, and lockup garages were to be seen on every side, with metal shutters, some of which displayed the names of firms, whether printed on or stencilled. There were also a good number of repositories for hire, running from 2,000 to 10,000 square metres, their presence attested by a large hoarding that read "Flexibility at the Service of Logistics". Additionally there were two or three small factories that looked as peaceful as could be, as though working at only a quarter of their capacity, and there was a filtering station, all this distributed along a spur of road that appeared to be nameless.

This is a neighbourhood that is even emptier than anywhere abouts in the height of the summer, and practically silent – the only perceptible sounds come in the form of a soft undertone with dull shudders, echoes of heaven knows what. During the year, at a pinch, an elderly couple or two may stroll there with their dog. The occasional driving instructor has homed in on the place and spread the word, making the most of the absence of traffic to put their pupils through their paces at smaller risk, and sometimes too a cyclist passing through will put his bike on his shoulder and take advantage of the little bridge that crosses the Seine to Ivry. From this bridge there is a view of several other bridges flung in all directions across the water. Just above the confluence with the Marne a vast Chinese commercial and hotel complex has drawn up its Manchu architecture on the verge of the stream, and of bankruptcy.

But today there was nothing and nobody. Nothing except for a small refrigerator van parked in front of one of the storage depots, nobody except for Le Flétan at the wheel of this van equipped with a Thermo-King unit. Baumgartner had parked the Fiat alongside the van and wound down his window without getting out: it was Le Flétan who eased himself out of the van.

Le Flétan was much too hot, Le Flétan was complaining of the heat. Perspiration rammed home the message of his unkempt appearance: his hair was a greasy, straggly mass, patches of sweat overlaid the various stains on his logoed T-shirt, dirty streaks creased his face like a premonition of wrinkles.

"O.K.," said Le Flétan, "it's all there. What now?" "You pick 'em up," Baumgartner replied, handing him the key to the lockup. "You stack everything in there. And gently does it, handle with care." "You know, in this heat . . . " persisted Le Flétan, but "Get cracking," Baumgartner repeated.

Baumgartner stayed behind the wheel and did not leave the driving seat; he kept a regular watch to ensure that nobody was looking, and pulled on a pair of supple sheepskin gloves, linen-stitched and light to wear, while he supervised the transfer of the crates into the lockup. It was scorching, not a breath of wind, Le Flétan was dripping with sweat. His muscles, atrophied by substance-abuse, still managed to ripple a little beneath his T-shirt and Baumgartner did not care for this, he didn't care to look, at least he didn't care to take pleasure from watching. With his work completed, Le Flétan returned to the Fiat. "There we are," he said. "D'you want to come and see? Oh, you're wearing gloves." "It's the weather," said Baumgartner, "it's me, with this heat. My skin, you see. Don't let it bother you. Have you got everything out?" "The lot," said Le Flétan. "Wait while I check," said Baumgartner and got out of his car and inspected the contents of the lockup.

Then he looked up with a frown. "There's one missing." "One what?" "One crate. There's one that's not there." "You're joking," exclaimed the crack-head. "There were seven at the start and there are seven now. It's fine." "I don't think so," said Baumgartner. "Go and double-check inside the van, you must have forgotten one."

Le Flétan shrugged sceptically and climbed into the back of the refrigerator van, whereupon Baumgartner promptly slammed the doors. Muffled voice of Le Flétan, at first playful then irritated, then anxious. Baumgartner shot the bolt, went to the front of the van, opened the door and slid behind the wheel.

From the driving cabin the voice of the young man was completely inaudible. Baumgartner slid open a small panel behind the driving seat, released a catch then opened the rectangular window that gives onto the temperature-controlled storage area. This spyhole was the size of a packet of ten cigarettes: big enough to glance into the back but not big enough to pass a hand through.

"There," Baumgartner said, "that's the end of that." "Wait," said Le Flétan, "what are you doing? Come on, now, stop horsing around." "It's over," Baumgartner said again. "Now you're going to get out of my hair at last." "I've never given you any grief," Le Flétan ineptly observed. "So let me out." "I can't," said Baumgartner, "you're a nuisance. You're liable to become a nuisance, so you are a nuisance." "Let me out," Le Flétan persisted, "if not, you'll be found out and then you'll be in real trouble." "I think not," said Baumgartner. "According to the public records you don't exist, if you follow me. Nobody's going to notice a thing. It won't even be of interest to the cops. Nobody knows you except for your pusher, and he has no interest in running to them. How d'you expect anyone to notice that you quite literally don't exist any more? Who's going to notice the absence of an unknown person? So pipe down. It'll be over in a jiffy – just a touch of hot and cold."

"No, no," said Le Flétan, "will you please now just pack it in!" He made a further attempt to convince Baumgartner before evidently running out of arguments. "Another thing," he tried to put forward as a last resort, "what you're doing is too pathetic for words. This is the way people are killed in all the soap operas, there's nothing all that original about it." "You're not wrong,"

Baumgartner conceded, "but I don't mind admitting I'm influenced by soap operas. The soap opera is an art form like any other. Anyway, enough of that."

Then he hermetically bolted the aperture and, once he had started the engine, he switched on the compressor. The thermodynamic principle that is carried into effect in a thermostatically controlled vehicle, and more generally in every refrigerator, is well known: in the walls a gas circulates that absorbs the heat contained within. Thanks to the little motor situated above the driver's cabin and thanks to the compressor that allows this gas to circulate, this heat is transformed into cold. Moreover there are two temperature settings for a vehicle of this kind: five degrees above and eighteen degrees below freezing. It was this latter option that Baumgartner had taken care to book by telephone the previous day.

23

THE DISAPPEARANCE OF THE ANTIQUES NATURALLY represented a heavy loss. The financing of the expedition to the Arctic, no small investment for Ferrer, was all money down the drain and represented a net loss. And since, what with a stagnant economy and a lean season, the time had come when nothing was selling any more in the gallery, this was of course also the time when his creditors chose to remind him of their existence, when the artists claimed the balances in their accounts and the bank manager started getting edgy. Then, when the end of the summer hove into view, as each year at this time all manner of taxes would crop up, along with threats of reassessment, one kind of duty and another, divers subscription renewals, as also the renewal of the lease on the gallery accompanied by registered missives from the letting agent. Thus Ferrer began to feel the devil at his heels.

First of all he had had to report his loss, of course. As soon as the theft was noticed, Ferrer had called the local station and a tired officer from the CID had turned up within the hour. The man had taken note of the damage, logged the complaint, and requested the name of his insurers. "Well, the thing is," Ferrer had explained, "the way it's turned out, these things haven't yet been insured. I was just on the point of doing so, but ... " "You're a complete idiot," the detective had rudely interrupted him, castigating him for his negligence and explaining to him that the fate of lost objects was as haphazard as could be, that the chances of recovering them were absolutely minimal. This sort of business, he had explained, was very seldom cleared up, given how highly organised was the traffic in stolen art; at best the thing was likely to drag on for ages. One would see what could be done but the prospects were poor, very poor. "Anyway, I'll be sending a man along from Criminal Records," the detective concluded, "to see what he can find. Meanwhile of course you're not to touch anything."

The technician arrived a few hours later. He did not introduce himself straightaway but spent a moment in the gallery looking at the art on display. He was a scrawny, short-sighted little man with very fine fair hair, and a fixed smile; he did not seem in any hurry to get down to work. Ferrer had taken him at first for a prospective buyer – "Are you into modern art?" – before the man identified himself, showing his card: Detective Inspector Paul Supin, Criminal Records Division. "That must be interesting as a calling," observed Ferrer. "You know, I'm only a laboratory technician; take away my electronic microscope and I see precious little. But it is certainly true that I find it interesting." Going into Ferrer's back room he unpacked his small stock of equipment, a tool-case containing the classic accessories: camera, phials of transparent liquid, powder and brush, gloves. Ferrer watched him at work until the man took his leave. He was discouraged, he was going to have to make good very fast, things were beginning to feel too hot by half.

The summer moved slowly along, as if the heat made the weather viscous, its progress seemingly slowed down by the chafing of its molecules raised to a high temperature. Most of the working population being away on holiday, Paris was more supple and more thinned out, but scarcely more breathable under the motionless air rich in toxic gases like a smoke-filled bar at closing time. Here and there all over the city advantage was being taken of lower traffic density to make holes in the streets and repair them: clatter of pneumatic drills, whizz of borers, spin of concrete mixers, streams of fresh tar in the sun veiled by these emanations. To all of this Ferrer paid scant attention – too many other things preoccupied him as he crossed Paris by taxi from one bank to the next, trying without much success to raise a loan, beginning to think he might have to mortgage the gallery. Thus it is that we next find him at eleven o'clock in the morning, with the heat fit to kill, in Rue du 4-Septembre.

This Rue du 4-Septembre is very broad and very short, and it is money that makes it tick. Its Napoleon-III buildings are all more or less alike; they house banks, international or otherwise, head offices of insurance companies, brokers' offices, temping agencies, financial press offices, foreign-exchange bureaux, chartered accountants', probate administrators' offices, trustees for co-operatives, estate agencies, lawyers' chambers, rare-coin shops, and the burnt-out wreck of the Crédit Lyonnais. The only neighbourhood brasserie is called L'Agio. But the offices of Polish Airlines are located there too, as well as photocopy shops, travel agents, beauty parlours, a world champion hairdressers', and the wall plaque in honour of a Free Frenchman fallen for his country at the age of nineteen (lest we forget).

Moreover there still are thousands of square metres of reconditioned office space to let and sites in the throes of reconstruction under the eye of strict surveillance cameras, on Rue du 4-Septembre: the old buildings are gutted while preserving their façades, pillars and caryatids, their sculpted crowned heads overlooking carriage gateways. Each floor is renovated in accordance with the prevailing byelaws so as to obtain spacious accommodation, picture-windowed and double-glazed, the better thereby to accumulate more and yet more capital. As all over Paris in the summer, the helmeted workmen beaver away, unfolding plans, munching sandwiches, speaking into their walkie-talkies.

It was the sixth bank in two days that Ferrer had visited to solicit a loan, he came out yet again empty-handed, his damp fingers leaving their impression on the documents with which he had furnished himself to support his applications. After these had once again come to nothing, he reached the ground floor where the lift gates slid open on a vast lobby empty of people and furnished with numerous settees and low tables. As he was crossing this space Ferrer had no inclination, no strength to return home straightaway, he preferred to sit down a moment on one of the settees. How was anyone to tell from the look of him that he was weary, despondent and discouraged? From the fact, for example, that he kept his jacket on even though it was sweltering, that he studied a speck of dust on his sleeve with no thought of brushing it off, that he did not even flick a lock of hair out of his eyes, but especially, perhaps, from the fact that a woman crossed the hall and he took no notice.

Given this woman's appearance, that is what is the most surprising. In all logic, from what little one knows of him, Ferrer ought to have shown an interest. She was a tall, slender girl, handsomely shaped, with well-defined lips, wide pale-green eyes, her hair in auburn curls. She wore high heels and was dressed in a loose-fitting black outfit very low-cut at the back, and set off with little bright facings in a herringbone pattern at her shoulders and hips.

As she passed close by him, it would have occurred to anyone else, or indeed to him in his normal state, that those clothes were only there to be taken off, indeed ripped off, her. Besides, the blue folder she held beneath her arm, the pen that pensively brushed her lips, seemed to be accessories only there for the form – she herself could have passed for an actress in the opening scenes of a hard-porn movie during which one comes out with any old nonsense while waiting for things to hot up. This said, she wore no make-up. And Ferrer only had time to take in this detail, while according it no more attention than he did to the decor of the hall, when a general prostration took hold of him, as if every part of his body were suddenly short of breath.

A 500-kilo weight seemed to descend upon his shoulders, his

skull and his chest all at the same time. A taste of acid metal and of dry dust invaded his mouth, laid siege to his forehead, his throat, the back of his neck and produced an asphyxiating mixture – the start of a sneeze, a violent hiccup, a deep nausea. He was quite unable to react, his wrists seemed to be clamped in handcuffs and his whole being smothered in a sensation of stifling, of utter anguish, of imminent death. A pain tore his chest, penetrating from throat to groin, from navel to shoulders, while radiating through his left arm and leg, and he saw himself falling off the settee, he saw the floor rise up quickly towards him, while at the same time in slow motion. Then, once he was lying on the floor, at first he was simply unable to move, then he lost his sense of balance, then he lost consciousness – how long for there is no way of telling, but it was just after he remembered for a second what Feldman had warned him of, about the effects of extreme temperatures on heart cases.

Anyway, he soon came to, even if it was now impossible for him to utter a single word. It was not the blackness that invades the screen of a television set that has been switched off, no, his field of vision continued to function just as a movie camera continues to record images after it has been knocked to the ground on the sudden death of its operator, filming quite fixedly whatever lies before its lens: an angle where the wall meets the floor, a badly squared-off skirting board, a length of piping, an ooze of glue at the edge of the carpet. He tried to get up but fell only the more heavily in the attempt. People other than the young woman in black must have hurried along for he sensed people leaning over him, his jacket being removed, being turned onto his back, someone was making for a phone, then the emergency services arrived quickly in a van.

The ambulance men were handsome young lads, calm, reassuring and well muscled; they were in blue uniforms, with leather accessories and clasps at their belts. Gently they laid Ferrer on a stretcher, meticulously the stretcher was loaded into their van. Ferrer felt protected now. Without stopping to think that this was remarkably like the February incident, although frankly less agreeable, he tried to recover a rudimentary use of speech in the ambulance, but was kindly bidden to keep quiet till they reached the hospital. Which he did. Then he blacked out again.

24

WHEN HE OPENED HIS EYES, HE SAW AROUND him nothing but white, as in the good old days on the ice pack. Ferrer was lying in an adjustable single bed with a firm mattress, and was tightly tucked in, alone in a small room, with no other colour but the emerald of a far-off tree standing out against the sky in the squared frame of a window. The sheets, the counterpane, the walls of the room, and the sky were all equally white. The single green note, the distant tree, could be one of the 35,000 planes, the 7,000 limes, or the 13,500 chestnuts planted in Paris. Unless it belonged with those one may come across in the outlying patches of waste ground, the kind whose name one always forgets, maybe it doesn't even have a name – this type is nothing but a weed on a giant scale, clandestine flora monstrously overgrown. Although it was too far away, Ferrer still tried to give it a name but this slight effort was enough to exhaust him, and he closed his eyes again.

The next time he opened them, five minutes later or the following morning, the surroundings were unchanged but Ferrer, this time, forbore to reconsider the tree question. It is difficult to establish whether he was striving to think of nothing at all or whether he was in no condition to bend his mind to anything. As he felt and vaguely distinguished a small foreign body attached to his nose that made him squint slightly, he tried to raise his hand to it to identify it but his right forearm would not respond. On closer inspection he found that this forearm was secured palm-upwards to the bed-frame by a strap and pierced by a fat transfusion needle held in place with a large translucent sticking plaster. Ferrer was beginning to grasp what was happening, it was only for the form that he checked with his left hand that the foreign body fixed to his nostrils was dispensing oxygen. Then it was that the door opened on a young woman, also dressed in white but with a black skin; on putting her nose round the door, she turned back to someone who must have been another nurse, asking her to tell Dr Sarradon that No. 43 was awake.

Alone once more, Ferrer made a further tentative effort to identify the tree in the distance but, if he still did not succeed, neither did he go back to sleep: we were thus making progress. It was with caution, however, that he inspected his surroundings in greater detail, turning his head to distinguish the various pieces of equipment at the head of his bed, screens and monitors which must have been keeping tabs on the state of his ticker: numerals in tremulous liquid crystal that kept undergoing modi-fication, sine curves moving from left to right, ever starting again, as similar and as different as a wave train. A telephone stood at his bed-head, a reserve oxygen mask hung from a hook. Ferrer endured his malady with patience. Outside, the daylight was fading, turning all the whiteness in his room into beige and deepening the colour of the distant tree towards a bronze-green, then to a deeper green still. Finally the door opened again and this time it was Dr Sarradon in person, wearing a bushy black beard and a bottle-green gown, with a silly little cap of the same colour: so we were staying with green.

As he examined his patient, Sarradon told him that on his emergency admission they had had to perform a triple bypass on him without his recovering consciousness, it all seemed to have gone off all right. And in fact, once the bedclothes were pulled back, as the dressings were being changed, Ferrer saw that he was entirely sewn up the full length of his left arm and leg as well as up the central line of his chest. It was as pretty a piece of needlework as you could wish, consisting of very regular long and thin sutures reminiscent of the lacing you get in English Renaissance lacework, or the inside of a seamed stocking, or a line of handwriting.

"Not bad," concluded the doctor when he was finished. "It's healing quite nicely," he added as he glanced through the medical notes hung at the foot of the bed, while the nurse dressed Ferrer in thoroughly disinfected pyjamas. The patient, according to Sarradon, would need to spend another three or four days in intensive care before moving to a normal room. Then he should be ready to leave in a couple of weeks. He was allowed visitors. Night was falling.

In fact the next morning Ferrer felt a little more like his old self. He spent a moment wondering who, among his entourage, he could inform of his situation. It was as well to forget about telling Suzanne, who had had no news of him for more than six months and who might not respond all that well to such a call. He preferred also not to risk upsetting his family, who seemed to him anyway to have become a very scattered and remote archipelago, little by little overwhelmed by the rising tide. Which did not, truth to tell, leave all that many people, and Ferrer promised himself at least to call the gallery in the course of the afternoon. Although Elisabeth had soon grown accustomed to his brief impromptu absences, and would have opened up shop as usual and seen to matters in hand, there'd still be no harm in her knowing where he was. But there was no hurry for that. Besides, it would be better to close the gallery until he was recovered, indeed it would be no bad thing in this hollow season. Tomorrow he would call her to this effect. He was going to try for the moment to get back to sleep when the nurse unexpectedly announced a visitor. Instinctively he tried to sit up, but no, still too weak, not possible.

Then a young woman appeared whom he had all the more difficulty in recognising in as much as she had changed her outfit since Rue du 4-Septembre: what she was wearing now was a blue tanktop with rust-coloured stripes and a skirt split up to the thigh in a stronger shade of blue. And flat-heeled shoes. And one of her shoulder straps was inclined to slip. But she was still just as bereft of make-up. Once he finally recognised her, after a few nonplussed seconds, he felt not at all presentable in his pyjamas: he made a mechanical gesture to smooth down his dirty hair which was coated here and there with the conductive gel of the routine ECG which he had been given on admission.

In spite of the shoulder straps, in spite of the split skirt, and even though this girl's deportment was decidedly of the kind that would put ideas in your head, Ferrer felt from the outset that things were not going to work out between the two of them. While he may to some extent have been able, in his enfeebled condition and through half-closed eyes, to size up the nurses and speculate on the presence or absence of other textile elements beneath their uniforms, he derived no more spontaneous emotion from this woman than he would have done from a nun doing her rounds – and there was, besides, something nun-like about this absence of make-up. Unless subconsciously he considered that she was out of his league, it's been known to happen, but no, that was not his style.

She did not stay for more than five or ten minutes, in any event, she explained that she had got the address of the hospital from the ambulance crew, that she had just wanted to see how he was getting on. "Well, you can see how we're doing," said Ferrer for lack of anything else to say, and smiled thinly, with a vague gesture towards the oxygen dispenser and the drip. After which they didn't have all that much to say to each other; she didn't look the type who ever had much to say, as she waited by the door as if constantly poised to leave. Before she did leave she offered to stop by again and see how he was, if he felt like it. He accepted unenthusiastically: at bottom he was pretty indifferent to this girl, he couldn't really see the point of her visit, he couldn't work out just what she was after.

Thus during the three days that Ferrer was to spend in Intensive Care, the young woman would come and visit him, always at the same time in the afternoon, never for more than fifteen minutes. The first time, she installed herself in the heavy armchair which she dragged across to the bed; it was a grubby-looking object, its seat supported with livid plastic straps. Then, when she got up again, she'd stand for a moment by the window which continued to frame the distant tree – bird song emanated from it and arrived through the open window, briefly making the emerald green shiver and sparkle. On the second and third days she sat at the foot of the bed, the bedclothes tucked in really much too tight – for the whole of her visit, Ferrer would not dare move his clamped extremities, insteps tightly arched, big toes cramped by the sheet which was taut as a tent canvas.

However, on the third afternoon, before she left, he asked her her name. Hélène. Hélène, good. Not a bad name, that. And what did she do in life? She was to take a moment before answering.

25

MEANWHILE BAUMGARTNER WAS TRYING TO PARK his car in front of a big seaside hotel at Mimizan-Plage, in the north-west of the Pyrénées-Atlantiques, on the edge of the territory that he was usually scouring at about this time. The hotel did not look all that terrific, but at this season it was not easy to find anywhere; moreover, this one too was all full up: its vast car park was cluttered with foreign number-plates. Baumgartner had done well to book.

So he drove very slowly along the rows of parked cars, passing couples and families dressed in short, colourful outfits, heading for the seaside. The sun beat down on the scene, the tarmac was smouldering, and the children who went barefoot hopped about protesting. Every parking space was taken, none became free, it was all turning into a drag, and Baumgartner could have found his temper fraying, but he had lashings of time, in fact the search for a parking space enabled him to kill time. He took care not to park in the bays marked on the ground with a picture of a wheelchair, which indicate that these are reserved for the handicapped. Not that Baumgartner was all that public-spirited, not that he was all that sensitive to the lot of these folk, not a bit of it; in a funny way it was merely a question of not incurring some handicap of his own in return for God knows what, under the effect of some contamination or other.

With the parking question resolved, Baumgartner pulled his suitcase out of the boot of the Fiat and made for the hotel entrance. Its façade would have been repainted quite recently, milky constellations reached out discreetly in some of its corners, and the lobby was pervaded by the sour, fresh smell of whitewash, reminiscent of curdled milk. Around the building, traces of what was recently a building site were to be encountered – scraps of dirty plastic sheeting piled up in containers situated in the limbo of the car park, planks coated with cement stacked any old how in a forgotten corner. The receptionist for his part had his forehead spangled with red blotches, and feverishly scratched his right shoulder as he checked his register for Baumgartner's reservation.

The room was dark and uninviting, the fragile, bockety furniture had a factitious look like so many stage props, the bed offered a mattress hollowed out like a hammock, and the shape of the drawn curtains did not marry up with that of the window. There was a rigid and forlorn sofa, and above it a crappy lithograph proffered a few zinnias, but Baumgartner did not spare it a glance: he marched straight to the telephone, dropping his bag en route, lifted the receiver and dialled a number. It must have been busy because Baumgartner pulled a face, hung up, took off his coat and circled his case without opening it.

A few minutes later he went into the bathroom to wash his hands; turning the taps on and off produced seismic shocks in the entire establishment's plumbing, and on his way out he skidded on the slippery tiles. Back in the bedroom, he pulled open the curtains and took his station in front of the window to discover that it looked onto a well, a dark air-shaft, a stifling chimney of laughable diameter, its glassed-over roof all grimy. Enough is enough! Baumgartner, dripping with sweat, lifted the phone again, called Reception and demanded a different room. The receptionist continued to scratch himself as he gave Baumgartner the number of the only other free room, on the floor above, but as the hotel staff seemed decidedly inattentive, nobody came to pick up his case and he carried it up the stairs himself.

And on the floor above, he went through the same rigmarole

point by point: once more he tried to phone, but the line was still engaged. He looked on the point of losing his temper again but calmed down, opened his case and put his things away in the murky wardrobe and the pitch-pine chest of drawers. Then he inspected this new room which was the identical twin of the earlier one, apart from the lithograph above the despondent sofa: the zinnias had been displaced by crocuses. And if the window gave a mediocre view of the car park, at least it let in a bit of sunshine, at least Baumgartner would be able to keep an eye on his car.

26

"MEDIC, TOO, ACTUALLY," HÉLÈNE ANSWERED AFTER a moment's pause, "though not exactly. And anyway, not any more, I mean I no longer practise." Besides, she had never tended anyone, she'd preferred basic research to minding an endless string of patients; and even her research she'd been able to throw up a couple of years earlier, thanks to an inheritance plus an allowance. Her last job had been at the Salpêtrière Hospital, in Immunology. "I was researching into antibodies, looking to see if there were any, calculating how many there were, trying to see what they looked like, I studied their activity, see what I mean?" "Of course, at least I think I do," ventured Ferrer who, following Baumgartner's example and in accordance with Sarradon's instructions, would himself switch rooms two days later, going two floors down.

The room looked more or less like the previous one but was more than twice the size because it had three beds. It was less cluttered with medical impedimenta, its walls were in pale yellow and the window did not look out on any tree but on a drab brick building. Félix Ferrer's neighbours were, on his left a fellow from Ariège built like a pillar and evidently bursting with health – Ferrer never would discover what brought him into the ward – and on his right a Breton, a punier creature who looked like an atomic scientist with hyperopia, forever lost in a magazine; his complaint was arrhythmia. It didn't happen all that often that anyone called in, twice Arrhythmia's mother (inaudible whispered palavers, news value non-existent), once Ariège's brother (booming commentaries on one hell of a match, news value negligible). The rest of the time, the commerce that Ferrer held with them was limited to negotiations concerning which television programme to watch and the sound level.

Hélène returned each day to visit him, but he continued to afford her an unenthusiastic welcome, and never evinced the slightest pleasure when she pushed open the door. Not that he had anything against her, but his thoughts were elsewhere. From her first appearance, on the other hand, the girl had his room-mates evidently galvanised. In the days that followed they watched her each time with greater lust, each in his own manner – Ariège frontal and voluble, Brittany allusive and oblique. But even his neighbours' concupiscence did not manage to rub off on him as is sometimes the case – you know what I mean: you're not particularly taken with a person whom a second person is craving for in your place, but that in itself gives you the idea, nay the authority, nay the injunction to want her, things like this can happen sometimes, they've been known to happen, but not in this case.

At the same time when a person's inclined to take an interest in you, there's nothing to prevent her running the occasional errand, she can take the initiative of bringing you the day's papers, which you then pass on to the Breton. If they were autho- rised under the hospital rules, perhaps she would bring flowers too. On each of her visits Hélène would enquire after Ferrer's health, scrutinising with a practised eye the curves and diagrams hanging from the end of the bed, but their conversation never went beyond such clinical issues. Aside from her erstwhile profes- sional activities, she never breathed a word about her past. Thus the notions evoked a moment ago about an inheritance and an allowance, for all their potential in biographical terms, did not offer a starting point for any further development. Nor was Ferrer ever struck by a wish to tell her his life story which, at this junc- ture, did not seem to him all that enviable or worth the telling.

So to start with Hélène came each day as if that was her calling, as if she were invested with a mission as benevolent visitor, and when Ferrer began to ask himself precisely what she was after, of course he dared not put the question to her. She was neutral, almost cool and, although she appeared to be entirely at his disposal, she never gave him an opening. Not that availability is everything, it does not necessarily stimulate desire. In any case, Ferrer was weary and largely preoccupied with impending ruin, more inclined to worry about bankers than about doctors; he was all up in the air – scarcely the frame of mind in which to engage in seduction. Blind he was assuredly not, he could see well enough that Hélène was a pretty woman, but he always looked at her as though through a pane of bullet-proof glass, proof against sexual impulses. Their exchanges were all somewhat abstract or else entirely concrete, they left no room for feelings, left them under lock and key. A bit frustrating, but at the same time quite restful. Before long she no doubt had to face the fact herself, for she spaced out her visits, coming only every second or third day.

But after three weeks when, as anticipated, the question arose of Ferrer going home, Hélène offered to oversee his departure. It happened one Tuesday, towards the end of the morning; Ferrer was rather weak and wobbled on his pins as he clutched his little bag. She arrived and off they went in a taxi. And Ferrer, incorrigible as ever, despite the silent company of Hélène on the back seat, was already eyeing up the girls on the pavements through the taxi windows, all the way back to his place, or more precisely to in front of his place, as Hélène did not go in. But it wouldn't be too much to ask if he invited her out to supper the next day or the one after, sometime in the week, I mean, I don't know, but I'd call it the done thing. Ferrer thought so too. All right, let's make it tomorrow, get it over with, and then it was a question of deciding which restaurant to meet up in; after some hesitation Ferrer suggested one recently opened in Rue du Louvre, next door to Saint Germain-l'Auxerrois, don't know if you know it? Yes, she did. O.K. tomorrow evening?

27

B UT FIRST, THE NEXT MORNING, FERRER RESUMED
his activities. Elisabeth, who had reopened the gallery
the two days previously, informed him of the few things
that had happened in his absence: not much new work coming
in, not much post, no telephone calls, not a fax, not an e-mail.
Normal out-of-season stagnation. The habitual collectors had
not yet shown up, everyone must still be on holiday, except for
Réparaz, who had just rung to say he was on his way, and by
golly here he was – the glass-fronted door opened and in he
stepped, in his inevitable navy-blue flannels with his initials
embroidered in small letters on the front of his shirt. Some time
since he'd last shown up.

On arrival, he shook hands and remarked on how happy he
was with the Martinov he'd bought in the New Year, you remember, the big yellow Martinov? "Of course," said Ferrer. "They're
all more or less yellow, in any case." "And have you anything
new, meanwhile?" the tycoon asked anxiously. "Haven't I just!"
said Ferrer. "Odds and bits, but I haven't yet had time to hang
them all, the thing is I've only just reopened. Most of what's here
you've already seen." "Still, I'll take a look around," declared
Réparaz.

And off he went to loiter about the gallery with a mistrustful
air, pushing his glasses up the bridge of his nose or nibbling at
the earpieces as he made a quick tour past most of the pictures
only to draw rein in front of a large oil on lined canvas, 150×200,
representing a gang rape, hung at the start of the summer in a
thick metal frame heavily meshed in barbed-wire. After twenty
seconds' contemplation, Ferrer went to join him. "I thought

this would say something to you," said he. "There's something about it, isn't there?"

"Well, yes, could be," mused Réparaz. "Know what? I wouldn't mind having it at home. A bit on the large side, of course, but what really bothers me is the frame. Couldn't the frame be changed?" "Hang on a second," said Ferrer, "you've noticed that the picture is a wee bit on the violent side, I mean you have to agree it's a shade brutal. Well this frame, the artist had it made specially for that very reason, if you follow me, because it's part of the thing. It absolutely belongs with it." "If you say so." "Stands to reason," said Ferrer. "Besides, it's not expensive." "I'll think about it," said Réparaz. "I'll have a word with my wife. It's the subject, too, you know, she's pretty sensitive. As it's a bit what-you-call-it, I wouldn't want her feeling . . . " "Quite understood," said Ferrer. "Think about it. Talk to her."

After Réparaz left nobody else pushed open the gallery door until closing time, which, in consultation with Elisabeth, was brought forward. Ferrer, a while later, was to meet Hélène at the agreed restaurant, a vast shady room dotted with little round tables with white tablecloths, intimate copper lamps, and artistic little bouquets, nifty service by exotic lovelies. Here Ferrer often ran into people he knew a little without necessarily exchanging greetings, but he always took pleasure in having a friendly word with the exotic lovelies. Come to that, he would do well this evening to mind his ps and qs, at the risk of getting a trifle bored by Hélène, as short of conversation as ever, and this time wearing a light grey suit with thin white stripes. If this suit regrettably offered no plunging neckline, Ferrer could nonetheless observe that round the girl's neck a slender white-gold chain supported an arrow-shaped pendant that pointed very pointedly in the direction of her breasts, there's something on which to focus the attention, something to maintain one's vigilance.

Whether it were innocence or manipulation, Hélène never spoke much but at least she knew how to listen, get the other going again with the appropriate monosyllable, bridging a sudden silence by asking just the apposite question at the crucial moment. Regularly resting his eyes on the arrow to recharge himself but never wholly succeeding, any better than when she came to visit him in hospital, in generating some solid lust – and I myself find this hard to fathom for I'm the one to testify that Hélène is highly desirable – Ferrer kept the conversation going by talking about his work: the art market (pretty quiet at the moment), current trends (it's a bit complicated, it's all so fragmented, we'll have to go back as far as Duchamp), and current debates (the thing is, Hélène, when art and money come into contact, they don't pull their punches), collectors (getting more suspicious all the time, perfectly understandable), artists (more and more out of touch, all quite understandable), and models (they no longer exist in the traditional meaning of the word, which strikes me as no surprise). Preferring to avoid making a fool of himself, he abstained from describing his voyage to the Arctic and its lamentable sequel. But if his observations were all superficial and he kept charging at open doors, he evidently failed to bore Hélène to whom Ferrer, out of force of habit, suggested going out to have one for the road.

Well, it often happens at this juncture – leaving the restaurant, having one for the road – that a man who has been at pains to avoid ingesting garlic, red cabbage or too many stirrup cups, will attempt to kiss a woman. It is customary, the done thing, and yet, there again, nothing of the sort occurred. And there is still no way of knowing whether Ferrer was bashful, whether he was afraid of being repulsed, or whether it was simply that he was not all that set on it. We must not rule out – Feldman would have told him, Feldman who started out in psychiatry before switching to cardiology – that the heart attack followed by the spell in hospital will have provoked in Ferrer a momentary loss of self-esteem, without any radical psychological discontinuity, rest assured, but liable to generate a small measure of inhibition. Low self-esteem my foot! Ferrer would have answered as he sidestepped an embrace and still proposed to Hélène that she stop by at his gallery one of these days, as this kind of thing seemed to interest her.

The day she came by, at the close of a rainy afternoon, no longer any blue-green or light-grey suit, no low-cut outfit, just a white blouse and jeans, also white, beneath a fairly roomy mackintosh. They had five minutes' conversation. Ferrer, still somewhat ill at ease, commented on one or two of the exhibits (a small Beucler, four Esterellas hillocks), then left her to pursue her visit on her own. She ignored the small-format Martinovs, devoted a lot of time to the Marie-Nicole Guimard photographs, placed two fingers on a component of Schwartz's closed-circuit bellows on display right at the back, then barely slowed her pace in front of the gang rape. Without completely losing sight of her, Ferrer leaned on the desk and pretended to be supervising the lay-out of the next Martinov catalogue with Elisabeth when Spontini popped up from nowhere. "Why Spontini!" cried Ferrer brightly. "How are you getting on with the temperas?"

From the back of the gallery Hélène thought she understood that the said Spontini had not come to present his work, his temperas or anything, but his grievances. The word contract was pronounced. The word rider was invoked. Percentages were challenged. Not close enough to follow the conversation, Hélène seemed to take a sudden interest in the most recent works of Blavier hanging behind the desk. "You understand . . . I," Ferrer was saying, "I have a certain notion of my work, I reckon it is worth fifty per cent of the work's value. If you're now reckoning that it's worth say forty, we are not going to have a meeting of minds." "I find that too high," said Spontini, "I find it enormous.

Honestly I find it enormous. It's out of all proportion. Frankly I have to ask myself whether I wouldn't do better to go and talk to Abitbol, that's all he's waiting for, Abitbol, I saw him only the day before yesterday at Castagnier's preview."

"Besides," said Ferrer wearily, "this is not the first time you've tried this on me. You've taken advantage of working with me for ten years to get to know everybody, and you've made sales behind my back, I know it, even while you were exhibiting your work here. So what I'm saying to you is this, when people treat me this way, never mind Abitbol, in principle I show them the door. I mean really, you have no idea! The difficulties we have working in France at the moment." "But, what about Beucler?" Spontini objected. "After what he's done to you, he's still here."

"Beucler," said Ferrer, "he's quite a different matter. Beucler's an altogether different kettle of fish." "Even so, don't forget," Spontini insisted, "he's really taken you to the cleaners. He's left you with ten per cent on one work, this Beucler of yours, he's pocketed ninety per cent, and everyone's in on the secret. And here he still is, and here you are in the middle of setting up this deal for him in Japan. I've been told. I know, everyone knows." "Beucler's a different matter," Ferrer repeated, "and that's a fact. I wanted to end our association, perfectly true, but he's still here. It's as illogical as that. Let's change the subject, if you don't mind."

Running out of arguments, they soon had nothing else to say to each other, and Spontini left, muttering complaints interlarded with threats. Ferrer, all done in, dropped into an armchair. Hélène, who had returned for another look at the Schwartz, was smiling at him from a distance. He repaid her with a thin smile as he stood up then, going across to her: "You heard, I suppose you have understood. You must find me loathsome." "Not at all," said Hélène. "I can't stand this sort of situation," observed Ferrer, rubbing his cheeks, "it's the worst thing about this business. How I'd love to be able to delegate to someone else on these occasions. I used to have this assistant, Delahaye, I've mentioned him to you, he was beginning to get the hang of it very well, to fill in for me, then he went and died, blast him! A pity, because he was a good man, Delahaye, he was very good at smoothing things out."

He was massaging his temples now, he looked tired. "You know," said Hélène, "I don't have all that much to do at the moment, I could give you a hand if you wanted." "It's kind of you," said Ferrer with a sad smile, "but I really cannot accept. Strictly between you and me, the way I'm placed at present, I'd be unable to pay your salary." "As bad as that?" "I've had a few problems lately," Ferrer acknowledged, "I'll tell you about them."

And tell her he did. The lot. From the beginning. When he had finished the account of his misfortunes night had fallen. Outside, at the top of the building site the two yellow cranes flashed winking lights at the end of their jibs while up in the sky an airliner, Paris–Singapore, blinked from its wingtips at the same rhythm: thus winking in an earth-sky synchronicity, they signalled their presence to each other.

28

PERSONALLY THIS MAN BAUMGARTNER'S BEGINNING to get up my nose. His daily routine is too tiresome. Apart from living in a hotel, phoning every other day and visiting whatever comes to hand, he really does precious little. I mean how flabby can you get? Since leaving Paris for the southwest, he's spent his time driving aimlessly about at the wheel of his white Fiat, a basic vehicle bare of optional extras or ornaments, nothing in the way of window stickers, nothing dangling from the rear-view mirror. He's preferred to take the byroads. One morning, a Sunday, he arrived in Biarritz.

As the ocean was powerfully churned up, as it was a Sunday of the mellowest, hazy sunshine, the inhabitants of Biarritz had stepped out to look at the waves. They were standing in rows, layer upon layer, along the beaches but also on the esplanades, the piers, the balconies, vantage-points and other promenades offering a view over the rippling, muscular ocean, they lined up along everything that overlooked it and watched it going through its turbulent routine. This spectacle will leave a person dazed and paralysed, he can look at it indefinitely without wearying of it, no reason to stop – fire also has this effect on him, rain sometimes has this effect, watching the world go by from a café terrace may also induce it.

At Biarritz, this Sunday, near the lighthouse, Baumgartner noticed a young man venture to the water's edge, at the extreme tip of a rocky prominence, at risk of getting completely soaked by the vigorous storm of spray, which he avoided with a matador's twitch of the hips. Moreover it was in the language of the bullring that he commented on the power of the wave-trains, saluted (*Olé*) a particularly spectacular explosion, allowed a promising, thunderous wave (*Torito bueno*) to approach (*Mira mira mira*) and build up (*Toro toro*) – all language used to encourage, solicit and summon rampaging beasts in the arena. Then, once the wave had charged savagely in all directions, had shattered in a great explosion, when this monster of the deep came to lie down and die at his feet, the young man, arm outstretched and hand raised as though to stop time, addressed it with the gesture of the matador to the bull in the occasionally long-drawn-out interval during which the beast, after receiving the *coup de grâce*, remains standing while life drains away before it collapses, often on its side, legs jutting stiffly out at right angles.

Baumgartner did not stay for more than two days at Biarritz, time enough for the ocean to gets its breath back, then he was off inland. More even than during his previous visit, he tended to steer clear of the towns, simply passing through them or taking the bypass when there was one. He preferred to stop in villages, he'd spend a moment in the café-tabac without addressing a word to a soul.

He preferred to listen in to the conversation (*four men with time on their hands were comparing their weight and substituting it for the number of the corresponding French département. Thus the scrawniest said Meuse, the more or less average put in for Yvelines, the one on the corpulent side admitted that he was within a whisker of Belfort, the fattest overshot the Val-d'Oise*), to read the notices scotch-taped to the mirrors (*TOP BANANAS: HEFTY VEG. COMPETITION. 8h to 11h, Registration of Produce. 11h to 12h30, Judging. 17h, Prize-giving followed by Reception. The following produce may be entered: Leek, Salad Greens, White Cabbage, Kale, Cauliflower, Red Cabbage, Tomato, Melon, Pumpkin, Pepper, Courgette, Beetroot, Carrot, Celeriac, Swede & Turnip-cabbage, Turnip & Parsnip, Radish, Potato, Mangelwurzel, Sweetcorn, Garlic, Onion. All growers may compete. No more than nine vegetables per grower. One specimen per vegetable. To be entered with leaves, stalks and roots if possible. Judging will be made on the basis of weight and appearance)*, or look up the weather forecast in the local papers (*Background of broken sky, rain and showers will fall, sometimes accompanied in the afternoon by a clap of thunder*).

The weather indeed was breaking, nevertheless Baumgartner seemed to be growing less fussy about the quality of the hotels in which he stayed. He would spend the night in more primitive establishments than hitherto, he seemed not to care. Those first days he would scrupulously obtain the local and national papers and run through the Culture and Society pages without ever finding a mention of even the smallest antiques theft. Once it had become unlikely that his would be noted, Baumgartner reduced his consumption of newsprint, eventually limiting himself to leafing through the papers absently at breakfast, making them all sticky with butter and jam, underlining passages with coffee, creating interlaced circles in orange juice all through the salmon-pink financial pages.

One evening of driving rain, between Auch and Toulouse, he was motoring through the night, which was falling earlier and earlier. Beyond the windscreen wipers switched to their fastest setting, the headlights could barely manage to light his way: he noticed only at the last moment a silhouette making its way along the edge of the road on his right, slightly below the road-level. Swallowed up in the wet and the darkness, indeed just about to dissolve in it like a sugar-lump, the silhouette did not wave nor even turn round at the approach of vehicles whose headlamps and engines were in any event muffled in the rainstorm. If Baumgartner made to stop, it was less out of charity than as a reflex action, or because he was getting a little bored with his own company: he flicked on his right-hand indicator, braked a hundred metres further on, and waited for the silhouette to reach him.

But it did not press its pace, as though it had not made a connection between itself and the Fiat's coming to a halt. Once it had come up with the car, Baumgartner saw through the fog of the streaming window that it was a girl, it would seem, a girl who opened the door, got in without the normal preliminary observations between those offering and being offered a lift. She heaved her rucksack onto the back seat and sat down without a word, cautiously slamming the door. She was so streaming wet that the windscreen slightly misted over at once – Baumgartner hated to think what the seat would be like once she had left. Besides, she was not only soaked through, she looked on the grubby side and in a world of her own. "Are you heading for Toulouse?" Baumgartner asked her.

The girl did not answer at once, her face was not all that easy to make out in the dark. Then she announced in a monotone, in a slightly mechanical and vaguely disturbing delivery, that she was not heading for Toulouse, she was going to Toulouse, that it was regrettable and curious that this distinction was ever more seldom drawn, that there was no excuse for it, the misuse was anyway all part and parcel of a general abuse of language about which all that it is possible to do is to voice one's objection, that she at any rate objected most strenuously, after which she turned her soaking head of hair against the headrest and fell asleep. Plainly gaga.

For a moment or two Baumgartner was stunned and slightly irritated, then he gently engaged first gear as though he were pondering before moving off. A half-kilometre further on, as the girl had started gently snoring, he felt such a surge of irritation that he was almost ready to stop the car and put her out again in the dark and the wet, but he got the better of the impulse: she was sleeping peacefully at present, her whole body relaxed, limp, strapped in by the seat belt, it would be unworthy of the gentleman he had decided to become. The sentiment does him credit but it was chiefly something else that prevented him: it was above all her voice that reminded him of someone. Concentrated on the task of driving in these hostile elements, he scarcely had the opportunity to give her sidelong glances, and in any case the young woman was slumped against the side-window and had her back to him. But suddenly Baumgartner recognised her, realised who she was, it was all too unlikely, but there was no disputing it. All the way to Toulouse he drove as though on eggshells, holding his breath and avoiding the smallest rut, the tiniest jolt that could risk waking her. The drive took not less than an hour.

Reaching Toulouse at dead of night, Baumgartner dropped the girl off in front of the railway station without putting on the courtesy light; he kept his face turned away while she unfastened her seat belt and got out, thanking him twice almost inaudibly. Instead of driving off at once, Baumgartner watched her in his rear-view mirror as she disappeared in the direction of the station buffet without turning round. It was dark and as this girl – who seems to me off her rocker – had not given him so much as a glance, everything points to her not having identified him, at least this is earnestly to be hoped for.

The ensuing days, Baumgartner pursued his random itinerary. He was well acquainted with the drabness of roadside diners, the sour awakenings in hotel rooms in which the heating has not yet come on, the numbing impact of rural developments and building sites, the bitterness of impossible relationships. This continued for some further two weeks after which, towards mid-September, Baumgartner finally noticed that he was being tailed.

29

THE WHOLE OF THIS SAME FORTNIGHT HÉLÈNE continued to stop by quite often at the gallery. As at the hospital, she would come at any old time but never for more than one hour, once every two or three days and, as at the hospital, Ferrer would welcome her with polite reserve, with a strained courtesy and rather forced smiles, the way one tries to humour a frail relative.

The long account he had given her of his recent difficulties had not brought them all that much closer, in the end. She had made no particular response as she listened to him, neither one of admiration at Ferrer's Arctic exploits nor one of commiseration, if not amusement, at the dismaying conclusion to the matter. And if she had made no further offer to help him in the gallery, this did not seem to be for financial reasons. The fact remains, they had not made much progress, they kept hunting for things to say without always finding them, and this could produce silences – which could have been no bad thing, there are times when silence is golden. Accompanied by the right look and smile, silence can produce excellent results, a rare intensity of feeling, subtle perspectives, an exquisite aftertaste, a secure resolution. But not in this case: these silences were only spongy, ponderous taciturnity, as cumbersome as trudging through wet clay. After a moment neither of them could stand it. Soon Hélène was coming less and less often, then scarcely at all.

At first Ferrer had been relieved, true enough, but it was no less true that this development inevitably created rather quickly a little void that he had not expected, and here he was soon catching himself waiting for her, glancing casually up the street, and needless to say she had never given him her address nor left him anything by way of a phone number, seeing that the idiot has never asked her for one. And now it was a Monday morning, which is not often all one could wish for: shuttered shops, overcast sky, muggy atmosphere, squalid underfoot, in a word the whole place was shut, it was as depressing as a Sunday without the alibi of having the day off. Little scattered groups were crossing the street outside of the studs marking the pedestrian crossings towards the only discount store open, and Ferrer's humour was of the same bilious, rancid colour as the cranes on the building site opposite and the electric sign on the supermarket. Spontini chose a poor moment, stopping by at around eleven in order to remind him that they were still in disagreement over the percentages.

He did not have much leisure to pursue the discussion: "Listen," Ferrer broke in, "now let me tell you what I think. You're not putting in enough work, that's what it is, your work has not evolved. Strictly between the two of us, the stuff you're turning out doesn't hugely interest me any more." "What d'you mean by that?" enquired Spontini anxiously. "What I mean is simply that all right you've made sales in two art houses and to three individual buyers, but that doesn't mean you exist. For me, you're zero. Wait till you have regular collectors abroad, then you may be able to talk of a career taking off. What I mean is that if you're not happy, there's the door."

Framed in which stood a fellow with whom Spontini almost collided as he left the gallery, a fellow in his thirties, in blue jeans and bomber jacket, not exactly an artist's outfit in this day and age, and still less a buyer's, one might rather have called it the outfit of a young copper, and this is precisely what the man was. "You remember me," said Supin, "I'm from Criminal Records. I'm here about your loss report."

Without going into all the technical details, the situation

according to Supin was as follows. Good news and bad news, I'd as soon start with the bad, which is that under the electronic microscope the analysis of samples taken from the workshop had got them nowhere. But parallel to that, the good news was that in the pockets of an unfrozen corpse, discovered by chance and not all that well preserved, something had come to light in a wad of stiffened, crumpled old Kleenexes, compact as flat pebbles or miniature cakes of soap at the end of their life, to wit a scrap of paper with a car registration number. After identifying this number, a cross-check left open the possibility that the Fiat in question had some connection with the theft reported by Ferrer. So they were looking out for it. That's where matters rested.

Ferrer was straightaway in a much better temper. Before closing the gallery, at the end of the afternoon, he received a visit from a young artist called Corday, who put forward certain plans, sketches, models and assembly prices. Unfortunately he did not have the funds to realise all his aims. "But it's good, all this," said Ferrer, "it's very good, I like it a lot. Tell you what, we'll mount a show." "Really?" said the other. "Yes indeed," said Ferrer, "of course, of course. And if we make a go of it, we'll do a second one." "So shall we sign a contract?" Corday imagined. "Take it easy," said Ferrer. "Hold on. Contracts don't get signed just like that. Come back and see me the day after tomorrow."

30

THE SCHENGEN TREATY CAME INTO EFFECT IN 1995.
It brought about, as we all know, the free circulation of
persons within those European states subscribing to it.
The suppression of internal border controls, as also the establishment of a reinforced surveillance along the external borders,
allow the rich to travel among the rich, comfortable among their
own kind, opening their arms all the wider to each other the
better to close them against the poor who, being treated like
dirt, only grasp the extent of their misery the more keenly. True,
the Customs & Excise continue in office, and thus John Citizen
is no more authorised now than he was before to traffic with
impunity in what he wishes; but the said John Citizen is now free
to move about without waiting for an hour at the frontier so his
passport can be given the once-over. This is what Baumgartner
was on the point of doing.

By dint of patrolling the area, the smallest eco-museums,
curiosities, panoramas and viewing points situated in the lower
left-hand corner of the map of France held no further secrets
for him. Lately he had not left the south-western extremity, never
more than one hour from the border, as if he were some sort of
stowaway aboard a leaky vessel, skulking cautiously about near
the lifeboats, concealed behind a ventilator shaft.

But Baumgartner had no need now to notice the same motorcyclist more than three times in three days, dressed and helmeted
in red, to decide on a change of air. This individual first loomed
up in his rear-view mirror, in the distance, on a twisting mountain back-road, appearing and disappearing as the hairpin bends
dictated. Another time, at a motorway toll booth, not far from

two police motorcyclists in black, it was the same one, it seemed to him, leaning against his machine as he munched a sandwich – the helmet did not seem to get in the way of his jaws as they chomped. On the third occasion, the man had apparently broken down by the side of a main road in the rain, which had returned; he was hooked into an emergency telephone box. As he passed him, Baumgartner took care to aim the near-side wheels of his vehicle at a deep and broad puddle; he laughed on looking in his mirror and seeing the man jump at the muddy splash, but was a bit disappointed not to see him shake a fist.

Baumgartner's life, which had been a little ragged, silent, felt-padded like a pea-souper these last weeks, recovered a spot of zest with the apparition of this motorcyclist in red. This presence, and its attendant anxiety, took the edge off his loneliness, thus attenuating the echo produced by his every gesture in the hotel rooms. His only remaining line with the world was his daily phone call to Paris, which mitigated his isolation, and it was by phone that he announced his departure for Spain. And then in any case autumn had certainly arrived, he said, the evenings were becoming chilly. "It's simple. It never stops raining. I'll be better off over there."

From his present location, that is today Thursday morning in Saint-Jean-de-Luz, there is a choice of two routes for reaching Spain. Either Autoroute 63 where the frontier consists of rows of arches and columns punctuated by hoardings and old yellowing cut-out symbols heat-applied to the asphalt and coming unglued, booths that are closed because no longer in use, barriers forever raised above a scattering of officials, three of them with nothing to do, dressed in vague uniforms, turning their backs to the traffic as they wonder what they're supposed to be there for. Otherwise there's the option of the trunk road numbered 10: this is what Baumgartner chooses.

On No. 10, Béhobie is the crossing point, in the shape of a

bridge over the Bidassoa. Great juggernauts are parked in front of the last French building, which is a bank, and Customs now consists of abandoned, vandalised blockhouses, their blinds sagging at an angle. Such window panes as they have left are filthy and to some extent hide the rubble and detritus that's piled up – all rather heart-breaking but it won't be long before it's all torn down: mindful of the state of the installations, the government in Madrid has given the go-ahead to the project initiated by the local authority and now it is only a question of days, the bulldozers are straining at the leash as they await the order to wreak destruction on the local buildings as on the local economy, then the decree may be signed authorising them to blow the whole place to smithereens.

The entire zone, moreover, has already the feel of a building site about it. Many of the houses whose walls have collapsed have been invaded by a parasitic vegetation that has grown up unstintingly through their stove-in roofs. An assortment of blackened textiles and plastic sheets dangle from the windows of those newer buildings that have not yet been bricked up. There is a pervasive acid smell of rust, and the sky itself also has a rusty or excremental hue, barely distinguishable behind the ink-dark rain. Some of the factories hemmed in by mounds of scrap, distinguished by derelict scaffolding and all daubed with slogans, look as if they've been run into the ground without waiting for the receivers. Beyond the bridge, the vehicles are parked any old how as they await their drivers who have gone off to buy duty-free alcohol and tobacco. Then, once they're on their way, the road ahead is a chronic snarl-up, a thick peppering of red lights, the traffic jolts forward by fits and starts, like a cough.

Baumgartner did like everyone else: he left his car and ran through the rain towards the cut-price shops, his coat collar pulled up over his head. One of the shops was offering small nylon rain-hats lined with tartan for thirty-five francs, which were just the job: Baumgartner tried on several. Size fifty-eight was too small, sixty a bit on the large side, so he took a fifty-nine without hesitating or trying it on, it was bound to do the trick, but after he had tried it on in the car, in front of the vanity mirror, it didn't look as though it fitted all that well either, but never mind, it was too late, the Fiat crossed the frontier without hindrance, and Baumgartner breathed a little easier after that.

Crossing a frontier, the body changes, it is a well known fact, the eye changes focus, the air-density is not what it was, the smells, the sounds are more concentrated, even the sun has a different look about it. The rust has a different way of eating away at the road signs, and these suggest an unfamiliar concept of bends, speed restrictions or hump-backed bridges, added to which, some of them are hard to make out, and Baumgartner felt he was becoming another person, or rather at once the same and another, as when one has had a complete blood-transfusion. Once he had crossed the border, what's more, a gentle breeze unknown in France sprang up.

Three kilometres beyond the old border-post a new tailback had formed. A van bearing the message POLICIA was parked facing the oncoming traffic, which was being filtered by men in black uniforms and further on, every fifty metres, other men in camouflage fatigues, sub-machine-guns held at an angle across their chests, watched the sides of the road. Baumgartner thought nothing of it but, three kilometres further down the road, while he was driving at a moderate speed, a navy-blue Renault van overtook him. Instead of pulling back into lane the van fell into step beside him, and from a lowered window, an arm appeared in a sleeve of the same colour as the van, and extended by a long, pale hand whose slender fingers waved slowly up and down, the fingertips drumming the empty air rhythmically, keeping the tempo as they pointed to the shoulder of the road, onto which, calmly but firmly, Baumgartner was obliged to pull in.

His progress aborted in this civilised manner, Baumgartner switched on his indicators, urging himself not to sweat, braked slowly and came to a halt. Once the blue van had overhauled him to come to a gentle stop some ten metres from the Fiat, two men climbed out. They were Spanish Customs officers, smiling and clean-shaven; their hair still held all the furrows of the comb, their uniforms were neatly pressed, they approached Baumgartner with dancing steps, a song still on their lips. One of them spoke French with barely a trace of an accent, the other said nothing. "Flying Customs, sir," said the one who talked, "just a small formality, your vehicle's papers and your own documents, and will you be kind enough to open your boot."

It took less than a minute for the contents of the boot to be inspected by the one who did not talk, and found to be of no interest: bag, change of clothes, toilet kit. The officer who never spoke shut the boot as delicately as a watchmaker, while the other, with Baumgartner's ID in his hand, tiptoed off to the van whence he emerged three minutes later, no doubt having made a phone call or tapped into a terminal. "Perfect, sir," he told him, "please accept our apologies and our best thanks for your co-operation which redounds to our credit and serves only to make us all the more absolute in our respect for a fundamental morality which is indissociable from the mission that has happily been entrusted to us and to which a lifetime cannot be dedicated other than quite unreservedly, making no allowance even for family ties ("Yes," said Baumgartner) and this regardless of any obstacle which daily, by its very consequence and brutality, even goes to uplift and create the élan that inspires us each day to fight this cancer which is the violation of the principles of dutiability ("Yes, yes," said Baumgartner) but which does permit me amid a hundred other things to wish you, in the name of my people in general and of our Excise Department in particular, a most excellent journey." "Thank you, thank you," said Baumgartner, bewildered, but then he crashed his gears, stalled, after which he was off again.

He was back on the road, now, and autumn had certainly arrived, in fact it was quite well advanced since at this moment a flight of storks crossed the sky following the line of the road. They would be migrating storks, it's the season, they're on their little annual shuttle, Potsdam–Nouakchott via Gibraltar almost non-stop, often following the line of existing roads. They make but a single stop, practically at the halfway mark, on the interminable straight line that connects Algeciras with Malaga, this road being lined with pylons on the tops of which a thoughtful authority has taken care to install huge nests fit for storks. There they rest up a little, take the time to catch their breath, to exchange a little gossip, to snap up native rats and vipers, or even maybe a nice little carcass, you never know – while upstream the two handsome Spanish Customs men looked at each other and burst into giggles. "*Me parece, tío,*" said the talking one to the silent one, "*que hemos dado tiempo al Tiempo.*" And they both fell about laughing. The breeze sprang up.

And twenty minutes later, shortly before noon, Baumgartner drove into a seaside resort. He parked his Fiat in an underground car park in the centre, went to book in to the Hôtel de Londres et d'Angleterre, which overlooks the bay, then he left the hotel and strolled along for a while with no particular end in view, in the broad, bright streets of the town centre, where several clothes shops, be they luxury or not, are situated. He knew enough Spanish to try on a pair of trousers in a boutique, but not enough to explain why he did not want them. Then he made for the old town, its streets lined with an uncanny number of bars. He went into one and pointed at the display of little objects, some in a sauce, others poached or grilled, and he gobbled them down standing there at the counter, then returned to the hotel by the promenade running the length of the bay.

And two weeks later it was very cold for early October. On the promenade everyone was already in anoraks and overcoats, furs and scarves, the push chairs were smothered in eiderdowns as they were pushed along at a fast clip. From the window of his room in the Hôtel de Londres et d'Angleterre Baumgartner saw a woman with the magnificent build of a sea lion, dressed in a black one-piece bathing costume as she went into the grey-green ocean the mere colour of which was enough to make one feel cold. She was all on her own in the bay, beneath a muddy grey sky which didn't help; people stopped on the promenade to watch her. She waded into the freezing water until it was up to her ankles, her knees, her crotch, then to her waist at which depth, before stretching her arms forward and plunging in, she crossed herself and Baumgartner envied her. What has she got that I haven't, to do such a thing? Perhaps it's simply that she can swim. Which I can't. Crossing myself I can manage, but swimming, no.

31

"WHAT ABOUT THIS CONTRACT, THEN? ARE WE going to make it?" Corday pressed him feverishly the following morning. "Oh the contract, the contract," said Ferrer, the previous day's enthusiasm already abated, "not just now. We'll not sign it just now. For the moment let's say that it is I who will see to the reproduction side, that'll be my responsibility. And I shall reimburse myself once the thing's sold. Then we have to see if it takes off, if we can find you some other place in which to exhibit. In Belgium, in Germany, that sort of thing. If it doesn't take off, then we'll have to stick to France, we'll try to find something in the arts centres, for example. After that we shall try to get an item picked up by a national or provincial arts trust, right? – then we could get that piece displayed somewhere, which could already get things moving. Then New York."

"New York!" gasped the other, echoing him. "New York," repeated Ferrer, "New York. It's always a bit more of the same. And then if that works out we can see to whatever needs doing about the contract. Excuse me a minute."

Near the entrance to the gallery, hovering bemused in front of a recent work, a gigantic bra made of asbestos (which had come Ferrer's way on the recommendation of Schwartz's mistress's husband), stood the Detective Inspector, once again. He looked such a stripling, young Supin, always dressed in his standard-issue copper's outfit, an outfit he found unappealing but it went with the job. He seemed particularly happy to be there at the Ferrer Gallery, modern art, that's more in my line.

"The Fiat," said Supin, "just to let you know it seems to have been sighted close to the Spanish frontier. Flying Customs, routine check, a stroke of luck. They tried to hold up the driver for a moment but, being Customs, of course, their hands were tied. They passed the news on pretty quick, fact is, that lot and us – we're thick as thieves. Of course I'm going to try to track the fellow down, I have some colleagues there whom I'll put on the case, but I can't make you any promises. If I turn up anything I'll give you a call. I'll get back to you this evening or tomorrow in any case. Tell me, just out of curiosity, what sort of price-tag is there on the big bra?"

Once he had bowled him over with the price and Supin had tottered out, and despite the news that might possibly move things forward a little, Ferrer was overtaken by a black mood. He got rid of Corday as fast as he could, and was no longer even confident of keeping his promise to him, we should have to see. He had to pull himself together before this momentary depression left him totally deflated, above all before it contaminated the whole of his professional life and generally his outlook on the art world. Looking around in a fit of disgust at the works he had on show, he was seized by doubt which led him once again to close the gallery ahead of time. He gave Elisabeth the rest of the day off before locking the glass-paned door, pressing the switch to lower the metal grille, then setting off on foot, leaning into the wind, which was quite violent that day, to the Saint-Lazare Metro station. Change at Opéra, get off at Châtelet, whence the Palais de Justice is not two minutes' walk once you're across the Seine. Ferrer's various professional and financial worries were not the only reasons for this depression, for his bowed posture and stony face: it was also because today was 10th October, and getting divorced is never all that much of a lark.

He was of course by no means the only person in this situation, not that there is much consolation in that: the waiting room was crammed with couples whose marriages had hit the buffers. In spite of the litigation that brought them there, some of them did not seem to be getting on together all that badly, they'd be talking peaceably with their lawyers. The session was fixed for 11.30 and at 11.40 Suzanne had still not shown up – always late, mused Ferrer with a grin of vexation, but then the Family Division judge was late too. The waiting room was furnished with uncomfortable plastic seats stuck to the four walls, surrounding a low table covered with an assortment of dog-eared publications: law periodicals as well as art reviews, health magazines, and weeklies devoted to the lives of celebrities. Ferrer picked up one of these latter and started leafing through the pages: it consisted as usual of photos of stars, stars in every sphere, be they opera singers, television or sporting personalities, politicians, even celebrity chefs. The centre spread offered the picture of a superstar flanked by her latest conquest, and in the background, somewhat out of focus but still perfectly recognisable, Baumgartner could be descried. Ferrer was about to reach this page and this photo in another four seconds, three, two, one, but Suzanne chose this moment to arrive and he closed the weekly without regret.

The judge was a grey-haired judge, calm and tensed up at the same time, calm because she liked to think that being a judge was second nature to her, tensed up because she realised it was a nature she'd never got to grips with. Although she forced an air of visible aloofness, Ferrer imagined her being considerate when left to her own devices, reassuring and perhaps even affectionate, yes, certainly a good mother even though there would not be a barrel of laughs every day. It was quite conceivable that her husband was a clerk of the court and attended to the domestic tasks when she was going to be late home for supper, over which they would argue about points of civil law. As she first saw the couple together, Ferrer, taking it that her questions were only for the form, kept his responses to the minimum.

Suzanne was just as reserved for most of the time, giving only such answers as were required, saving her breath. "No, no," said Ferrer, when the judge asked them, for the record, to confirm that they had no children. "So your mind is made up," said the judge addressing the remark to Suzanne – and, turning to Ferrer: "You, sir, do not look quite as sure of yourself as the lady. "No, no, I am perfectly sure, no problem," said Ferrer. Then she was to have a word with them individually, the one after the other, madame first. As he waited his turn, Ferrer did not pick up the same magazine and, when Suzanne left the judge's office, he got up, trying to catch her eye, but she avoided his gaze. He bumped into a chair as he went in. "You are quite sure you want a divorce?" the judge asked. "Yes, absolutely," Ferrer answered. "Good," said she as she closed the file, and that was that.

On leaving the building, Ferrer would readily enough have suggested to Suzanne that they go out for a bite together or simply stop for a drink, maybe in the place across the street, the Brasserie du Palais, but she left him no time to do so. Ferrer shuddered, expecting the worst: the scathing insults, dire warnings which he had evaded in January, but no, there was nothing like that. She merely raised a finger to command silence, opened her handbag and took out a set of duplicate keys for the gallery, which had been left at Issy, handed them to him without a word, then moved off southwards towards the Pont Saint-Michel. Five motionless seconds later, Ferrer resumed his way northwards towards the Pont au Change.

When the afternoon was over Ferrer closed the gallery as usual at seven o'clock; it would soon be dark, the sun was no longer on view from this part of the earth, all that was left was the purest blue-grey sky across which a distant aircraft gleaned the sun's last rays, no longer visible from down below, to draw a straight line in a shocking pink. Ferrer stood rooted a moment longer, glancing up the street before setting off. The local tradesmen were pulling down their metal shutters as he had done. The workmen on the building site opposite had also stopped work once the cranes' jibs had been providently turned downwind for the night. On the façade of the big building next door every other window was blocked by a satellite dish: when there was sun, those dishes must stop it getting in, giving instead a welcome to the pictures destined for the television which duly replaced the window.

He was about to move away from the gallery when a woman materialised at the end of the street – her silhouette reminded him of someone, but it took him a moment to identify her as Hélène. It was not the first time that Ferrer had had some trouble placing her straight off: even in hospital, when she came into the room he underwent the same spell of latency, knowing perfectly well that it was she even while he needed each time to reconstitute her, starting again from scratch as if her features did not spontaneously fall into place on their own. And yet they were beautiful, those features, no two ways about it, harmoniously distributed; Ferrer could admire them singly but it was the way they related to each other that kept changing, never producing quite the same face. In unstable balance, as though they entertained a shifting relationship, one could believe that they were in perpetual motion. So each time Ferrer saw Hélène again it was never precisely the same person confronting him.

She turned up on the spur of the moment, with nothing particular in mind. Ferrer suggested they have a drink, reopened the gallery and, while going to fetch champagne from the cool of the workshop, he determined to study Hélène's face this time, patiently, meticulously, much as one learns a lesson by heart, so as to recognise it once and for all and be rid of the embarrassment it kept provoking in him. But his efforts were all the more hopeless in that today Hélène for the first time had put on make-up, thus altering and complicating the whole procedure.

The thing is that make-up masks the sensory organs even as it embellishes them, at any rate, be it noted, those that have several uses. The mouth, for example, which breathes and speaks and eats, drinks, smiles, whispers, kisses, sucks, licks, bites, blows, sighs, shouts, smokes, grimaces, laughs, sings, whistles, hiccups, spits, burps, vomits, exhales, gets painted not least to honour the many noble functions it fulfils. The neighbourhood of the eye is also painted for it looks, expresses, weeps and closes to sleep, which is just as noble. The nails are painted too, for they enjoy pride of place amid the immense and noble variety of manual operations.

But one does not apply make-up to those organs providing only one or two services. Neither the ear – which serves only for listening – to which one merely fastens an ear-ring. Nor the nose – whose only task is to breathe, to sniff and which sometimes gets bunged up – to which, as to the ear, one may attach a ring, a precious stone, a pearl or even, in certain climates, an actual bone, while in our climate we are content to dab it with powder. But Hélène did not flaunt any of these accessories, she had merely applied some ruby lipstick, some mascara which hailed from somewhere around Sienna, colourwise, and a deft touch of eyeliner. It seemed to Ferrer, as he was engaged in opening the champagne, that this would make the whole thing all the more complicated.

But no, this would not have time to complicate anything because at this moment the telephone rang: "Supin here, I'm calling sooner than expected, I think I'm onto something." Grabbing the nearest pencil, Ferrer paid him the closest attention, jotting down a few words on the back of an envelope, then profusely thanking the Inspector. "Don't mention it," said Supin, "just a lucky stroke. We are on good terms with the

Spanish Customs people," he reminded him, "and I have a top-notch colleague in the gendarmerie, a motorcyclist, over there, who took it upon himself to do a little tailing on his own account. So you see, all the stuff you hear about the various police forces being at daggers drawn . . . " Once he had hung up, Ferrer nervously filled two glasses to overflowing. "I'll have to be off rather quickly," he said. "Meanwhile, perhaps we're going to be able to drink to something at last, you and me."

32

WHETHER ONE CROSSES THE FRONTIER AT Hendaye or at Béhobie by the motorway or the main road, heading for the south of Spain, one has to pass through San Sebastián. Once Ferrer had crossed some drab industrial wastelands, skirted oppressive ribbons of 1930s architecture, and asked himself from time to time what he was doing here, suddenly he'd arrived in this large, luxurious and quite unexpected seaside resort. It was built on a narrow tongue of land, straddling a river and a hill which separated two almost symmetrical bays, this double indentation tracing out an approximate omega, a woman's chest which projected into the hinterland, two oceanic breasts corseted by the Spanish coast.

Ferrer parked his hired car in the underground car park close to the principal bay, then put up at a small hotel in the town centre. For a week he scoured the broad, airy, peaceful avenues, carefully cleansed and lined with bright, solemn buildings, but also short narrow streets, these, too, carefully swept, but dark and hemmed in with narrow buildings, all sinew. Palais and palaces, bridges and parks, Baroque, Gothic and neo-Gothic churches, spanking new arenas, vast beaches flanked by the Royal Tennis Club, the casino, and an institution offering thalassotherapy. Each one of the four bridges was more portentous than the last, and paved in mosaic and decorated in stone, glass, cast iron, embellished with white and gold obelisks, wrought-iron lamp-posts, sphinxes and turrets inscribed with royal monograms. The river water was green before shading to blue as it entered the ocean. Ferrer often lingered on these bridges, but still more frequently he strode along the promenade which lined the conch-shaped bay, in the centre of which there was a tiny island crowned with a small castle.

As he ambled about in this way for days on end with nothing in particular in view save for a stroke of luck, trying to make an inventory of each quarter, he began to weary of this town – it was at once too big and too small, one was never sure where one was, even while one knew it only too well. Supin had given no clue beyond the name of San Sebastián along with a somewhat dubious hypothesis. It was no more than conceivable that this was where the art-thief was hanging out.

To begin with, at mealtimes, Ferrer tended to haunt the bustling little bars in the old quarter where one could stand at the counter and eat all manner of dishes without being required to sit at a table for a solitary meal, something that can be pretty dispiriting. But of this too Ferrer was beginning to tire: eventually he spotted down by the harbour an unassuming restaurant where the solitude was less oppressive. He would call Elisabeth at the gallery late afternoon, and in the evenings he would go early to bed. But after a week he felt he was on a hiding to nothing – here he was in a strange town, looking for a stranger, which really did not add up, and he grew discouraged. Before determining upon a return to Paris, Ferrer was to spend a couple more days in this town, but instead of scouring it to no effect, he preferred to drowse away the afternoon in a deckchair on the beach when the autumn weather allowed, then kill these final evenings on his own in a leather armchair in the bar at the Maria Cristina hotel, before a glass of *txakoli*, as also a full-length portrait of a doge.

One evening when the whole ground floor of the Maria Cristina was taken over by a rowdy party here assembled for a congress on cancer, Ferrer chose to go across to the Hôtel de Londres et d'Angleterre, an establishment which was scarcely less chic than the other, and with a bar that enjoyed the advantage of overlooking the bay through great airy picture windows. That evening the place was much quieter than over at the Maria Cristina – three or four couples of indeterminate age sitting in the room, two or three men standing alone at the bar, not much activity, very little coming and going; Ferrer settled himself right at the back of the room by one of the big windows. Night had fallen, the lights along the shore were reflected in blurred columns on an oil-smooth ocean, upon which rested in peace, by the harbour, twenty-five pale silhouettes of pleasure boats.

Now these window panes, depending on one's angle of vision, permitted one not only to look out but also to observe the interior of the tranquil room, by dint of reflection. Soon a movement was to be noted at the far end of the bar: the revolving door had started turning for a moment, allowing Baumgartner to emerge from it, who came and propped his elbows on the bar next to the single men, turning his back on the bay. Those shoulders and that back, distantly reflected in the glass, made Ferrer's brows pucker and as his gaze focused on them ever more closely, he eventually rose from his chair and made a cautious approach to the bar. Stopping two metres short of Baumgartner, he seemed to hesitate for a second then went up to him. "Excuse me," he said, placing two fingers lightly on the man's shoulder, and the man turned round.

"Fancy!" said Ferrer. "Delahaye. I thought as much."

33

NOT CONTENT WITH NOT BEING DEAD, WHICH IN the end occasioned in Ferrer only mild surprise, Delahaye had changed a great deal in a few months. In fact he had reinvented himself. The jumble of vague obtuse angles which had always defined his person had given place to a nexus of sharp lines and acute angles, as if all of this had been the object of a reorganisation carried to extremes.

Now that he had become Baumgartner everything about him was made up of impeccably ruled lines: his tie, when he wore a tie at all, had always been worn with its knot at half-mast and off-centre beneath the left or right point of his collar, the pleat of his trousers was never visible except as a faint wraith, thanks to the baggy knees, even his smile which once upon a time never survived for more than a moment then quickly faded, rounded out, melted like an icicle in the tropics, his haphazard side-parting, his diagonal belt, the earpieces of his glasses, and even the look in his eyes – in a word all the sketchy, muddled, unfinished, mixed-up segments of his body had been put to rights, straightened up, starched. The irrepressible wisps of his shapeless moustache had themselves been scythed, to be replaced by an impeccable straight line, perfectly marked out, as if traced with a fine Latin brushstroke across his upper lip.

Ferrer and he considered each other for a moment without speaking. No doubt to give himself a countenance Delahaye began imparting a slow spin to the glass he held in his hand, then stopped the movement: the contents of the glass pursued their rotation before returning to quiescence. "Right," said Ferrer, "perhaps we could find somewhere to sit down. That will make it easier to talk." "O.K.," sighed Delahaye. They left the bar for the groups of deep armchairs disposed in threes and fours around low tables with mats on them. "You choose," said Ferrer, "I'll follow you."

As he did so he observed his former assistant's attire from the back. In this domain, too, things had changed. His double-breasted suit, charcoal-grey flannel, seemed to be doing duty as his tutor, to judge by his erect carriage. As he turned to sit down, Ferrer noticed a tie in midnight blue on a shirt with thin pearl stripes, on his feet Oxfords the colour of antique furniture, and his tie pin and his cuff links emitted dull flashes, reticent, muffled tones of opal and old gold, in a word he was dressed the way Ferrer would always have wished him to be, at the gallery. The only thing that spoiled the picture was when Delahaye dropped into an armchair and his trouser legs hitched up a little to reveal that his sock suspenders were not pulling their weight. "You're looking pretty well turned out," said Ferrer. "Where d'you go for your wardrobe?" "I had nothing left to wear," said Delahaye. "I had to buy the odd item here. You can make some pretty good buys in the town centre, you'll never believe how much cheaper things are here than in France." Then he sat bolt upright, straightened his tie, no doubt carried slightly off-centre by shock, and hauled up his socks that had slumped round his ankles.

"It's my wife who gave me these socks," he went on absently, "but, you see they have this way of slipping down. They have a tendency to slip." "Well," said Ferrer, "that's not unusual. Socks that you're given do tend to fall down." "Quite right," said Delahaye with a nervous smile, "you never said a truer word, can I get you a drink?" "Gladly," said Ferrer. Delahaye summoned a white-coated waiter, they paused in silence while the drinks were brought, then without a smile glasses were discreetly raised, they drank. "Right," proffered Delahaye, "how are we going to sort this out?" "I don't really know yet," said Ferrer, "that will largely depend on you. Shall we go and stretch our legs?"

They left the Hôtel de Londres et d'Angleterre and, instead of heading towards the ocean, for a wind was now getting up, they went in the opposite direction. The days were drawing in more and more frantically, the night darkened more and more quickly. They followed Avenue de la Liberté towards one of the bridges that spanned the river. This powerful current vainly pours itself into the Cantabrian Sea, but when the sea proves overpowering, it comes flowing upstream, stems the current and invades it, and the fresh water is smothered beneath the onslaught of so much sea water. Then, as its waves wash in against the current, they break first against the piers of Zurriola and Santa Catalina Bridges, then ease off upstream of Maria Cristina Bridge. Nonetheless they continue to convulse the river, stirring it to a greater depth, imparting to its waters a succession of peristaltic traumas all the way up to Mundalz Bridge and no doubt beyond. At the middle of the bridge they stopped, and as they briefly contemplated the battle engaged beneath their eyes between the fresh water and the salt, as Delahaye fleetingly remembered that he had never learned to swim, an idea crossed Ferrer's mind.

"Fact is, I could get rid of you, once and for all," he said softly but not really believing it. "I could drown you, for instance, no problem at all. In fact maybe that's what I should do, considering all the trouble you've caused me." The other hastened to object that such an action was bound to get him into worse trouble, but Ferrer remarked that as Delahaye had already disappeared officially, this new disappearance could not but pass unnoticed.

"For the records, you're dead," he reminded him, "you no longer exist in the eyes of the law, that's what you wanted, wasn't it? So if I do you in, what do I risk? Killing a dead man is not a crime," he ventured, little realising that he was reproducing the argument that Delahaye had earlier put to Le Flétan. "Come on," said Delahaye, "you're not going to do it." "No," Ferrer agreed, "I don't think I am. Besides, I don't know how I'd go about it, I'm not all that familiar with these methods. You have to admit, though, that you're really screwed." "I agree," said Delahaye. "You might put it more delicately, but I agree."

None of this got us a great deal further forward, so for a few moments silence ensued, for lack of anything to add. Ferrer was wondering what had got into him to have used such coarse language. Occasionally a stronger wave exploded noisily against one of the bridge piers, throwing up spray onto their shoes. On Maria Cristina Bridge the street lamps in the shape of sugar loaves emitted an intimate light. Downstream the lights on Zurriola Bridge could be seen; they are in the shape of ice-cream cones with three or four scoops, but they give a better light.

"So," Ferrer supposed, "I could get you into trouble for theft or fraud, breach of trust, you name it. But just take theft, that's against the law. I think that passing yourself off for dead is not all that above board either, is it?" "I wouldn't know," Delahaye assured him; "it's not a matter I've really looked into." "What's more, starting off down that road," said Ferrer, "I suppose you haven't stopped there, I expect there'll be other little nasties in the woodwork." Thinking of Le Flétan's unhappy end, Delahaye abstained from comment. "O.K., I played my hand wrong. Fair enough, I scuppered it. These things happen. But what am I going to do now, have you thought of that? You're the one who's coming out of this on the credit side," he added brazenly, "it's you again who are going to be all right."

Then Ferrer pushed Delahaye, bending him backwards across the parapet, insulting him at first inaudibly, and made to throttle him without pause for thought. "Why, you little bugger," he continued more distinctly and abandoning all restraint – but not before taxing himself for coming out with too many obscenities for one evening – "you dirty little shit," while the other, his head forced backwards over the frothing river, tried to emit some expletives of his own, assorted with protests, but could only gurgle, "Don't, don't, please don't!"

We have been in Ferrer's company now for about a year, but we've never yet taken the time to give a physical description of him. As this somewhat intense scene does not lend itself to a lengthy digression, let us get it over with: let us say in short that he is in his fifties, on the tall side, dark hair, green eyes, or grey depending on the weather, let's say he's not a bad-looking specimen, but let us point out that, despite the problems he has with his heart (be it the organ or the affections) and even though he is not particularly robust, he can pile on a good deal of muscle when he gets worked up. Which is what seems to be happening at the moment.

"You dirty little scumbag," he therefore continued while perilously constricting Delahaye's larynx, "you pathetic little crook." Cars were crossing the bridge, a fishing smack was passing beneath it, showing no lights, four pedestrians unmindful of their fight loomed furtively on the opposite pavement, no-one stopped despite the noise even though it boded no good. "No," Delahaye was now hiccupping, "please don't." "Shut up, you turd," Ferrer swore at him, "just watch and see how I'm going to sort you out." And as the other was going into convulsions, Ferrer felt his carotids pulsing frantically behind the angle of his jaw as precisely as he had watched his own arteries, a few months earlier, on the echocardiogram. Well heaven help me, he was wondering all the while, I mean what's got into me this evening to be swearing like this?

34

THE DAYS, THEREAFTER, TRICKLED BY, FOR LACK OF alternative, in the customary order. There would be a whole day on the road, to begin with, Ferrer having decided to return to Paris at his leisure. He stopped for a long lunch break around Angoulême, and afforded himself a detour with no particular bit of sightseeing in view, merely to take time to recapitulate and look ahead. In the car, for lack of an RDS system it was necessary to adjust the wavebands of the FM stations every hundred kilometres. In any case he kept the volume low and listened with but half an ear, the radio serving as nothing more than a sound-track to the film of the last twenty hours that he kept rescreening in a continuous loop.

Things had worked out almost too easily with Delahaye. After his moment's irritation, Ferrer had calmed down and they had moved on to negotiations. Delahaye was nailed, he had no way out. He had built huge hopes on selling the antiquities under the counter, and was looking forward to enormous profits; thus in a few months he had run through all his savings, spending them on comfortable hotels and designer clothes. Today he was practically down to his last pennies. These hopes of his had been dashed by the arrival of Ferrer who, once he had recovered his wits, had dragged him off to a bar in the old town to put a deal to him. The discussion had been more composed, thought had been given to the future, Ferrer had recovered a measure of politeness in addressing his ex-assistant.

Delahaye wished, for lack of anything better, to keep for the future, humbly and definitively, this name of his, Baumgartner, which he must have intrigued a great deal to obtain. He would assuredly make the most of it. The fact is, he'd had to pay the going rate, false identity papers that stand up to scrutiny do not come cheap, and anyway now there was no going back. But he had, even so, tried to negotiate, he would undertake to tell Ferrer where the antiquities were being stored – for a consideration. Ferrer considered the figure to be modest enough, but still took pleasure in revising it downwards, accepting to pay him a little less than one third of the sum requested, which was still sufficient for Delahaye to look forward to spending a little time in a foreign country of his choosing, preferably one with a weak currency. The other not being in a position to bargain, they left it at that. The parting had taken place without rancour, and Ferrer reached Paris in the early evening.

The day after he was back, the first thing to do in the morning, on the strength of the indications furnished by his ex-assistant, was to go to Charenton to recover the objects, then to rent a large safe-deposit at the bank and hasten to stash them there, once they were insured. This done, in the afternoon, as he was on his way back to see Jean-Philippe Raymond and pick up the expert's definitive report, he was hardly in the secretary's office than he found himself face to face with Sonia. The same as ever, with her Bensons and her Ericsson, which inevitably conjured up the Babyphone in Ferrer's mind. She seemed to glance at him with indifference but, as he followed her into the corridor leading to Raymond's office, she turned round sharply and started to abuse him for never having called her. Obtaining no reaction from Ferrer, she proceeded to insult him under her breath and when he tried to create a diversion by escaping into the Gents, she joined him there and flung herself into his arms crying, "Ah . . . take me!" As he resisted, attempting to remind her that this was neither the time nor the place, she turned violent and set about trying to scratch and bite him then, abandoning all restraint, to kneel down and unzip him with a view to doing heaven knows what, don't be daft, you know perfectly well what. But, heaven knows why, Ferrer put up some resistance. After restoring a measure of calm, he was able to slip away, though not without mixed feelings, from these assorted molestations. Luckily a little later, back at the gallery, it turned out that in his absence things had taken a turn more or less for the better. Business seemed to be picking up a little but, all that afternoon, Ferrer was hard put to concentrate.

Sonia was undoubtedly not the answer, but Ferrer who, as we know, finds it hard to live without women, tried two days after his return to stoke up one or two adventures. They were potential affairs, flirtations left on the back burner, baited traps that needed checking, files already opened, files pending that offered a greater or lesser degree of interest. But none of these initiatives came to anything – the people who might have breathed life into them turned out to be unobtainable, moved away, or otherwise engaged. Only the cases of minor interest seemed capable of being put back on track, but this time it was he who was no longer all that keen.

There was always Hélène, of course, although Ferrer thought twice about resuming contact with her. He had not seen her since the day she'd put on make-up; he had there and then headed off for Spain, and even now he still did not know exactly how to behave towards her and what to think. Too distant and too close, too available and too cold, too opaque and smooth, she offered very few hand-holds allowing Ferrer to claw his way up to heaven knows what summit. He resolved nonetheless to call her again but, even with Hélène, he had to wait a week for a rendezvous. The week went by, and three times Ferrer decided against cancelling the meeting; everything went as predictably as could be, that's to say they had dinner then slept together, it was not a complete success but they saw it through. Then they had another go. This time it went a bit better, and so they carried on with it until it started becoming not bad really, the more so as between these grapplings even their tongues were loosened. They even found themselves laughing together. Progress, maybe this was progress.

Let us also continue to make progress, now, let us speed up. In the weeks that followed, not only did Hélène come to spend more and more time in Rue d'Amsterdam, she spent more and more time at the gallery. Soon she had a duplicate set of keys to the flat, soon Ferrer did not renew Elisabeth's contract and naturally it was Hélène who took over; she also inherited the keys to the gallery which Suzanne had handed back outside the Palais de Justice.

Hélène learnt the ropes fast enough. The art of smoothing things over came to her so readily that Ferrer left her, part-time at first, to handle the bulk of his dealings with the artists. She was entrusted, for example, with overseeing the development of Spontini's work, to boosting Gourdel's morale, or moderating Martinov's requirements. This role was all the more necessary as Ferrer was largely absorbed with attending to his recovered antiquities.

Very soon, as a matter of course, Hélène moved in at Rue d'Amsterdam without even much need to discuss it, then, with business picking up well, she was soon working full-time at the gallery. Evidently the artists, and Martinov especially, preferred dealing with her than with Ferrer: she was calmer, more balanced than he was; and each evening in Rue d'Amsterdam, he'd get a rundown of the day's news. While never actually planned that way, their life was beginning to resemble that of a married couple. They were to be seen in the morning, she in front of her tea, he in front of his coffee, discussing figures and publicity, production schedules, exchanges with other countries, and they'd end up both giving the thumbs-down once and for all to the plasticians' budget.

Moreover Ferrer was now thinking of moving house. It had become altogether possible. The objects found on the *Nechilik* had paid handsome dividends and the market was now picking up, what's more, the telephone was starting to ring again, the collectors were reopening their saurian eyes, their chequebooks were coming out of their pockets with the zest of leaping salmon. Pulling the rug from under the plasticians had made no difference to the bank balance, while Martinov, for example, was on his way to becoming an official painter: ministry lobbies in London, factory entrances in Singapore, stage curtains, theatre ceilings here, there and everywhere, add to that, he was being given more and more retrospectives abroad, it was O.K., it was going all right. Beucler and Spontini, much to their surprise, were now attracting a solid following, while even Gourdel, the also-ran, was starting to sell again a little. Thanks to all this lovely money coming in, Ferrer concluded that it was possible, nay, obligatory, to change flats. He was now perfectly capable of buying: so it was a question of finding something bigger, something brand-new, a penthouse apartment giving onto the sky, just being completed in the VIIIe, and which would be ready in the first fortnight of January.

While waiting for this accommodation to be completed in every detail, the Rue d'Amsterdam apartment was thrown open to visitors. Cocktails were organised, and dinners; collectors like Réparaz were invited – he turned up without his wife; art critics came and fellow art dealers, one evening even Supin was invited, and he brought his fiancée. To thank him for his help, Ferrer solemnly presented him with a small lithograph by Martinov, which Hélène persuaded Ferrer to let him have at a knockdown price. Supin was bowled over, he declared at first that he could not accept it, but eventually he left with his fiancée on one arm and his lithograph wrapped up under the other. It was now November, the air was crisp and the sky blue: perfection.

When there were no guests they would sometimes go out to dinner, then drop in at the Cyclone for a drink, or the Central, or the Soleil, bars where people in the same line of work tended to hang out, art dealers or critics they'd had round just a couple of nights ago.

In the weeks that followed, until the end of the month, Ferrer occasionally ran into some of his old flames, sometimes at close quarters but especially at a distance. One day near the Madeleine he happened to notice Laurence at a pedestrian crossing waiting like him for the light to change; she was across the street from him, but Ferrer, recalling their somewhat acrimonious parting, would just as soon she didn't spot him, and moved along to the next light to cross. Another day, in Place de l'Europe, he was suddenly caught up in a cloud of Ecstatics Elixir and inhaled it cautiously, but without being able to identify the woman who was leaving it in her wake. It is not certain that it was Bérangère, for it seems that the subscribers to this perfume have increased in number of late. He forbore to pursue this scent-trail, not being one he had ever appreciated anyway, he even evaded it by making off in the opposite direction.

One evening Ferrer stopped in for a drink with Hélène at the Central, where whom should he run into but Victoire, whom he had not seen since the beginning of the year. She had not changed all that much even if her hair was longer and her eyes more distant, as if their focus had receded in order to take in a wider angle, a more panoramic view. And she did look a bit tired. A few sweet nothings were exchanged. Victoire seemed abstracted, but addressed to Hélène as the latter moved away – "I'll leave you for a moment" – the smile of a freed slave or a defeated Amazon. Apparently she knew nothing of Delahaye's disappearance. Ferrer supplied her with the official version, accompanied by a woebegone look, and offered her a glass of dry white before making off after Hélène.

This was the time when he and Hélène were making every-thing ready with a view to moving in: their conjugal bedroom and their separate rooms when they preferred to sleep on their own – everything must be allowed for – the offices and the guest rooms, the kitchen and the three bathrooms, the terrace and the utility rooms. Several times a week Ferrer went to visit the building site; the work was almost completed. He trod on raw concrete and inhaled plaster dust which clogged the palate as he thought through the finishing touches, the decoration, curtain colours, relationship between pieces of furniture, ignor-ing the estate agent, who tripped and stumbled about among the joists as he unfolded inaccurate plans. On such days Hélène preferred not to accompany Ferrer. She would stay at the gallery and take care of the artists, notably Martinov who needed close watching – success is such a fragile thing, it requires such constant attention, it's a labour every instant – while Ferrer, from the terrace of his future penthouse, watched the clouds arrive.

These clouds boded no good, in their serried ranks, resolute as a professional army. The weather, furthermore, had taken a turn for the worse, as if winter were getting impatient, herald-ing its onset in a very ill-tempered way; it jostled autumn with menacing storms in order to take its place as quickly as possible, choosing one of the last days of November to empty the trees noisily in less than an hour of their leaves, all hunched up like the remnants of yesterday. Where the weather was concerned, a degree of pessimism was justified.

35

S O WINTER HAD COME, AND WITH IT THE YEAR'S END, and with that the last evening of the year, in anticipation of which everyone had taken care to invite themselves to visit each other. As a rule the thought of this evening always put Ferrer a bit on edge, but not this time, not in the least. He had laid his plans well, he was going to bring Hélène with him to Réparaz's, where one hell of a party was anticipated: a huge crowd, twelve bands, fourteen buffets, three hundred celebrities from every sphere you could think of, and two ministers at the dessert stage, it all threatened to be rather fun.

On New Year's Eve, a little before the television news, Ferrer was cheerfully laying out this programme for Hélène when the doorbell rang and the postman was there, accompanied by an assistant postman; they were stopping by for their Christmas box with their job lot of calendars necessarily featuring dogs pointing, cats snoozing, birds roosting, seaports and snowy peaks, in a word an embarrassment of riches. "Of course," enthused Ferrer, "come on in."

Hélène seemed to be in agreement with him about the picture for the calendar, they chose a pair of bouquets shown recto-verso, one per semester, then Ferrer in high good humour gave the postmen three times their usual tip. The delighted postmen wished the couple every possible happiness, Ferrer overheard them commenting the event on the stairs as he shut the door, this done, Hélène announced that she had something to say. "Of course," said Ferrer, "what is it?" Well, she said, the fact of the matter was, as to this party chez Réparaz, she would prefer, all things considered, to give it a miss. Martinov was also giving a party with a dozen of his friends in his new studio, the fruit of all his recent sales, its dimensions were more in keeping with his present status, and the thing is, that is where she would rather go. "If you don't mind."

"Not in the least," said Ferrer, "it's as you wish." Of course it would be a wee bit delicate, given his relationship with Réparaz, but he'd sort it out, there'd be no problem for him to make his excuses. "Well no," said Hélène, turning away, "that's not what I meant." On reflection, it would be better for her to go on her own. And as Ferrer pouted and frowned, "Listen," said Hélène, turning back to face him, "listen to me." She gently explained that she had been thinking it over. And this new flat. All this furniture. This idea of living together with all this open sky above them, she really didn't know. She was not quite sure she was ready, she needed to think about it, they'd have to discuss it another time. "I'm not saying to drop the whole thing, you see, all I'm saying is I need to think about it. Let's talk about it again in a few days." "Very well," said Ferrer as he inspected the tips of his new shoes – new in the last few weeks, all his shoes were – "all right, so be it." "You're sweet," said Hélène, "I'm going to dress. You'll tell me how it went at Réparaz's." "Yes," said Ferrer, "I don't know."

She set out from Rue d'Amsterdam a little on the early side, it seemed to him, for this kind of party. Left on his own, he wandered for a moment round the sitting room, turning on the television only to switch it off again, spontaneously cursing Feldman for having made him cut out the cigarettes. Then he tried three or four half-hearted phone calls which, this being a bank holiday, only picked up answering machines. He no longer had any great wish to go to Réparaz's – he had taken a shine to Hélène ever since she started at the gallery, and would be bound to wonder at her absence. Of course he had not made any alternative plans for the evening, so it was a little late to be improvising some fall-back arrangement. The more so as he had turned down other invitations, and to ring up casually now and accept at the eleventh hour seemed a tricky one: here too, people were going to raise an eyebrow, ask him questions to which he would not have the tiniest wish to reply.

He had to make further calls, none too few of them, but still drew a blank. He put on a CD, at once turned down the volume, then changed disc, but switched off before turning on the television again and standing in front of it for a good while without changing channel or taking in what he was looking at. He also stood for some minutes in front of the open refrigerator, in the same cataleptic trance, and without taking anything from it. And two hours later, we see him walking down Rue de Rome on his way to the Saint-Lazare Metro station, where there is a direct connection to Corentin-Celton. On New Year's Eve at around eleven at night the Metro trains are not packed. It is not unusual to be able to take one's pick of seats and Ferrer was well aware that at this moment he may have been opting for the worst of all possible solutions.

He knew that Suzanne, abandoned exactly one year ago give or take a couple of days, was absolutely in her element when it came to organising New Year's Eve parties. He was well aware that he was exposing himself to the worst and that this worst would be fully merited, he was even more aware that Suzanne might go off the deep end at the very sight of him, that he was taking a huge risk. There might even be something a touch suicidal about what he was doing, but he didn't seem to care, as if there was nothing else for him to do, I know it's idiotic but I'm doing it anyway. Besides, who's to say? – it could be that Suzanne herself has changed, perhaps she has grown civilised since they first met. The thing is, she had always had this propensity to a Neolithic violence, and Ferrer sometimes asked himself if he hadn't first gone up to her at the mouth of a cave.

Suzanne, holding a club in her hand, a flint axe stuck in her belt, that day she'd been dressed in a suit made of a pterodactyl's wing under a trench coat cut from an ichthyosaur's eyelid, and on her head an iguanodon's claw made to measure. Those next five years had not been easy, it had been one battle after another, but things had perhaps moved on, one would see.

The house, anyway, no longer looked quite the same. The front-door knob and the letter box had both been repainted in red, the card no longer bore the name of Ferrer nor Suzanne's maiden name. There were lights showing at all the windows and it looked as if the house was now occupied by new residents who were throwing a New Year's Eve party. At a loss, Ferrer dawdled a few moments by the front door without the slightest idea of what he was going to do or of what he felt like doing, until the door opened, releasing a blast of loud music at the same time as a girl who stopped in the doorway and showed no inclination to move, apparently all she wanted was a breath of air.

She looked a nice enough girl who made a little sign to him when she saw him, and smiled. She held a glass in her hand and must have been around twenty-five or thirty, not bad looking, there was a touch of Bérangère about her though without quite the class, it was conceivable that she might be a tiny bit tipsy, but only a tiny bit, a trifling matter on a night such as this. As Ferrer remained rooted to the spot, she spoke to him, "Are you a friend of Georges?" Ferrer was too nonplussed to answer right away. "Would Suzanne be there, by any chance?" he finally asked her. "I don't know," said the girl, "I've not seen any Suzanne but maybe she's here, there's quite a crowd, I don't know every-one. I'm the sister of one of Georges's colleagues, he's just moved in. The house isn't bad, but the heat is something, in there." "Yes," said Ferrer, "it looks O.K." "Would you like to come in for a drink?" the girl kindly suggested.

Behind her, through the open door, Ferrer saw the redecorated entrance hall, different furniture, a chandelier he did not recognise, pictures hanging or pinned to the wall, ones which would never have suited Suzanne nor him. "I'd be glad to," he answered, "but I certainly don't want to intrude." "Not in the least," said the girl, smiling, "come in." "I'm terribly sorry," said Ferrer stepping forward cautiously, "this is not at all what I had been expecting. It's a bit complicated to explain." "It doesn't matter," said the girl, "I'm here too by accident. You'll see, there are some marvellous people here. Come on in." "All right," said Ferrer, "but honestly I'll only stay a moment. Just a quick one then I'm off."

ONE YEAR

VICTOIRE AWOKE ONE FEBRUARY MORNING, recollected nothing of the previous evening, found Félix dead beside her in bed, packed her bag, stopped in at the bank, then took a taxi to the Gare Montparnasse.

It was cold, the air was pure, every bit of dirt had sought refuge in the corners, it was cold enough to add width to the intersections and paralyse the statues. The taxi dropped Victoire at the foot of the station approach.

At the Gare Montparnasse, where it froze even harder than anywhere else, it takes just three notes in grey to make a thermostat: the polished charcoal grey of the platforms, the concrete overhead – raw steel – and the metallic pearl of the expresses, enough to turn the customers to stone in this morgue-like atmosphere. Like stiffs pulled out of refrigerated drawers, a label tied to the toe, these trains slide towards tunnels that will make short work of your eardrums. Victoire looked on the screen for the first train capable of taking her as fast as possible as far as possible: one, due to leave in eight minutes, had Bordeaux for its destination.

When this story began, Victoire was wholly unacquainted with Bordeaux as indeed with the entire south-west of France; but she was well acquainted with February which is, with March, one of the worst months for Paris. So while it was all to the good to escape at this time of year, she would sooner have done so in different circumstances. Now, having no recollection of the hours preceding Félix's death, she feared she might be suspected of having brought it about. Above all, she did not wish to have to furnish an explanation; moreover, she would have been hard put to do so – she was not convinced, after all, that she had had no hand in it.

Once the tunnels had been negotiated, Victoire, her ears ringing, closeted herself in the toilet to count the sum she had withdrawn from the bank; she had liquidated the greater part of her current account. The sum, in large-denomination notes, amounted to almost FF 45,000, enough to get by on for a while. Then she scrutinised herself in the mirror: she saw a young woman of twenty-six, lean and nervous, with a determined look, a green glint in the eye at once wary and truculent, black hair worn in a bob albeit skew-whiff. She had little difficulty in erasing all emotion from her face, clearing it from view, for all that she was feeling far from confident. She returned to her seat.

This was a window seat in a smoking compartment, facing the direction of travel. Here, Victoire strove to put her memories of the previous evening in order, but remained unable to reconstruct the events as they had happened. She knew she had spent the morning alone after Félix had left for the studio, then had lunched with Louise before bumping into Louis-Philippe at the Central in the late afternoon. It was always by chance at the Central, and often at the end of the afternoon, that Victoire would run into Louis-Philippe, whereas he always knew how to find her the moment he felt like it, wherever she was and no matter when. She remembered having taken a glass or two with him and then returning home maybe a little later than usual: after that, decidedly, nothing. Anyone else in Victoire's shoes would have sought the advice of those close to her in a case like this, but not she: she had no family, all her bridges were burnt.

What had occurred would no doubt return to her memory sooner or later, no point pressing the matter, no harm in simply looking out of the window at the vaguely industrialised country-side in its bland uniformity, with never a feature to catch the eye, even when the view was not anyway masked by a cutting.

Pylons, high-tension wires, motorway interchanges, silos, allotments adjacent to quarries. Lost out in the sticks amid non-existent livestock some technological centre would crop up with no obvious connexion to anything about – the occasional factory making heaven knows what. Even the trees, of limited species and variety, were as hard to tell apart as the cars on a trunk road that for a moment ran parallel to the railway line.

Nothing, in fact, to contemplate without fatigue, but the interior of the train, half empty at this season, afforded barely more by way of entertainment. An elderly couple, three single men including a dozing masseur, two single women one of them pregnant, plus a team of teenage girls in ponytails, dental plates and sports bags on their way to the nil-score game. The masseur's index finger, thrust inside a tome on anatomy, trembled intermittently, evidently tired of forever marking the same page. Victoire got up and, brushing the backs of the seats to keep her balance, made for the buffet car.

There, alone with her quarter of Vittel, she watched through the picture windows this drifting panorama, a landscape that divulged nothing beyond its identity, no more a landscape than a passport is a person, distinguishing marks or features nil. The surroundings seemed to have been left there *faute de mieux*, a stop-gap until they hit upon something better. The sky consisted of a uniform cloud in which anonymous dusky birds drifted hither and yon without conviction like so many underpaid walkers-on and the sun conceded a mute light redolent of a waiting-room without the ghost of a magazine to help pass the time. Returned to her seat, Victoire dozed off like everyone else until the station at Bordeaux.

She had thought to proceed at Bordeaux just as she had done at Montparnasse and jump aboard the first train she came to, but several were leaving at the same time, one for Saint-Jean-de-Luz, another for Auch, a third for Bagnères-de-Bigorre. In order to cover her tracks, scarcely knowing from whom, Victoire tossed up three times between these destinations then, as Auch came up each time, in order to cover them even better in her own eyes, she settled for Saint-Jean-de-Luz.

Saint-Jean-de-Luz station gives straight onto the town centre, near the harbour. Leaving her case in the lockers, Victoire bought a street-plan at a newsagents' and set off to scour the streets. It was mid-afternoon, the shops were reopening, including the estate agents', and she paused in front of them to study the To Let notices. Each advertisement was illustrated with a photograph and suggested a decor fit for a television film, the makings of a screenplay, but Victoire did not feel like trying an estate agent's – sky-high fees, identity checks, forms to sign and thus written traces which since this morning she preferred not to leave. She was going about it this way only to give herself an idea of the prices. This done, she reclaimed her bag and chose a hotel in a street that did not fetch up at the harbourside.

She was to spend only one night there. The next day she looked at the customers' small ads scotch-taped to the glass-paned doors of the shops. Fairly quickly, towards the end of the morning, she found an offer that could suit her. On the telephone the landlady sounded agreeable enough and they arranged to meet within the hour. The rent was FF 3,600, which Victoire proposed to settle in cash, there and then, if the place suited her. It was to suit her. She was to spend three months there.

Victoire made her way to the address and found a cramped, dejected little suburban villa, out where there was plenty of air and the residents were retired couples. A neglected garden surrounded this lacklustre building whose back windows gave on to a golf course and the front ones on to the ocean; the door and the shutters seemed to have been closed for a good while. Victoire sat on her suitcase and awaited the arrival of the landlady, imagining her to look no different to the house itself.

Wrong: this landlady was the opposite in each particular. Her face was bright, her clothes were bright, her lips smiling, and she drove a coral-pink two-tone convertible. Her name was Noëlle Valade, and she seemed to float an inch or two above the ground despite her imposing bosom – but that is the way with imposing bosoms – some weigh you down as ballast while others lift you up – sandbags or helium balloons, and her translucent, luminous skin argued a strict vegetarianism. Her prematurely white hair was secured only by a tortoiseshell clip, innocent of any coiffeur's ministrations. Noëlle Valade did not wish to live in this house, which she had inherited from a female relative, she explained as she tried to open the door, but neither did she want it to go to rack and ruin. The lock was sticking.

The place comprised a living room that had given up the ghost, a kitchen with not much to say for itself and two bedrooms upstairs separated by a narrow bathroom – a rather forsaken place, it would seem, cluttered, damp, dingy, and emitting an odour of mildew that was not entirely unpleasant. Evidently no one had been living there for quite a while, but it was habitable and nothing was missing; indeed too much furniture contained too many objects flung together cheek by jowl. Decorative objects for the most part, the kinswoman's other effects having been given away to charity. It looked as if life had quit the place on a sudden, in a precipitate movement, abandoning all these objects from one second to the next, leaving them to gather dust, to congeal for ever behind shutters quickly slammed to. It looked as though at the last moment a book, a bowl, a cushion had been provisionally displaced, transferred to a sideboard, a shelf, the arms of a sofa, notionally for a moment or two but in fact for all eternity.

The wallpaper no longer joining at the seams, the evidence of furring in the bathtub, the rusting metal, Noëlle Valade indicated these things with a sweep of her fingertips that stopped short of making contact with them, and Victoire could not at first make out whether this was because the place inspired a special repugnance in the lady or whether it represented a settled attitude towards material objects. However, Noëlle Valade seemed to have taken to her tenant; she showed no distrust and reduced the formalities to a minimum – no papers, no deposit, simply three months' rent in advance in banknotes that flitted placidly, like so many blue-green dragonflies, from the tenant's handbag to her own.

These three months fixed by Noëlle Valade traced out Victoire's immediate future, so she didn't have to give it a thought, and spared her the worry of having to take a decision no doubt pricked with hesitations. She was grateful for this to her landlady (Call me Noëlle), who described the salient features of her life. Working in a bank but barely, for form's sake, one day on two days off, she lived for all practical purposes off her maintenance allowance; she had certainly considered remarrying but no, it is I, she said, who am my best friend. She was only happy in her own company, she explained as she returned to her car, a gift from her latest husband (I never thanked him, I told him you know perfectly well I'm incapable of saying thank you), and which, once she had turned the key, was flooded with an unearthly sound of organ music and waves. Then she lowered the window on her side. "Well, I'm happy to have stumbled on you," she told Victoire with a smile. "I can't stand ugly women, they're always forcing me to prove something." And as she put the car into reverse, Victoire could verify that it was indeed a question of a settled attitude – Noëlle laid not so much as a fingertip on any material object, she drove her car by dint of magnetic induction.

While Noëlle Valade had been speaking, Victoire filled the gaps with only the sketchiest information about herself. Not out of – at all events not only out of – any particular mistrust, but such was her habit, and Louis-Philippe had often taxed her for it.

But that is how Victoire was: as words must be spoken when one meets people, she got out of it by asking questions. While the answer was being supplied, she took it easy and prepared her next question. That is how she always proceeded, and nobody noticed, or so she believed.

After the landlady drove off leaving her alone in front of the villa, Victoire looked at the place as if it were a person, guardedly, defensively, the way she often confronted men even when there was nothing to threaten her; thus she would suggest the possibility when in fact it had not crossed anybody's mind. No doubt such a look had played its part in the brevity of her employments hitherto, in the non-renewal of her fixed-term contracts. In fact, these last months, Victoire had been looking only evasively at the job market, not so much looking as biding her time, counting less on her savings, currently gathered in her bag, to live on than on Félix, who until the previous evening had seen to everything.

Later, she had inspected the house in detail, opening the empty wardrobes in which the clothes hangers banged together, and the drawers full of incomplete objects: decommissioned photo albums, unlabelled keys, keyless padlocks, handles without their accessories, door knobs, candle stubs, fragments of bedsteads, a watch lacking its minute hand. Empty candlesticks and table lamps without plugs stood on side tables, as well as what must go by the name of a photophore, a singleton flower vase sitting on needlepoint doilies, on squalid lace napkins. Two exotic statuettes attested a colonial past.

In a cupboard, amid the nests of dust, Victoire placed her hand on two old boxes of sugared almonds; the boxes had faded pink and blue braiding extended by pompons and tassels; they still held little sugared balls, the silvery coat flaking off. On the wall she straightened a portrait, sitter unknown. In the bathroom, toothbrushes without bristles and wafers of soap, sanitary accessories, ancient and mouldering, tacky and disintegrating, repulsive, moulded in first-generation plastics. It would take several days with every window thrown open for all this lot to lose a bit of its smell, without ever being completely aired.

Victoire settled in quickly, changing nothing on the ground floor, and in the bedroom she chose upstairs using only a chest of drawers for her clothes. She laid out her personal effects – two books, a Walkman, a little pewter elephant – on a bedside table. But her money she would conceal in a cupboard in the other bedroom at the bottom of a large drawer containing folded linens. Stiff and damp like everything else, these linens had not been unfolded for ages, and a yellowish grey-brown streak ran the length of their pleats.

She emptied her room of all furniture and accessories, so that apart from the chest of drawers and the bed, pulled over to face the window (its curtains taken down), nothing remained but a large mirror fixed to the side wall. Thus, during the day, as Victoire lay abed she would have nothing before her but a rectangle of sky like a blank page – white, grey or blue according to the weather – divided by a centre margin with a full stop one third of the way down in the form of a window-catch. The first days she remained often in that posture, stretched out in bed, whether she was vainly trying to think about her life or whether she was trying equally in vain not to think about it at all. The all-pervading silence that lorded it round the villa did not favour these attempts.

On the one side, the golf course was quite busy: groups of silhouettes were to be seen, motionless or dissolving into movement. On the other side, the ocean could be seen but was too far away to be heard. Nor did any echoes emanate from the surrounding dwellings even though Victoire did, after some time, begin to notice occasional faint sounds in the vicinity of the house. The sounds were of a quiet fall or thud, barely audible, varying in nature and degree, muffled or dulled, sometimes followed by a rebounding echo; once it was the noise of shattering glass, another time the impact of a bass drum, or a brief creak, a firecracker taking its time, and once only a stifled cry. They came without rhyme or reason, once or twice each day, some days not at all. Eventually Victoire would listen out for them without being able to determine where they came from. If they gave no hint of their presence for two days in a row and she forgot all about them, it only took one of them to come popping up unexpectedly and remind her of the whole series. At least they never happened at night, so they never disturbed her sleep.

Those first days, she set out each morning to read the local and national press by the ocean, always at the same spot, weather permitting. The weather often did permit, and the spot, separated from the shore by a narrow coast road, was a sloping esplanade undergoing improvements; it had been furnished with new benches and recently planted with languid shrubs shod in plastic film. Those first days, she looked in all the papers, under news items or death notices, for any information regarding Félix's death, but to no avail. Once it seemed probable that the matter would go un-noted, Victoire reduced her purchase of daily papers: eventually she no more than glanced through them, leaving them open on her lap as she brooded on the ocean.

On this ocean there drifted at all hours, whatever the sky, the heads of surfers, like so many buoys or tossed balls, waiting for the wave. When this appeared, each one would heave himself up on his board to catch it and hurl himself at an angle onto its slope, remaining poised there for a few seconds before tipping over in a fluorescent parabola, immersed in the foam, and all was begun again. Meanwhile on the little road edging the shore, their ever-patient girlfriends awaited the surfers in specially converted minibuses; passing them on her way home, Victoire would hear the car radios crackling.

Soon she began to go out during the day, in the afternoon and even in the evening, but cautiously, like a convalescent, and as if treading on eggshells. There were not many tourists at this season, not many young loafers, simply a few elderly couples, occasionally foreigners, who took pictures of the scenery, photographed each other against the background or asked a stranger to take their picture together against the background. Then they would smile at their camera while keeping a watchful eye on it, their smile slightly strained by the thought that the stranger might suddenly make off with their camera. Sometimes this service was requested of Victoire, who readily obliged, but who usually kept herself to herself, for she avoided getting in the viewfinder as she would an area of radio-active contamination. Even so she must often have been photographed all unwittingly in the background to one of those couples with the circumspect smile, and no doubt the prints were still in existence.

On sunny days she might also spend a moment on the beach; this, like every beach in winter, was a vast abandoned area serving no purpose, deeply rutted by the powerful tractors from the cleansing department – in spite of which there still remained, buried between two layers of sand, no shortage of organic or manufactured jetsam, abandoned by the warm-weather bathers or brought in by the tide. Not many people walked on the beach: young couples tightly arm-in-arm or imported pensioners, flanked by big dogs gnawing a branch or smaller sausage dogs snug in their woollies. Victoire would settle herself in a sheltered spot, well away from the cold water, spread out a towel, then a newspaper and, sitting on the former, would leaf through the latter as she plugged in to her Walkman. Thus she continued for some while to run through the papers, but she stopped buying them the day after a person came and rang at her door.

The morning was young, about ten o'clock, some three weeks after her arrival, and Victoire was of course not expecting any-body. She had passed without transition from her bed to the bathtub, and continued to snooze in the water, now adjusted to the temperature of her bedclothes. The hoarse rattle of the bell downstairs by the front door failed to make her open an eye. The person insisted – two sharp knocks – then appeared to give up. The bell's ring had disappeared without leaving an echo and Victoire, submerged, was not even all that sure she'd not dreamt it; twenty seconds later she'd forgotten about it.

That same afternoon, while she was busy in the kitchen around teatime, a draught threw open her bedroom window then slammed it noisily shut. She climbed the stairs to go and close it properly but first, leaning against the latch bar, she considered the empty sea.

It was not empty for long since at the right side of the frame, in the distance, there appeared the prow of a red-and-black freighter. The ship's radio officer was at that moment taking a breather as he leaned on the ship's rail, and viewed the shore through his telescope – the villas dotted about, the drooping flags hoisted on the beach flagpoles, and the dinghies with their flapping sails that sagged like old curtains. Then, plumb in the middle of the sky, the radio officer observed the twin-engined propeller plane towing a publicity streamer, surrounded by sea-birds tracing figures against a background of cloud ever dissolving and reforming its shape. On a sudden, though, the wind got up and made the flags snap drily, the sails belly out, a dinghy capsize, the figures split up, the streamer undulate in a spasm and the window almost slam again while at the door somebody rang once more. Holding the casement, Victoire leaned silently out but did not straightaway recognise the intruder, who had tipped back his head and was looking up in her direction. "But what are you doing here?" she asked. "Let me in," replied Louis-Philippe.

Dumbfounded, Victoire looked at him without stopping to wonder how he had picked up her trail, then went downstairs and opened the door. Louis-Philippe had changed a bit since the last time. True, he was still the skinny little fellow with an apology for shoulders, eyes drowned in worries behind his thick glasses, brow furrowed with regrets, but he had less of a hungry look than usual and he was turned out a little more smartly. His carefully chosen outfit – doubtless not chosen by himself – hung inertly on his frame, all clean and ironed like a Japanese banknote. "You're looking like a million dollars," exaggerated Victoire. "Well, I'm eating a bit better," he offered. "I'm on a better diet."

One evening at the Central he had been told of Victoire's disappearance, so Louis-Philippe had set off in search of her, and there he was. "I don't need to tell you why I'm here." The fact was, as he explained to her, on the information he had managed to glean Victoire was not really suspected of Félix's death, but it was just as well, in case of doubt, for her to watch her step, keep a low profile, not go flaunting her presence more than she had to. It could not be taken for granted that none of the responsibility would rest with her. Louis-Philippe would keep her abreast of developments. He would continue to keep track of the situation. Tonight he was going back to Paris. Another week and he'd have news for her. "Don't make a move till I give you the signal." After he left, Victoire had gone back up to her room and lain down to try and think. Here she perceived one of those discreet thumps she had earlier noticed, followed by a couple more. This time it sounded at first like a gong, then like a small splash, then like the rustle of crumpled leaves. But she was no better able this time than on the preceding occasions to determine their source.

Over the next few days, to keep herself busy, Victoire often considered spring-cleaning, but that's as far as she got, the size of the task discouraged her. Then she tried to occupy herself with the garden, rake the gravel, mow what must once have been a lawn or collect in a basket the dead stems of overblown geraniums – but in the first place she did not know how to go about it, and secondly some tool was always missing.

After another month, then she began to miss the menfolk. Neglecting the advice of Louis-Philippe, who had never shown up again, Victoire left the house more frequently, letting herself be seen in public. Café terraces, hotel bars, seafood restaurants whose basins of oysters gave off a leathery tang. But all to no effect: men inevitably approached her, but not a single one of them met her need. She had to await a fine evening, by the harbour, to find one.

Gérard. He was twenty-two, handsome, slim, with a ready smile of variable geometry, dressed in a supple midnight-blue leather coat that had seen some wear, black corduroy trousers, tight rollneck, and elasticated ankle-boots. He was hanging out with a crowd of youths called Fred or Carlo, Ben and Gilbert and his borzoi, and the girls were called Chris, Gaëlle and Bille – the one Gérard was closest to. They met every day at one o'clock on the same bar-terrace. Gérard introduced Victoire to them, and she spent a few evenings with them but, seeing the look on Bille's face, soon preferred to stop at home while waiting for the young man to join her, quite far into the night.

Victoire would leave the front door open and, as Gérard climbed the stairs, his black corduroys would make a soft rasping noise as they rubbed together, for all the world like an asthmatic pigeon trying to coo, and the faster Gérard climbed the higher the pitch. He would find her awake in the dark and they'd fall asleep an hour or two later. The next morning, Gérard being the first one up, Victoire would be caught offguard and bury her face in the pillow, trying to reclaim sleep, much as on a station platform a person sprints after a moving train. But while he was dressing by the window, his dark silhouette outlined against the light oblong, Victoire would open an eye for an instant and hold this profile imprinted on her retina, white-on-black like a negative, and would fall asleep again watching this photo of Gérard against her, behind her closed eyelids.

In spite of everything, the young man would always address her with polite formality – a greater intimacy in speaking to her did not come easily to him. Even at night in bed when he was making out voluptuously in the second person singular, it took a mere nothing, a pause or diversion, to jolt him back into the plural. Among all the pleasures he brought her, those car trips also had much to recommend them. He was not bad as a mechanic, and maintained an elderly Simca Horizon, beige in colour, which offered neither the charm of a classic car nor the comfort of a modern one. Gérard would take Victoire for a spin around the locality, to the beaches and the Pyrenees, on day trips to Spain, meals in mountain diners threaded along the pecked line of the border. It was on of one of these runs that the car was once stopped by a routine police check: he had to show the vehicle's papers. While Gérard searched his pockets, Victoire slumped down in her seat a bit, looking straight ahead of her, one hand clasping the door handle. Then, once they had been allowed to continue on their way, Gérard turned to her and noticed the new expression on her face. "What's the matter?" "Nothing." "Just look at you! Was it the police?" "No, it's nothing." Gérard smiled one of his smiles and they lapsed into silence for the next two kilometres before talking of something else.

Louis-Philippe reappeared in April but didn't stay for more than a few minutes. He didn't even risk coming indoors, preferring to talk to Victoire by his car, an unassuming little white Fiat; he kept the door open and the engine running. He looked absent and apologised for not having shown up sooner; he was taking advantage of being in the neighbourhood, he told her, to bring her news. This added up to pretty little. It seems that there had been no further developments, that Félix's death was still unresolved and that Victoire was in the meantime to stay calm and be discreet. This said, as they exchanged the odd remark about the weather for lack of anything better, they heard a sharp crack followed by the sound of cascading glass at the back of the car. They turned round and saw that the back window had just been embellished with a circular cavity of some five centimetres' diameter and a crazing all round it. On the back window shelf, amid the debris of the shatterproof glass, there now rested a golf ball: a Titleist No. 3. Louis-Philippe uttered a brief curse, pocketed the ball, then slipped grumbling into gear.

At last understanding the origin of those anonymous sounds that had been perplexing her ever since her arrival, Victoire in the weeks to come discovered further balls in the garden, escaped from their territory over the blocks and barriers of bushes bordering the golf course. Once her eye was used to making out the little white spheres with their pockmarked skin, each one seemed thenceforth to engender another as if their form, once identified, allowed them to go on being recognised indefinitely; later she was picking up plenty more of them. They were to be found scattered like haphazard Easter eggs in the streets and the neighbouring gardens, stuck in the meshes of wire netting, squatting in the hollow of a gutter, agonising at the foot of a bank.

These stray balls also fell from time to time onto the cars, leaving them dented, and even occasionally onto the neighbours themselves, knocking them senseless. Victoire got into the habit of collecting them up, stuffing them into her pocket, then piling them up in the wardrobe of the unoccupied room, on top of the linens beneath which she concealed her savings. At first she collected those she chanced upon in the course of her walks; then this collecting became an end in itself, perhaps a little intrusive: Victoire no longer left the house without searching for them systematically as they landed hither and yon, some more or some less stained with grass and earth, marked as Hogan and Maxfli, Pinnacle and Slazenger, numbered from 1 to 4. She was constantly looking at the ground. Another fortnight went by, her days with the golf balls, her nights with Gérard, who disappeared as follows.

The first night he failed to show up, Victoire had not awoken at the time he normally came in, as if she had foreseen this absence. She registered merely surprise: when she opened her bleary eyes that morning and confronted the iron-grey rectangle of window, alone, there was a touch of surprise but also of relief; indeed she was all the more surprised to be feeling relieved. She made herself a coffee which she drank on her own sitting beneath a shawl on a straw-bottomed chair dragged out into the garden, her eyes glazed or half-shut beneath the stormy sky. This sky discouraged any excursion, so she spent the day at home, heating up a meal out of a tin and retiring to bed with a book at ten-thirty.

This time, she was to waken in the middle of the night, try to read the time by her watch in the dark before switching on her lamp: twenty-five past three. She switched it off only to turn it on again, knowing that she would not get back to sleep, nor would she have recourse to the book, the Walkman, anything. Victoire got up, went into each room in turn, which did not take long, went through them twice, pushing two chairs back into position and folding a garment tossed over the back of one, shifting a flower pot, moving three plates in the sink. At this time of night every sound is magnified, the slightest click becomes a twang, and when she set her hand to washing the dishes struck up a symphony orchestra, the vacuum cleaner made a full opera. Thoroughly on edge, Victoire set to cleaning everything item by item, one side at a time, a proper spring-clean.

Two hours later it was still dark, but under the electric light everything had taken on a new sheen, Victoire having scanted nothing save for the windows which could only be done properly by daylight. She was still too tensed up, however, to return to bed, so she then undertook a systematic inventory of the house. As she did this she realized that she was all jumpy, which was worrying, but she mocked herself for her feverishness and gave vent now and then to brief bursts of laughter. She opened the cupboards and drawers one at a time and cleaned them after she had emptied out their contents, which she put back in the drawers once these too were cleaned. Downstairs first, then upstairs: her bedroom, then the other, right to the wardrobe with her golf balls in the bottom drawer and her cash under the linens. By then it was about six in the morning.

But once she had the linens out, she stood rooted for almost half a minute, trying to understand what it was she was seeing. Then she ran her hand across the bottom of the drawer, several times, as if only that could convince her that, if not a single ball was missing, there was not a single banknote left. The money was all gone.

Bathed, made-up, perfumed, Victoire settled herself a little before noon on the terrace of a harbourside café. The sky was overcast as on the previous day, the air damp and fresh, the tables starred with droplets, and she was the sole occupant of the terrace. Victoire appeared calm even though she kept replaying in her mind the scene before the wardrobe with the empty drawer. At that moment the domestic clatter had given way to a silence altogether more deafening. She had leant towards the wardrobe, then slowly straightened up only to stoop over once again and pull out the empty drawer completely and take another look into the depths, as if the banknotes could pass through solid oak. She had even turned the drawer upside down and shaken it, but nothing fell out but a slow cascade of dust particles. Then, holding it by its handle as if it were a suitcase, she had gone into her room and made for the window through which the coming of daylight was already overdue. As she passed in front of the mirror she had stopped and, catching the reflection of her face in the glass, dropped the drawer, in its reflection, at her feet.

But Victoire had now recovered her self-possession, and was waiting patiently for Gérard to make his usual appearance around one o'clock, but he did not. The others arrived in dribs and drabs, more or less awake, more or less glad to see Victoire; she took the time for a coffee before asking them, equably, where she might find Gérard. But Fred, Chris, Gaëlle, none of them knew the answer, they'd not seen him for three days; anyway Carlo, it seemed, had disappeared at the same time. Bille was not letting on – the beam in her eye spelt revenge. The others, though, looked honest enough, and Ben, the emotional Ben, was clearly worried. Later on Gilbert, who had been harder to get hold of, gave the same answer as the others to Victoire's question, but his smile as he caressed his borzoi boded no good.

Back at the villa by the golf course, Victoire took a quick stock of her situation, then of her finances. Her situation first: there was no absolute proof that Gérard had had any hand in the disappearance of the money, any more, after all, than Victoire herself had had in that of Félix, but neither could the suspicion be discarded in this case, or a serious presumption be ignored. Of course going to the police was not an option, as Gérard seemed to have understood. So the only answer was to leave and find somewhere less expensive. The three months' rent were anyway running out with the end of winter. She rang Noëlle Valade to return the keys. The landlady did not seem to notice how clean the place was, she even ran a finger along the mantelpiece but as usual without actually touching it. Victoire was close to telling her all that had happened.

Then her finances: having counted out FF 2,200 in her wallet, Victoire went to the local branch of her bank where she took the precaution of not addressing herself to any of the cashiers. A cash-dispenser delivered a badly printed statement of her balance, which added up to FF 7,939. As she tapped in her code, she felt a touch apprehensive at the thought that, being on a wanted list, the code could signal her presence at once as it went through. But no hand dropped onto her shoulder, no car door was flung open to block her passage along the pavement as she left the cash-dispenser. As of today, then, her balance amounted to FF 10,000 and some loose change, which is not to be sneezed at and yet which, in the absence of other prospects, is zilch.

However, instead of spreading this sum across the largest number of days to come, making it last as long as possible, Victoire chose not to reduce her lifestyle too drastically. She preferred to count on things sorting themselves out and set forth in search of a decent hotel where she could hole up and watch developments. Then she would see. In the worst case, she might always land a job as sales assistant or check-out girl, or find herself a lover with more of a conscience than Gérard; in the worst case, she might even take to streetwalking, we'd have to see. We were not in a hurry. We'd only consider this possibility as an absolutely last resort. In the meantime we took a room at the Hotel Albizzia.

Three hundred francs including breakfast, at first glance the ideal room, not too big, fairly low ceiling, a silky light coming in through a pair of lancet windows with window boxes. Polished parquet floor, hip-bath, wall-mounted television, spare eider-down, and a view onto a garden taken over by warblers, planted out with *pittosporum* released on parole, and edged with domestic plane trees. Of course at this price the nest egg would be disposed of in less than three weeks, but the lady in reception seemed reassuring: with her warm smile and benevolent chignon, she seemed to imply that they could come to some arrangement once Victoire, put at her ease, told her how matters stood, leaving out a number of details. Well, the first morning, after being awoken by a congress of blackbirds, Victoire went down to breakfast and froze on the dining-room threshold on observing, seated by a French window, plunging a croissant into a bowl, Louis-Philippe immersed in a newspaper folded in front of him, shoving his glasses up the bridge of his nose.

There was no explaining the presence of Louis-Philippe at the

Albizzia, and it was none the less disturbing for that. When he had stopped by the golf course villa a few weeks ago, Louis-Philippe had muttered, as he gathered up the shards of glass in a Kleenex, that he was going back to Paris that night and had said nothing about returning here. Now if he was stopping here in town, evidently at least since the previous day, it was not like him to have neglected to pay a call on Victoire. True, he could be simply passing through on a different errand and he might have postponed such a visit until later. Perfectly true. Possibly he had stopped by the villa after the young woman had left, and had found the door shut, and possibly he would exclaim in delight if Victoire, now crossing the room, caught him by surprise as he read. Possibly. A discreet retreat, however. Victoire went back up to her room, shut the suitcase she had barely unpacked, left the hotel and took a bus northbound up the Atlantic coast.

This road runs far from the beaches, there's no sign of the sea, which is a pity. One wouldn't mind watching the waves, watching them as they were born, grew to maturity and toppled over, to see them in their endless succession, each propounding its own version, its own interpretation of the ideal wave; one might compare their gait, their conception, their succession, the sound they made, but no . . . Victoire left the bus round about three at Mimizan. Why Mimizan? Why not? But in the end not: two hours later she boarded another bus for Mimizan-Plage.

Mimizan-Plage. No offence intended, but it's not a patch on Saint-Jean-de-Luz. At all events, the hotel wasn't. The room price was barely less and it looked out on the parking lot, the receptionist had eczema, the staff were distrait, the plumbing noisy: a battering ram kept the pipes shuddering at all hours. As the back of the building was being repainted, the scaffolding – two lengths of planking obliquely connected by a ladder to make a Z across the window – kept out the daylight. No one on the lower platform, but on the upper a man was at work: all one saw and heard of him were the lower limbs up to the thighs, and the transistor. This way at least the parking lot was not all that visible, but Victoire was quick to realise that – with spring on the way – she'd prefer to be out and about as much as possible.

On foot at first. But the Landes are so flat that the thought of a bicycle becomes irresistible. After reckoning up her finances once again, Victoire allowed herself to invest in one for somewhat less than a thousand francs from a dealer-repairman who welcomed her, in this slack period, as a saviour. The better to secure her things Victoire asked him to install a carrier bigger than the standard version and, carried away by his enthusiasm, the man made her a gift of it. It was one hell of a fine English bike with seven gears, ruby reflectors, gleaming spokes, silky smooth chain, dropped handlebars, Olympic frame, drum brakes and butterfly nuts. And a retractable pump. And the *grand tourisme* saddle that fitted the rump to perfection. Plus the sun was shining.

Victoire would spend the entire day pedalling about. If it was at first with a view to going for rides that she had bought this machine, she also doubtless kept in mind the eventual need to put it to a more rugged use. The touring bike would give way to the utility vehicle. So it was necessary to get into training. After some experimenting with the gear lever, taking corners on gravel, and simply coming off, Victoire eventually got the hang of it pretty well and parked the thing in the hotel garage, whence the next morning she'd be off again and never mind the aches and pains.

Even so she was to spend some ten days at Mimizan-Plage, the time needed to get into practice for cyclotourism. Here she would keep herself to herself and had nothing to do with the commercial travellers nor with the other hotel guests, who in any case were furtive and rare at this time of year. Being out of season, there were days when the pallid sky and the silence made for a depressing ambiance in Mimizan-Plage, like an old avant-garde movie revisited after its expiry date. Victoire would daily scour the area until there was nothing left to discover and, as her resources continued to dwindle visibly, she ended by resolving on a change of scene.

The preparation for this departure took her a whole day. First she acquired a robust kitbag, medium size, with side pockets and zip fasteners, in which to cram her things. What took up most of the time was to assemble these things, a process that required a little sorting and making some reluctant sacrifices. In particular Victoire had to part with one dress, two skirts, three blouses, two pairs of shoes and other contingent objects, retaining only the indispensable, the solid, the practical and the waterproof. This sorting effected with difficulty, she shut her pretty clothes inside her suitcase, which without a backward glance she abandoned under lock and key in her bedroom cupboard. Then by bicycle, heading inland, she took the road towards Mont-de-Marsan; after some thirty kilometres this crosses the dual carriageway connecting Bayonne and Bordeaux.

As always by the side of motorway-type roads, there were two or three of those impersonal, cheap hotels with windows giving onto interchanges, toll booths, bypasses. Every operation, in the absence of human resources, takes effect by means of machines and swipe cards. The sheets are as scratchy as the towels made of disposable synthetic material. Victoire settled for the most anonymous, a see-nothing-hear-nothing building of the Formula 1 chain.

As there was no place for storing bicycles she took a room on the first floor so she could bring hers up conveniently. It quickly dawned on her, though, that in this room, even more than at Mimizan-Plage, she'd never be able to pass the time with only the bike for company, with the smell of the bike. Everything, every colour and accessory sealed to the walls as in a prison cell was rather an incitement to escape from the room with all speed, weather permitting. But as the weather did not, as the rain began to beat down the following days, Victoire found herself obliged to stay there often. A recluse in the hotel, she could for lack of anything better get some idea of its customers' profiles.

These profiles were three in number, according to the length of occupancy of the rooms. An hour or two: unmarried couples whose lawful wedded partners would sooner or later catch up with them thanks to their credit card details. A night or two: apprentice commercial travellers whose duties did not, however, prevent them from indulging in a spot of adultery when the occasion served. Longer stays, a week or two, a month or two: lone penniless vagrants such as Victoire and sometimes, crammed five to a room, even whole families of penniless vagrants. Like these latter, every evening Victoire updated her accounts, rounding up to the next complete franc, and waiting until she was down to her last three thousand before resolving on a more thrifty lifestyle. And thus at the end of one week, before turning in:

Albizzia: 310
Mimizan (280 × 11 days): 3,080
Bike: 940
Kitbag: 230
Formula 1 (165 × 7 days): 1,155
Food (50 × 19 days): 950
Sundries (toiletries, aspirin, cigarettes, repair patches): 370
Total: 7,045 francs.
Balance: 3,094 francs and it was time to act.

Victoire left the hotel the following day on the stroke of noon, taking advantage of her last shelter to the last moment.

The following days her daily round took a turn she had never before known. She slowly travelled the byroads on her bicycle; she did not risk a trip outside the vicinity, beyond the Landes, but stayed within the triangle delimited by Arcachon, Nérac and Dax.

By day she would stop in village squares, at fountains, buy cheese and cold cuts vacuum-packed in mini markets, along with fruit and slices of bread similarly plastic-wrapped then, in the evening, look for the cheapest lodging. But hotels below a hundred francs do not grow on trees, she had to make one or two supplementary purchases, a blanket and sleeping bag: FF 360; Michelin maps 78 and 79: FF 32.

The first time she had to sleep out in the open, Victoire had not made sufficient preparation: caught unawares by the early fall of night, she had to settle for an embankment under a knot of trees by a roadside, and slept very little and poorly. She spent all the next day looking for a possible shelter, which she found on the edge of a hamlet called Onesse-et-Laharie. At the back of an old hotel up for sale there was a badly padlocked door that gave on to a storage shed, its floor caved in; it was strewn with rotten mattresses and the frames of high metal beds projected crisscross patterns on the walls. Victoire was able to spend two nights in a row there, but in these villages the word gets round fast, just as well not to linger.

She rode, she wandered on plane rectilinear roads, at a perfect right angle to the trees. The forest, artificial as a pond, consisted of parallel rows of conifers, each one resembling its neighbours disposed on either side of the road, a geometric glacis. And as Victoire moved so did the rows, her eye defining a perpetual movement of perspectives, a fan forever opened and closed, each tree keeping station in an infinity of lines all fleeing at once, a forest set in motion by the turn of the pedals. And yet the conifers – each one its neighbour's equal and reduced to serfdom – had abdicated their very identity along with their independence; even their cast-offs left the floor in a condition that a qualified interior decorator would be proud of – wall-to-wall patterned carpeting, stain-proof, nonflammable, a satin bed of needles decorated with a dead branch here, a pine cone there. To bring the picture to life Nature laid on a minimal service of coypu, wood pigeons, squirrels and what-have-you which provided a few diagonals, a few calls and cries, the wind rustles the trees like a harpist's *glissando*, in the distance power saws moan.

So long as her three thousand francs permitted her to supply her needs, Victoire kept clear of the big towns. As the nights were growing milder, she grew accustomed faster than she would have expected to sleeping in the open, to finding quiet corners. In the early days she would find herself frequenting the least expensive restaurants for her meals, but she soon gave this up, not so much for the cost as for what followed: leaving a restaurant generally means going home – to leave with no home to return to is quite like finding oneself doubly out in the cold. So she also picked up the habit of eating on her own, turning her back on the world.

The day came when Victoire, aware that her resources were growing dangerously slender, had to envisage an early end to her wanderings from village to village across the forest. She saw she would be constrained ere long to make for bigger, more populous centres, where people congregate who have no fixed abode and manage to get by with less difficulty. Later on, though. She would stay in the countryside while she could still hold out. Until it so happened, as she was in a pharmacy and glanced in a mirror, that she saw something she had never been expecting: since she had virtually no change of clothes, no make-up, nothing with which to wash, nor indeed the money left with which to set this to rights, she was starting to look a real mess. She approached the mirror: although she had never yet given it a try, had kept putting it off, it was clear, the way she looked now, she'd left it a bit late to be looking for a job or something, and the very next day of course her bicycle was stolen.

The village, called Trensacq, inspired trust so this was the sort of thing one would not have expected here. Victoire had parked her machine in front of the village grocer's and left it there just long enough to buy a carton of milk. But when she came out the street was empty and the bicycle gone. Time was when Victoire would have kicked up a row, like going back into the grocer's shouting and waving her arms. Even now, though she could do with a wash and was no longer all that easy on the eye, the shopkeepers were generally ready to pass the time of day; she said little, but people talked to her. Yet seeing the way she was dressed, taking a look at her hair, she did not have the stomach to call anyone to witness. She continued her journey on foot.

As she would now be having to carry her baggage by hand, she needed to lighten her load once again. She would not get any cash for clothes that were too dirty and in some instances torn, nobody would want them, so Victoire abandoned them by a bottle bank. Then she was down to a pair of trainers, a pair of tough denim trousers and some layers of pullovers beneath a quilted parka, but she scarcely owned a change of underwear, which she washed whenever she could – and discreet watering places are not often met with. She began to hitch-hike her way about.

The first man to pick her up was a jovial type in a big Renault: thick black hair slicked back, matching moustache, dark-blue suit with a touch of green, light-blue-striped shirt and knitted tie, maroon in colour. His stylised sign of the Zodiac was clasped to a small chain and bobbed on his tie, while an oversized fluorescent nipple dangled from the rearview mirror. "Insurance," he explained, "I insure whatever anyone wants, I insure things people value, you'll find cigarettes in the glove compartment, you're not looking too hot." "I'm ok," said Victoire, "I'm fine." "Ah well," said the man, a shade disappointed, "so tell me, you going far?" The girl spread her arms.

"You're in luck, that's just where I'm going," a second driver told her an hour later as he sat behind the wheel of a black van with a cut-out of a deodorant pine dangling from the rearview mirror.

"You don't mind sitting beside me?" he offered, "I'd suggest the back but there's this coffin . . . but don't you worry," he bellowed, "I'm travelling empty today! Anyway, it's pretty quiet at the moment, medicine has been making strides, people no longer die. Where are you going on to?"

Now that is precisely what Victoire did not know. She could not yet bring herself to make for a big town, so she continued to take pot luck on the map, often choosing some modest population centre for no better reason than the sound of its name, somewhere to get a meal and shelter for a couple of nights. The result would be a random zigzag pattern; she might make real progress by resolving on a detour, but then she'd have to resolve upon a destination – and it was six of one and half a dozen of the other. Thus there was to be little evidence of coherence in her itinerary, it was more akin to the truncated flight patterns of a closeted housefly.

So she did not find it too difficult, at least initially, to stop motorists. As a rule it tended to be the men rather than the women who gave her a good welcome when they stopped for her, and readily struck up a conversation. In the course of this Victoire took note not simply of their characters but of the make, colour and internal disposition of their vehicle as it carried her onwards to an ill-determined goal. She was at first attentive to these details, but with time she paid them less and less attention.

There was a priest at the wheel of an R5 bereft of optional extras, no radio, nothing, merely a means of locomotion; the seats were stiff and there was a powerful doggy smell though no sign of a dog. The man was dressed in a creased charcoal-grey suit over a mouse-grey rollneck sweater, his lapel adorned with a small metal crucifix. He talked with a bluff military heartiness and drove as if he were at the console of a mighty organ, thumping the pedals with his great clodhoppers; beneath the rearview mirror a palm leaf withered. There was a mother and her three children, boisterously driving a Spanish Fiat. The windscreen, liberally plastered with the last six years' tax discs chronologically superimposed and assorted self-adhesive labels with a bearing on ecology or insurance, was thereby scarcely fit for its transparent role, and the less so in view of the windscreen wiper blades being at the end of their useful life. Victoire was jammed against the door by two creatures aged four and six intent on the performance of some bewildering gymnastics. Turned round and kneeling on the front passenger seat, his arms resting on the seat back, their elder brother gave the young woman a level stare. "Sit down properly, Juju, put your belt on," his mother told him, and went on to propose to Victoire, as she sized her up in the mirror, a few hours' household duties and babysitting. Victoire eyed the lady's progeny with disfavour and made a laconic reply. There were three youths, bashfully insolent, in split windcheaters, crammed into the front of a superannuated Ford Escort. In the back Victoire had a view of the shaven backs of the young folks' necks as they sat squeezed up against each other, not daring to turn round, save for the middle one, who was minded to carry on an ambiguous conversation with her but who was told by the others to belt up. There was a suffocating odour of petrol and dog but this time there was an actual dog, calmly installed beside Victoire; the looks he addressed her were polite and commiserating, as though he wished to dissociate himself from his masters' boorishness, to solicit her indulgence. On the rearview mirror this time there hung a fluffy white football with sky-blue panels.

There were others, then the money ran out once and for all, life became more and more horrible, and Victoire's appearance really began to leave something to be desired. Seeing the way she'd run to seed she found it all the harder to thumb a lift, and when she approached her age-group in the street they understood at once that it was for money. Some of them dipped into their pockets, most of them quite shallowly, and no one seemed surprised by this young beauty's poverty whereas poverty tends to be ugly.

With the bit of small change collected, Victoire lived off unlabelled ham, cheese spread and damaged fruit left over in the afternoon when the market stallholders had packed up. Everything she ate raw, cold and washed down with water from the street pumps. And, the nights becoming increasingly mild, she slept out of doors. She would find shelter in some isolated, abandoned spot, sometimes in ruins, and before she fell asleep she would tie the handles of her bag to her wrist with a piece of string. She was only disturbed on two occasions, once by a sedentary drunkard she managed to get rid of quickly, the second time by a tramp who at first sought to drive her away from what he regarded as his own pitch then, on second thoughts, preferred her to stay so he could take advantage of her. As he was weak and undernourished Victoire was able to get rid of him too.

But this incident, more than the previous ones, left her convinced at last that she must get back to a big town. The next morning the world under a leaden sky looked even more forbidding than usual and Victoire, coming upon a signpost that pointed to Toulouse, took her station beside it and started thumbing. Despite her morose demeanour a first vehicle stopped quickly; it was starting to rain.

This one was an old farmer, a man of few words, in his Sunday best and driving an old 605 in good condition; he carried her only twenty kilometres before dropping her in front of a notary's office where he was going to sell his smallholding. The prevalent odour in the car was a compound of ash and hot electrics, but not of dog even though there was one, lying on a plaid rug in the back. He was asleep and nothing would have betrayed his presence were it not for the frequent sighs to which he gave vent as he slept. The notary's house was deep in the country, beside a road little frequented except by tractors and farm workers on mopeds; the farm workers cast a glance at Victoire as they passed. She then had to while away a few hours before a Saab appeared, an unexpected arrival in this desert place; it was slate-grey with fawn leather seats, and its windscreen was adorned with a caduceus from the previous year. Its lone driver was no more talkative than the smallholder, but his silences may have betrayed a slight intoxication, or maybe sheer gloom. The finely tuned stereo delivered arrangements by Jimmy Giuffre in a faint aroma of throat pastilles, Virginia tobacco and a distant redolence of long-lost woman. He took her as far as Agen, where she got out at the end of the afternoon.

Then night began to fall, the rain likewise, the one more savagely than the other, and for hours no vehicle passed that way; soon Victoire was soaked through and blinded until a little white car appeared and braked beside her. She did not even notice it straightaway, then she mechanically climbed into its dark interior. "You going to Toulouse?" a man's voice asked. Victoire nodded without turning to him. She was haggard and streaming wet and a dumb wild thing and maybe not all there. In fact she was at that moment too weary, too lost to give this man as close a look as the others who had stopped for her. She did not take in the make of vehicle, she did not look at its interior fittings nor at what might this time be decorating the windscreen or dangling from the mirror. She fell asleep in her seat before her hair was dry.

An hour later she was wakened by the sensation of the car about to stop. Victoire opened an eye and saw through the streaming, misted-up window a heavy, graceless building reminiscent of a railway station. "We've reached Toulouse," the man's voice said, "here's the station. Will that do?" "Thanks," said Victoire. She shivered as she opened the door and pulled her bag out after her, still not looking at the driver. Then she slammed the door and said another perfunctory thanks and made for the station. She was quite sure, however, that she had recognised the voice of Louis-Philippe, who had stayed at the wheel of his Fiat without driving off straightaway, and who must be watching her through his newly replaced rear window as she disappeared in the direction of the all-night buffet, its window turgid with dirty yellow light. At the bar people were drinking beer; in a recess by the bar were two video games; posted up beside these games, a notice gave warning to the customers of the risk of epilepsy if the use was prolonged.

It was in Toulouse-Matabiau station that Victoire finally made some friends. But not at once. When force of circumstance first brought her to rub shoulders with homeless folk like herself she had preferred to keep her own company, not daring to strike up a conversation. Not that all that many of them haunted the countryside, they chose the towns; here they'd meet up in the squares and markets, in front of the stations and the big supermarkets. Victoire preferred to limit the exchanges when those folk started talking of solidarity, of sticking together, making a stand. It would happen that they'd hit the bottle, pick fights, it could also happen that they'd act drunk even when they'd not touched a drop. Often they looked flushed, spoke flushed, lashed out, but they seldom actually came to blows. They were naturally gregarious and seemed to take it amiss if one of their kind kept herself to herself.

In her isolation Victoire was finding it ever more difficult to keep body and soul together. One day she did consider street-walking, the possibility that had occurred to her a few weeks earlier, but she'd left it late: she was too scruffily dressed, too dirty, she was no longer sufficiently presentable to be the least bit attractive. No passer-by would let himself be tempted, of course, the only ones who might perhaps look for such a bargain would be her own kind, the very people who would have no money to pay her.

These folk stayed together in a group most of the time and compared plans, or manifested only bitterness and grumbles. They were lost, they did not have much to say for themselves. So long as she stood outside their circle, people were inclined to consider Victoire with mistrust, suspecting her of heaven knows what. Although she was on the street as they were, although on her uppers, there were doubtless things about her that did not accord with the standard profile of a tramp. As people kept pointing this out to her, making their own guesses and asking questions, she determined to put an end to it by becoming a joiner after all and thus put herself beyond suspicion. After studying the groups already constituted around the station, Victoire threw in her lot with a couple comprising a man answering to the name of Gore-Tex and his girlfriend known as Lightbulb. Gore-Tex seemed to have something of a hold over the others, however discreetly exercised, so maybe there'd be no harm in joining forces with them.

Lightbulb was a skinny girl with washed-out eyes, porous teeth, and skin so transparent that her veins, sinews and bones could be clearly made out. Her nails were decalcified but she had a ready smile. Gore-Tex, twice the girl's age, no doubt owed his nickname to his one prized possession, a warm and substantial parka lined with the eponymous material. He was an affable, sturdy fellow, on the tall side and not bad looking, but he was soft and this had its drawback: he would not bring himself to speak ill of anybody, which made him a bit of a wet rag to talk to. It was therefore with Lightbulb that Victoire was more inclined to see eye to eye. Gore-Tex's other possession was a dog. It had no name, and a rope for a lead. The dog was required to call the man papa: Come to papa, run along to papa, ask papa for a drink, go on, eat from that lovely tin of papa's. Now mind, papa will get cross.

From then on Gore-Tex, Lightbulb and Victoire slept together in their clammy clothes in makeshift shelters on building or demolition sites but also under a lorry's canvas top, a painted backcloth, a plastic sheet, and with practically never anything sexual between them. It was a mystery how, whenever hunger began to gnaw, Gore-Tex always discovered at the bottom of a pocket the same thirty-five francs that enabled Victoire and Lightbulb to go to the cut-price grocer's store.

They lived this way in Toulouse for two or three weeks, moved on to other neighbouring towns, then came the summer. Then, too, it came to pass that, in many municipalities the citizens, but even more their elected officials, got tired of seeing tramps, often accompanied by domestic animals, lay siege to their well-groomed towns, wander in their parks, their business quarters, their pedestrian precincts, selling their wretched magazines to the customers sitting outside their pretty brasseries. Several mayors therefore dreamed up ingenious edicts to outlaw begging, lying about in public places, newsvendors crying their wares, under pain of a fine; dogs without muzzles were caught and impounded, with consequent kennel costs. In short, efforts were made to encourage the down-and-outs to go hang themselves, preferably elsewhere. Whence the daily increased pressure exerted on Victoire and her friends to fall back on more modest towns or to leave for the countryside.

Since Gore-Tex's dog was twice within an inch of the dog pound, and as there was no way to meet the charges, they had to leave the town, after some deliberation. They took the roads westwards at Lightbulb's insistence, she having been seduced by Victoire's description of the Landes. Gore-Tex too said that the countryside had a great deal going for it – day labour in the fields could, he asserted, always be on offer. Lightbulb approved this notion but, once out in the sticks, they were never offered the smallest thing in this line. They continued their wanderings. For all Victoire's experience and her local knowledge, it was at present harder to find a square meal and shelter for the night: a group of three does not pass unnoticed through a village, it awakens caution without arousing the sympathy from which a girl on her own may benefit. The time came when, *faute de mieux*, the occasional theft was perpetrated with no intention to do harm.

The first was committed by chance, one night when Lightbulb and Victoire left to reconnoitre and look for shelter in a village of some thousand souls who all retired early to bed. They avoided the inhabited dwellings and sought rather to gain access to hangars and store sheds; they tried a door and it gave way to their shove. At the back of a grocer's belonging to the Guyenne and Gascogne regional chain, the door opened onto a stockroom. With no concerted plan, without a word exchanged, without a second thought, four tins of sardines and pâté were lifted along with two bottles of red wine, a wholesale round of cheese and four cartons of pasteurised milk. Then a quick getaway was made from the village to consume this fodder at a healthy distance, on the edge of a field in the dark. Never before had Gore-Tex or Lightbulb or Victoire carried things to such extremes, but the ease of the act was an incitement to continue. Thus they re-offended, even by day.

But prudently, in moderation, always following the same simple procedure: while Victoire circumvented the grocer, Lightbulb liberated one or two staple items, never more than one or two, and it always worked. It always worked, until that stormy evening when Lightbulb failed to get a good grip on two tins of ravioli secreted under her tunic and dropped one as she was crossing the threshold. "Well, what the hell!" cried the grocer as he raced round his counter. "God damn you!" he said, warming to his theme as he leapt after the girls who had dashed off in opposite directions as previously concerted for such an eventuality.

Among the neighbours and customers come to lend the grocer a hand Victoire was aware some moments later that two fellows heftier than the rest were still panting after her, mouthing curses, some fifty or a hundred yards behind. Noticing as she ran a bicycle leaning against a wall to her right, she seized the handle-bars as she passed, swung onto the saddle in a single movement and started pedalling frantically. She had got into training a few weeks earlier, and had perfected her cycling technique. But this was a clapped-out old bike the colour of verdigris with a death rattle for a bell, rusted wheel rims, flapping mudguards; the dynamo misfunctioned, the pedals did not match, the gearwheels were stripped, the fork was askew and the tyres were flat. And no pump. And the ruptured saddle left your backside in agony. And the rain fell.

Despite these handicaps, Victoire managed to get up enough speed to hear the insults and cries fade away before long at her back. Under the dark sky, under the pale streetlamps which splut-tered to life, she looked for a way out of the village, never mind in which direction. Soon she passed the final streetlamp and pene-trated into the darkness. Hers was no easy task: the front lamp's thin yellow beam proved quite useless and in a moment she could not see a thing. What's more, her hair kept falling into her eyes and the rain streaming down her face was to complete the impair-ment of her vision but she would continue to pedal – and kept course as best she could. She focused her attention on the road-side, more or less identifiable by a broken white line, half effaced.

On she went, a few cars dazzled her with their lights as they went by, splashed her as they overtook, but none of them seemed to be carrying pursuers. After a few hundred metres it was likely that they had given up, but Victoire did not slacken her pace. Her clothing was soaked right through to the seams and she was shivering, but continued to pedal like mad; so intent was she on this exercise that she failed to notice the triangular sign warning of a sharp bend on the left. Suddenly the white line merged into darkness and before Victoire could think of grasping the situation her front wheel was skidding on the rim of a shallow ditch, her cycle flipped over and she found herself shot across the ditch into a bramble bush; this was bounded by a barrier against which she cracked her skull. We all have to die one day, it might as well be now with everything up the creek, in the dark, the rain, the brambles, the cold, let's crash out as one smiles a welcome at the anaesthetist on the threshold of a futile operation. So it was that every sensation, all ambient noise – the snarled-up chain, the buzzing mudguard, the death rattle of the bell and the endless clicking of the free wheel – all of this cut out in a twinkling.

Victoire came to only a good while later; she did not open her eyes at once nor remember a single thing, just as a few months earlier she had woken to find Félix dead.

She found she was lying under a stiff, coarse blanket pulled up to her chin. She lifted her hand first to her forehead; it was covered with a damp cloth folded like a compress; then her sensations awoke, one after another, each in turn prompting the recollection of its origin; a small labour of association and cross-checking recovered her memory in full. A dull ache in her head reminded her of the barrier; and long burning streaks on her hands, her thighs and one of her cheeks reminded her of the bramble bush; then she raised an eyelid. The ambient light was feeble, a slightly rancid yellow, unless this impression owed more to the smell. Turning her eyes, Victoire made out two men sitting not far from her in unmatched armchairs; they were watching her from either side of a paraffin lamp.

One of them was bare-chested beneath a beige quilted anorak with a torn sleeve, the other wore a navy blue lorry driver's pullover; they were both dressed in ample jeans spotted with mud and grease, and great big clodhoppers. The man in the anorak was swarthy, dry, morphologically speaking; his look was sharp, unforgiving. The other had more substance, more flab to him; he was almost bald and his fat lips hardly smiled either; his face recalled that of Zero Mostel the film actor, and Victoire was surprised and briefly chuffed that in her condition the resemblance had struck her at once. The two men said not a word.

Victoire wanted to talk, but what was there to say? And moreover she felt sick the moment she tried to move her lips, which were anyway so desiccated they felt like a pair of hardened crusts, someone else's, not hers. "Quiet!" the wizened type said to her in an undertone, "keep quiet, relax. You're out of harm's way here." The other had moved away to pick a kettle off a hob on a butane gas canister wedged between a couple of canteens.

She nodded – all it took to pitch her backwards – shut her eyes – more wooziness with a vengeance – then reopened them; cautiously she inspected the place. She was lying on a mattress thrown straight down on a floor of beaten earth, in a little room with a low ceiling, a sort of cabin with walls assembled out of chipboard and plasterboard panels, all held together with fibrocement. Holy pictures and profane photos culled from geographical, pornographic or sporting magazines adorned their surface along with wallpaper samples. The furniture consisted of crates of one sort and another, a second, larger mattress shoved against the opposite wall, as also the odd armchair and small shelf, all knocked about and patched together. The floor was bestrewed with kitchen utensils and tools in equal measure, scraps of material hesitating between men's wear and dish rags, bags advertising shoes, an alarm clock stopped at eleven, a radio surmounted by a fork fixed by one of its prongs in the stub of the aerial.

Zero Mostel came back with a bowl and handed it to the wizened man, who held up her head and gently made her drink what was in the bowl, a sip at a time. It might have been broth made from a chicken cube, evidently flavoured with herbs. It was hot, and spread slowly and evenly through her system; Victoire fell asleep again almost at once. When she next opened her eyes, perhaps the next day, she was alone. A hole in the wall covered by a plastic sheet offered a hint of bright sunshine well up in the sky. The door opened at a push by the wizened man who stopped on the threshold; he held a dead rabbit by the ears. Victoire and this man exchanged a look then the man smiled, seized a long filleting knife and with a quick stroke beheaded the creature; its body fell onto his shoes and Victoire passed out again.

The wizened man's name was Castel, Zero Mostel's was Poussin. Castel and Poussin both answered to the first name Jean-Pierre, so it would be easier, Poussin considered as he plumped up Victoire's pillow on her next awaking, while Castel was cooking the rabbit, to call us by our surnames. Otherwise we'll get all confused. Poussin seemed less abrupt than Castel, his manners were not rigid: recovering her senses, Victoire found some measure of comfort in him.

The two men were about fifty and behaved like tramps, but they were precise in their speech and, in Poussin's case, a trifle affected. Castel's voice was somewhat brittle, freeze-dried, sharp as the exhaust of a motor starting from cold, while Poussin's came across all orotund and well oiled – his participles slippery and sliding like valves, his direct objects skidding in oil. They lived without money, remote from men, and fed off leftovers recovered at night from local rubbish tips and dustbins, and sometimes too from small game which they knew how to capture, rabbits but also hedgehogs, not to mention lizards. As for sex, they seemed to satisfy each other. "Which is so much the better for you," Poussin one day remarked to Victoire. "Because otherwise we would no doubt have raped you, and what could we have done with you after that?"

They had been leading this life for three years without disturbance. After their dismissal from the same outfit that made electronic components, where the functions they exercised were ill-remunerated, rather than wander about the Paris region in their unemployed state, they had decided to withdraw into the country. As a bourgeois lifestyle lay beyond their means, they took long walks and made a careful inventory of the region, whose climate suited them, before coming upon this isolated ruin. They had invested, consolidated, done it up as best they could, and even though at first, Poussin regretted, things had been a bit rough, they had taken a liking to it and then got used to it. Victoire drew inspiration from their story to invent one of her own that might justify her situation. Divorce, dismissal, the bailiffs, petty crime, rootlessness, a run-in with the Law and aimless wandering. "So there," she concluded. "I feel I've lost the way." "That is not necessarily worse," said Poussin. "If we didn't lose ourselves, we'd get lost."

It was with him that Victoire got on the best, at first; he was the one to have tended the wounds resulting from her fall off the bicycle, and then to have mended the bike. Those early days it was with him that she stayed indoors while Castel went off to fish, hunt, scavenge for basic commodities or scraps that Poussin had the task of accommodating. They would chat. Later it was Castel's turn to unwind and take Victoire with him on his expeditions; thus she acquired certain elementary skills, shooting blackbirds with bow and arrow, catching gudgeon barehanded, making traps with three large stones and a couple of twigs out of balance, all things proscribed by the Law. She informed herself about the precautions to take in the exercise of these pursuits engaged in without a permit, during the closed season, in reserved areas, and employing banned contraptions. Together they would make night-time forays to rubbish tips and building sites in search of a pot of paint or bag of cement, gas canisters, armchairs, shelving that Poussin would knock into shape.

Out of caution and thus on principle they seldom resorted to outright theft, which was strictly reserved for goods that had to be brand-new, those where second-hand substitutes would not do – not all that many when you stop to think about it, fewer than you would have supposed: basic foodstuffs, razor blades, candles, the odd bar of soap. For everything else one could get by with makeovers. Even cast-off footwear still almost new, indeed sometimes brand-new, though it might not necessarily be a good fit; even almost-new batteries from discarded remote controls. However, an exception was sometimes made for Victoire's needs and underwear would disappear from clotheslines. And in the evenings they'd play cards to the sound of the radio – music and sports repeats – they'd tune in to the news.

These last months Victoire had not read the papers much. At the villa by the golf course, all she had looked in them for, in vain, was news of Félix, and she'd stopped at the headlines. Later, with Lightbulb or on her own, she had continued to glance at them on the newsagents' stands, or sometimes she would spot a two-day-old paper sticking out of a bin or left on a bench – it would have been barely read seeing that in the summer months people follow the news less closely. Our masters know this (and we know they know it), which is why they profit from our being asleep to put in hand major changes that we can only accept as a *fait accompli* when we wake up in a stupor to kowtow to our new bosses and shell out at the new going rate. But Castel and Poussin, although not in the swing of things, kept an eye on the news. Hence they learned that the fishing season was now open. Early on the morning of the first day, Castel took Victoire to the edge of a small pond nearby, a limpid pool, oval as a hand mirror, prolonged by a narrow canal in the form of such a mirror's handle; they caught two tench.

The pond was hemmed in with giant poplars, their foliage a great compact, tousled mass. In the days that followed, Victoire went and spent several moments beside this pond; she would sit on the bank opposite. In summer, most of the time, there was not a whisper of wind to move these trees, whose doubles showed like so many playing-card Kings on the water, whose depths sustained a plentiful traffic of pike, black bass and pikeperch, creatures who threatened and pursued each other without truce, who coupled and devoured each other without quarter. Occasionally such traffic disturbed the surface and made ripples; the reflections of the trees would wave discreetly, as from a puff of wind – as if the pond could not endure seeing them so trans-fixed and took the sky's role in producing an illusion of breeze. On other occasions a real wind would shake the foliage and pro-duce the opposite effect: the pond surface was so ruffled that it was too clouded a mirror and sent back an image only of motion-less trees – as if there were no weather conditions in which these poplars could have a true understanding with their reflection.

In the middle of August, the wind shook the trees more often and more vigorously, it rained, Poussin remarked that it was like this every summer, the fifteenth brought a change of weather. It was in effect quite simply the coda, the conclusion of the summer, the season's last lap: if it was sometimes still very hot, there was a sense that the foot was off the accelerator, the ignition had been switched off, the heat was merely the tail of a comet in free fall, a car stalled on a slope, the sense that a new dotted line of readings had begun to cap the high temperatures; the shadows were visibly lengthening. As her life with the two men reminded Victoire of holidays, the first fruits of autumn suggested to her the beginning of term, raised the question of going back. She set this question aside, but a hunter gave the reply, most likely.

Most likely a hunter, fed up with constantly coming upon snares and nooses, began to keep watch, finally spotted Castel, and reported the matter to the authorities, for one fresh morning at the beginning of September, they had barely got up, barely exchanged a few words, and were preparing the coffee while deferring the moment to brush their teeth when the noise of the man's motor preceded the blue patrol van. Victoire was just dressed and still in the cabin when it appeared. Just time to pull on a jacket and shoes while the van was parking, just time to snatch up a bag while two men got out of the van, to cram two or three things into it, then to take advantage of their making first for Poussin, who was busy peeing against the sylvan backdrop, to leave the cabin by the nearest blind angle. Slipping through the door, skirting a wall, heart in mouth, tiptoe, she went into the adjacent woods. Not many dead leaves yet to risk betraying her footsteps, but she penetrated among the trees very slowly at first, holding her breath then, when she estimated that she was far enough away, she broke into a run, too fast and no doubt for too long, until she found a first road, and then another and then yet another, bordered by an old, worn, yellow-and-white milestone. On this milestone Victoire sat down and tied her laces.

The days that followed, in the absence of a map she got her bearings any old how, as the signposts dictated and with no precise goal. Sometimes she did her walking at night, slept in the afternoon, picked up discarded bread and unwanted vegetables, as also a plastic bag, tying the handles together the better to carry them. Victoire became dirty and in due course a regular slattern; there was an increase in the number of people with a diminishing inclination to offer her a lift, not least because when a lift was offered she no longer seemed to have much idea of a destination. And to pile it on so that she would be left in peace, Victoire began to behave like a mental case, as she imagined such a person would behave, and in fact she was often taken for one. She even took to talking to herself; often it was a matter of replies at an interview, an oral, an interrogation – the questions were inaudible but the answers were sometimes detailed, other times monosyllabic. She no longer thumbed lifts except after dark, imagining that the less visible she was, the less offputting her appearance.

On the third evening of her new solitude, Victoire happened still to be walking along the roadside and at the first sound of a motor raised a vague thumb without even turning round, a headlamp beam lightly warmed her back but the vehicle passed without braking. As she threw a glance at it she thought she recognised a rather old car, of the same make as Gérard's; but what with its speed and the darkness she could not make out the interior. She stopped walking, the rear lights quickly dwindled and disappeared in a sharp bend; if it was impossible for the driver not to have noticed her, it was not at all certain that he would have recognised her. Victoire resumed walking.

She tried not to slow her pace when, beyond the sharp bend, she came upon the Simca Horizon parked on the shoulder, side lights on, engine turned off. Victoire had to persuade herself to carry on at a normal pace, with her usual gait and absent look; but when she came up with the car, the window was lowered to reveal a smile of Gérard's. "I wasn't sure it was you," said Gérard, "I didn't brake at once." Victoire made no reply. "It did not seem possible," he pursued; "what a treat!" He nailed her with his look, but the smile that spread over his face was less one of pleasure than of amusement. Victoire turned away to continue walking, "But wait," said Gérard, "where are you off to, can I take you anywhere? Get in." She got in.

Apart from being new and of better quality, the overcoat Gérard was wearing was the same as before, same material and colour, and Victoire made a quick reckoning of what it would have cost, then the proportion of that sum to her own stolen money. Gérard moved off and kept going for some dozen kilometres before he slowed, parked the car at the entrance to a private drive, switched off, turned off the headlights and faced the girl. "Let's talk a little," he said, "let's chat." He rested a hand on Victoire's forearm and in the dark his smile was even more of an amused smirk. "Leave me alone," shouted Victoire pulling away her arm, and noted in passing that this was the first sentence she had uttered all day. "Come on," said Gérard. ". . . me alone," mumbled Victoire. "Don't keep saying that," he urged her. "My dough," said Victoire, and Gérard did not stop smiling except to whinny with astonishingly mirthful laughter. "What dough?" he cried again as he turned over his hands for her in waggish mimicry, and Victoire repeated "my dough, my money which you . . ." while he carried on chuckling. "No, not me, of course not," said Gérard with a reassuring smile, the sort specially designed for retarded people. "And even if it was me, what proof would you have?" "I know," said Victoire, "you know that I know." "All right," said Gérard, "go to the cops if you're so sure. Why don't you go to the cops, or are you better off with me than with the cops?"

As he said this he placed one hand on Victoire's shoulder and the other on her waist, pulling her towards him as he sought to pinion her arms, but before he had her quite immobilised she just had time to jab at his eyes with two fingers firmly spread as a V, then to fling open the door. Leaving the man to himself to yell and curse like a trooper, she fled for the trees again, vanished into the bramble thickets where she holed up till daybreak. She avoided the roads in fear and trembling lest she run into him once more, and realised only in the morning that she had left her plastic bag in the car.

Later, one damp Thursday in mid-September, when autumn had clearly arrived, after Victoire had got a lift from a vet, she was picked up by a kindly fellow, a dealer in sports goods. He had parked in front of a dimly lit bar back of beyond, and offered her a hot drink, whatever she felt like – milk, tea. After ordering something to keep her company he had driven off into the murky weather, and Victoire had stayed on by herself. The bar was dimly lit but already overheated: the gas-fired radiator by the bar was going flat out, striped oilcloths covered the tables, stiff curtains draped the windows, an incomplete collection of bottles bided its time back of the bar above six postcards (none of them posted from all that far away) pinned up then shat on by flies. In front of them stood a little row of trophies. The place smelled of home cooking, caustic soda, gingerbread and stale sausage.

Not many customers, an intermittent *patron* apparently on his own – he'd keep slipping out to the cellar or the yard at the back; apart from Victoire, there were just two other customers, one a structural pillar unremittingly propping up the bar, the other a transient, a seated one. Silence reigned. Now and then, to fill the silence, the prop would address a word to the *patron* who, when he was there, would not reply, then to the transient who made do with a nod. A clock saw to bridging the conversational gaps, while the thermostat on the gas-radiator recurrently triggered a short, muted burst of incandescence. It was baking, a woman came in and left, twice in a row, each time making some remark, maybe that it was too hot, though there was no knowing precisely what she'd said nor to whom. Eventually the bird of passage left and the permanent fixture belted up; he did not turn round even when the door opened and in stepped Louis-Philippe.

As he crossed the threshold and passed from the cold damp to the sudden steambath of the bar, Louis-Philippe's glasses misted up. He crossed the room without removing them to give them a wipe, so his eyes remained invisible, masked behind a portable fog. He reached the counter, quietly placed his order, then turned his blind lenses back to the room, zeroed in on Victoire, and walked to her table. He took a seat opposite her. Then the mist gradually began to clear symmetrically on each lens, starting from the centre; at first Victoire could distinguish nothing beyond the black dot of each pupil, then progressively the irises and the whites came into view. Louis-Philippe waited until both his eyes were visible in their entirety, right to the eyebrows surmounting his spectacle frames, before he began to speak.

The file on Félix was now closed, she was to understand, no need to give it another thought. In the end they had shelved the matter and absolved Victoire of any responsibility. Her disappearance had raised eyebrows at first, but no one had seriously thought of calling her to account. No suspicions, no suppositions even: she could by all means return to Paris. "I won't offer to take you back, I'm heading in the opposite direction, towards Spain." All the time he was speaking Victoire looked at Louis-Philippe with an air of indifference and gave no indication that she had fully grasped what he was saying. However, she got to Bordeaux that same evening, keeping to the back roads; here she took up her station by the motorway toll booths and ten hours later she was back in Paris.

A purple Scania semi-trailer dropped Victoire at the turn-off for the motorway to Metz, and from there she walked to the Porte de Bercy, then followed the arc of the Maréchaux northwards. At the Porte de Montreuil she turned left on Rue d'Avron towards La Nation whence, still heading north and keeping on the axis of the Métro, she followed the central strip of the succession of boulevards that took her past the Père Lachaise cemetery, to Belleville then Stalingrad.

After La Chapelle, occupied by the huts of a gypsy fairground, she followed Boulevard Rochechouart then Clichy without leaving the centre strip, a jetty between the opposing traffic flows. The jetty is furnished with benches and trees and peopled with males – unemployed, elderly, immigrant, sometimes all three – who sit on these benches, under these trees, and watch the dead leaves and crumpled papers fluttering about their feet. Where Boulevard des Batignolles passes over the tracks of the Gare Saint Lazare, an idea must have come to Victoire or taken shape in her mind because from that point on her pace quickened and gained assurance. She made another left turn in Rue de Rome, and followed it down, with a glance at the violins in the shop windows, as far as the station.

Beneath painted wooden ceilings, metal latticework and wired glass panes, the concourse in the Gare Saint Lazare is a long rectangle whose long sides are taken up with automatic ticket machines. Its short sides are taken up on the west by the Snack Saint Lazare Brasserie and on the east by a plaque commemorating railwaymen who gave their lives for France. The ticket hall for the main lines is located in front of the snack bar, beside a glassed-in booth containing two policemen dressed in black plastic and carrying mobile phones at their belts. Victoire went in.

The hall is embellished with a clock, two video screens, and a schematised map of France, its centre occupied by an engine in perspective. Victoire made for Window 14 where a queue was in a constant state of renewal, always the same yet ever changing, like a cloud. The ticket clerks were behind windows protected by a lavender curtain with a circular hole in the middle. The prospective travellers addressed this hole alleging an entire raft of fare-reductions in order to obtain return tickets at a cut price. Without according them more than a glance, the clerks would tap out their order on a keyboard then indicate the price on offer. Victoire joined the queue and, when it was her turn, murmured the name Louise.

On the other side of the window, a young woman looked up sharply and stared. "What are you doing here?" asked Louise. "It's ok," said Victoire, "it's quite ok." Considering Victoire's attire, the state of her hair and the expression on her face, Louise seemed on the point of making a comment but on second thoughts bit her tongue. "I'll explain," said Victoire. "Listen," said Louise, indicating with an eyebrow the newly formed queue behind Victoire." "I haven't got much time, what is it you need? Where are you going? D'you have a reduction?" "No," said Victoire, "I'm not going anywhere. It's more that I'm back. I'll explain," she promised again, "but could you put me up tonight, just for the night?" "That's not all that convenient," said Louise, "it's a bit difficult. I'm living with Paul at present, you remember Paul, you know how he is. Besides, you know what love is like, always the same, compassion or reflection."

It is surprising that this circular hole in the window – devised strictly for the transmission of railway travel information, and with a more regular circumference than the one that Victoire saw described six months earlier on Louis-Philippe's car – it is surprising that it could convey such opinions without the entire system exploding. "See what you can sort out with Lucien, why not?" suggested Louise; "you have the address?" "I think so. In the thirteenth arrondissement?" "I'll jot it down for you. It's at the bottom of Boulevard Arago. Do you have some money on you?" "Well, not really," said Victoire. "Here," said Louise.

Victoire took the Métro to Denfert-Rochereau then went down Boulevard Arago which in October looks like the picture of autumn from some old school textbook. It has the outline of a boomerang and is flanked with russet trees from which – when the weather is cool, the light grey and the sky lowering – the chestnuts drop and sometimes bounce on the cars like the negatives of golf balls. Lucien's flat was right at the end of the boulevard, towards the Gobelins. Victoire was to spend a fortnight here.

She barely knew Lucien, whom she'd met a couple of times at Louise's, but as luck would have it their hours did not coincide. They scarcely ever ran into each other in those two rooms; Victoire was still asleep when he left in the morning early, and he did not find her there late afternoon; and when Victoire came in late at night he was fast asleep. On waking up, Lucien would find by the edge of the bathtub a strand of Victoire's hair which was a line of handwriting, a long detailed signature, all her Christian names followed by a meandering flourish.

In the weeks that followed Victoire avoided the places she had frequented before. However, one evening in mid-November, once she had practically recovered her normal appearance, she risked a foray to the Central. She had never set foot in it since the day before her departure, but barely had she stepped inside than whom did she spot standing at the bar in the company of a pretty woman, but Félix.

Félix, who looked in the pink, did not seem to manifest any particular emotion as he saw Victoire approach. "Well," he merely exclaimed, "where on earth have you been? I looked for you all over, this is Hélène." Victoire smiled at Hélène and forbore to ask Félix how come he was not dead, which would have had its effect on the atmosphere; she preferred to order a *blanc sec*. "And Louis-Philippe," she asked, "have you seen him lately?" "Oh," said Félix, "so you haven't heard? I *am* sorry." "I'll leave you a moment," said Hélène. "I'm so sorry," repeated Félix in a murmur once she had gone, "I thought you knew. We never got to the bottom of what happened to Louis-Philippe, we never did find out, I think they found him in his bathroom some two or three days later. That's always the problem when you live alone. It happened just when you went off, that'll be what, one year, not quite a year. I even thought for a moment that that's why you left." "Heavens no," said Victoire. "Of course not."

The Silver Tassie
The Walworth Farce
Enda Walsh